The Mystery of the Campden Wonder

The Mystery of the Campden Wonder is a crime novel based on sensational events which occurred during the seventeenth century in the Gloucestershire market town of Chipping Campden.

They began one summer evening when the lady of the manor's steward vanished without trace or explanation. What ensued was described as 'one of the most remarkable Occurrences which hath happened in the Memory of Man'.

Investigation of the mystery was undertaken by Sir Thomas Overbury, an eccentric local magistrate. Whether or not he succeeded in unravelling it became another mystery, for his conclusions were never made public. The Campden Wonder has therefore remained one of the unsolved puzzles of English history.

Here, with the aid of his young servant, Ali John, Sir Thomas uncovers the truth—but only after a toll of violent deaths.

Like much of what passes for history, this story is a blend of fact and speculation.

Also by Jeremy Potter

Fiction

Hazard Chase (1964, reprinted 1989)
Death in office (1965)
Foul play (1967)
The dance of death (1968)
A trail of blood (1970)
Going west (1972)
Disgrace and favour (1975)
Death in the forest (1977)
The Primrose Hill murder (1992)

History

Good King Richard? (1983)
Pretenders (1986)
Independent Television in Britain, volume 3:
Politics and Control, 1968–80 (1989)
Independent Television in Britain, volume 4:
Companies and Programmes, 1968–80 (1990)
Tennis and Oxford (1994)

THE MYSTERY
OF THE
CAMPDEN WONDER

Jeremy Potter

Constable · London

First published in Great Britain 1995
by Constable & Company Ltd
3 The Lanchesters, 162 Fulham Palace Road
London W6 9ER
Copyright © 1995 by Jeremy Potter
The right of Jeremy Potter to be
identified as the author of this work
has been asserted in accordance
with the Copyright, Designs and Patents Act 1988
ISBN 0 09 474600 1
Set in Linotron Palatino 11pt by
CentraCet Ltd, Cambridge
Printed in Great Britain by
St Edmundsbury Press Ltd
Bury St Edmunds, Suffolk

A CIP catalogue record for this book
is available from the British Library

FOREWORD

This is the story of Sir Thomas Overbury, squire and Justice of the Peace, nephew to a namesake who had served as secretary to one of King James I's favourites and played a role in the government of England far above his station.

Pride and ambition were congenital in the Overbury family. The younger man shared to the full his uncle's self-esteem, restless intellect and thirst for place and fame. No cat was more inquisitive, no hedgehog more prickly, and he was famously quarrelsome—a brew which had brought his uncle to an early death by poisoning in the Tower of London.

For the young Thomas, a year at Oxford studying the works of theologians with mounting disbelief ended abruptly in a dispute with the Provost of his college over the nature—and indeed the very existence—of the Holy Trinity. Thus in 1642, at the age of eighteen, he was sent abroad in disgrace, consoled by the promise of an adequate allowance for as long as his face was not seen again in his native land.

Civil war broke out a few months later, and when his father espoused the royalist cause the rebellious son was minded to return and fight for Parliament. On reflection, though, the prospect of an extended Grand Tour seemed the greater attraction. After a leisurely journey through France and Italy he moved on to the Near East and explored the Levant before settling in Alexandria. There, comfortably ensconced as an English milord, he exercised his mind in Islamic studies and his body in brothels while waiting for his father to die.

Fifteen years of exile passed before news of that happy event brought him home to take possession of the family estates, where he quickly became as autocratic as his father before him. Reluctantly surrendering the joys of life as a bachelor, he did his duty by marrying an heiress of good child-bearing stock; but when she failed in hers by producing a daughter instead of a son he did not hide his anger or spare her his tongue.

The disappointments of his homecoming were public as well as private. To his chagrin, the Lord Protector's government had no post worthy of his talents which it was willing to offer to a returning exile who was openly scornful of Puritan ways.

Then came the Restoration and with it a reward for his father's loyalty and the happy chance that he himself was untainted by office under the Commonwealth. A knighthood and appointment as a magistrate enabled him to hold his head high among his fellow landowners in the county. Now a second Sir Thomas Overbury of Bourton on the Hill, Gloucestershire, was equipped to make a splash and take his place in the great world.

Events which began fifteen years earlier were to provide him with the opportunity.

1

Andrew Fettiplace, Robert Hayward and Daniel Perry were townsmen of Chipping Campden and conscripted pikemen in the army of the king. One spring day in 1645 they were lying on their stomachs behind a hedge, scarcely daring to breathe. The road beyond the hedge ran between the Parliamentary strongholds of Gloucester and Warwick, and they were waiting in ambush for an enemy force reported to be approaching from the south.

All three were praying for their own salvation in the forthcoming engagement and for the death of their colonel, Sir Henry Bard, the one-armed bearded monster who lay concealed with his musketeers a hundred yards ahead. As governor of the royal garrison at Campden House, he lived in style in the midst of deprivation and was the most detested man in three counties.

The fear and hatred which he inspired were not without good cause. Sir Henry's mercenaries, named by himself Bard's Angels, behaved like devils. On his orders supplies were requisitioned far and wide, and all without payment. Free billeting was enforced. Beds and bedding were stolen from honest citizens. Cattle and corn were lifted from the fields without so much as a 'by your leave'. Farmers were forced to pull their own ploughs, because Sir Henry had taken their horses. In a last twist of the screw he demanded taxes from those he had already stripped bare. Defaulters were threatened with having their homes fired and themselves hanged.

'Quiet!' The sound of marching men grew closer and the warning was whispered by Captain Hill, who commanded the contingent of Campden House pikemen. In a few moments, peering through their cover, the crouching men caught glimpses of breeches, orange coats and Monmouth caps passing by. A moment more and the peace and glory of a May morning were shattered by the opening fire of the colonel's musketeers.

Taken by surprise, the terrified enemy was overcome by confusion. Some at once fell wounded; some halted and stood rigid in dismay; others pressed resolutely on; others still turned in panic to flee. Their officers contributed to the shambles with contradictory orders.

Captain Hill leaped through the hedge, sword in hand, bellowing to his men to 'follow, follow, follow!' and block the enemy's retreat. In case they should feel disinclined to obey, Sergeant Coneybeare, his second-in-command, urged them on from behind: a wise precaution since some had been pressed into service and others were prisoners of war who had changed sides.

In the pecking order of the army pikemen were the lowest of the low, and among the garrison armour was in short supply. All available helmets, back and breast plates and tassets had therefore been issued to the musketeers, whose needs took priority. Buff leather coats were the pikemen's only protection, and that was precious little. But Andrew and Robert were stalwarts: they had the strength to wield the long-handled pikes and the grit to keep an enemy at bay while driving the steel head through his chest.

Not so Daniel: a small man and timid. Goaded into the attack at the point of the sergeant's halberd, he found himself confronting a fleeing Roundhead who brandished a weapon at his head. In parrying the blow his pike was knocked out of his hands and he was left defenceless: swords too were in short supply and none was to be wasted on the likes of Pikeman Perry. With the sergeant's eye no longer on him, he fell to the ground feigning death and then crawled quietly back behind the hedge.

The engagement was brief but fierce. The soldiers on either side had no quarrel with each other, but fate had placed them in opposing camps and it was 'kill or be killed' until all the

8

enemy lay dead or wounded or had surrendered or escaped. Andrew and Robert had accounted for four of them, who lay bleeding on the road until dispatched without mercy with sword thrusts or blows from the butt ends of muskets.

While the victors of the skirmish recovered themselves and set about disarming prisoners and plundering the bodies of the dead and dying, Pikeman Perry stole back to retrieve his weapon and join them, heart in mouth, trusting that his absence had gone unnoticed. He chose a moment when the sergeant's back was turned, but with Sergeant Coneybeare one could never be sure. He was reputed to be gifted with second sight, able to detect defaulters behind him without turning his head; and his punishments with the gauntlet or strappado were as much to be feared as any encounter with the enemy.

Andrew Fettiplace and Robert Hayward pretended to be unaware of their comrade's temporary desertion, and the three of them fell in together to be marched back to the regiment's headquarters. Sir Henry headed the column on horseback. He wore no badges of rank, but his richly embroidered uniform and the gold sash round his waist proclaimed his right to command. An empty sleeve testified to his heroism in the king's cause at Cheriton Down.

Immediately behind him marched an ensign proudly bearing the regimental battle standard. This displayed a crown and mailed fist surmounting the motto: 'Pro Rege et Gloria'. The background was white, the regiment's colour, chosen (as Sir Henry averred with a chuckle) to symbolise the purity of his angels.

Behind the ensign a dozen men wheeled a heavy cart which the enemy had been escorting. It contained two large barrels surrounded by piles of captured weapons and ammunition. Lest anyone should fail to notice this booty, it was accompanied by the regimental drummer beating time for the march and interspersing his usual repertoire with victory rolls.

The triumphal procession turned off the main road and wound steeply down from the brow of the hill to the street of the little town which nestled in a fold of the valley below. No cheers greeted them there. The shopkeepers, their customers and even the idle loiterers retreated hastily into the houses at the first sight of Sir Henry. The brave few who remained out of curiosity stared in silence.

Outside one cottage stood a woman holding two small boys by the hand. She was as dark as a Spaniard or a gypsy and her bold good looks attracted whistles from the ranks. Her eyes were smouldering with hate, but they lit up with relief as the column passed and she saw the three Campden men unhurt.

'The little one's a handsome lad, Daniel!' Andrew complimented him out of the side of his mouth. For this was Perry's family. Yet with a mere half-glance Perry himself paid them the curtest of heed. His mind was in a turmoil of terror, pondering whether his friends would save his skin by lying if he was charged with cowardice in the face of the enemy.

Robert Hayward's glance was to The Eight Bells on the other side of the street. The inn was kept by his father, who could be glimpsed at an upstairs window. Their eyes met in a momentary exchange of affection.

At Campden House the welcome was effusive. A messenger had brought the news. Major Hawkins, who had been left behind with a handful of men to guard the headquarters, ran down the steps full of flattery to help his commanding officer dismount.

'The prince will be pleased with you, sir,' he gushed when Sir Henry had had his helmet, cloak and boots removed and sat enthroned in the mansion's ballroom refreshing himself with the choicest of the cellar's wine.

Sir Henry grunted. The size of the force assigned to him by Prince Rupert rankled. Even a lieutenant-colonel was entitled to the command of a regiment of foot, whose full complement amounted to some thirteen hundred men. But recruits and arms were scarce and—ever the professional soldier—he was loth to swell his ranks, as others did, with rustics equipped with nothing more than pitchforks, scythes and flails. To deceive the enemy and disguise the fact that the men under his command were shamefully few to support the dignity of a full colonel, he had divided them into three so-called regiments. Yet in truth they numbered a bare three hundred in all. By way of compensation he abused them roundly and daily, but on this day—if on this day only—he was proud of them and showed it by making a short speech of congratulation before dismissing them to drink themselves into oblivion with stolen kegs of ale.

He was here because Chipping Campden, although unimportant in itself, lay in a strategic position, within territory controlled by Parliament. When the war began, each side in turn had seized the deserted house as a strongpoint. Then a royalist garrison from Oxford had been surprised and overwhelmed by a Parliamentary raiding party from Warwick castle. Since that time neither side had chosen to hold it until a few months previously, when Prince Rupert had decided that the enemy's line of communication must be rendered unsafe. He had accordingly dispatched Sir Henry to occupy and fortify the place, and Sir Henry had forced every able-bodied man in the town to set to work with spade, shovel and mattock and convert Viscount Campden's pleasure gardens into mounds of defensive earthworks.

Weeks had then passed without the expected assault by the enemy, and with his base secured Sir Henry had taken the offensive with harrying tactics. Thanks to a spy's intelligence and the negligence of enemy scouts, this day had seen his greatest success so far.

'Most especially will the prince be pleased with these, sir.' Captain Hill capped the major's congratulation as he entered the room with papers in his hand. They had been taken from a wallet found on the body of the enemy commander, whom Sir Henry had dispatched with a single pistol shot through the eye.

He took what was proffered with feigned indifference, which dissolved rapidly as he read. 'Oho!' he exclaimed with delight at the end. 'This shall go straight to His Majesty.'

The major studied the papers in turn and declared that the colonel had earned himself a barony.

The first document was a copy of an order from Parliament's highest military authority, rejoicing in the name of The Committee of Both Kingdoms. Addressed to Colonel Massey, Governor of Gloucester, it instructed him to remove the enemy from Campden by all means and thus end the ill consequences of having intercourse with Warwick severed. For this purpose he was empowered to take five hundred foot and five hundred horse from Gloucester, three hundred of each from Warwick, two hundred from Northampton, and two hundred horse from Worcester.

Major Hawkins turned pale when he read these numbers, but Sir Henry's chest puffed with pride that he and his small force could be responsible for denuding so many enemy garrisons.

The second paper was a copy of Colonel Massey's reply, addressed to the other garrison commanders for their information. In it the governor told the committee that he had labour enough guarding the town without being required to take over the county as well. If he beat the enemy out of Campden House, what next? he inquired: he had no men to garrison it and prevent their return. His letter ended with a formal notification of his decision to suspend any operation against the house pending receipt of further instructions.

Another bottle of wine was opened in celebration; then another; and another. When they had drained them all, Sir Henry invited his officers to join him in a victory jig. 'The Lord looks after His own, His own,' he trilled as they danced. Tripping merrily, he raised his eyes in thanksgiving to a galaxy of heavenly cherubs painted on the ceiling with hands outstretched as though holding up the chandelier.

'Amen,' intoned the major. 'Amen,' echoed the captain.

Their song and dance were interrupted by the appearance of Sergeant Coneybeare standing rigidly to attention in the doorway until given permission to speak.

'Where is your tongue, man?' demanded the colonel, casting jollity aside. This was his alternative to a rebuke for presuming to address him without permission. A subordinate of Sir Henry could do no right, as all under his command well knew.

The sergeant buried his anger under a silent vow to take revenge for all the insults suffered. 'The spoils are safely stowed, sir,' he said. 'They await your inspection, sir. And Mr Harrison craves an audience, sir.'

Hot on the heels of these words came Mr Harrison himself, escorted by an embarrassed guard who had failed to halt him at the outer door. As the steward of the house's owner, he was not inclined to beg for admission. To him Sir Henry was not a superior but a pestilential intruder. To Sir Henry he was an insolent retainer attempting to hamper necessary operations and therefore as much a foe as Colonel Massey.

Now in middle age, William Harrison had served the Campden family all his working life. In their absence he was in sole charge of a valuable estate which included not only the mansion but a large part of the town and many hundreds of surrounding acres. Not even the mayor was a higher dignitary than Master Harrison. But in time of war his was a thankless task, and the fighting had lasted almost three years. He had managed well enough, nonetheless, until this arrogant ruffian and his minions had descended on Chipping Campden like a pack of wolves on a herd of sheep.

Since then hardly a day had passed without cause for complaint about stolen livestock and wagons, barns burned for firewood, lead stripped from coffins to make bullets. Nothing was safe or sacred. Today he had come to confront the garrison commander about the condition to which his tenant farmers had been reduced, deprived of men and animals to cultivate their fields. He was, as always, plain-spoken, and Sir Henry was, as always, deaf to his pleas.

'Have I not told you often enough, Master Harrison, that had I money to pay for what must be taken, you would have it? But I am in great want of funds. If that answer does not satisfy you, let his lordship make a complaint to the prince, whose servant I am in all that I do.'

'This is not enemy territory. We are loyal to the king in these parts; yet you treat us no better than the rebels would. Neither the prince nor His Majesty himself would wish us to starve, I warrant. It is in obedience to your orders that your men behave like outlaws and savages.'

'I question the loyalty of any man who doubts what I do here in the king's name,' replied Sir Henry with a contemptuous belch. 'Let the Devil take him, I say. I am a fighting man and do King Charles great service. Have I not fought on the steppes of Russia and across the plains of Poland? Have I not served King Christian of Denmark? Gustavus Adolphus of Sweden? The Elector Palatine? The king of England has few commanders as experienced in battle and would not punish me if I chose to hang you like a dog. Which I have a good mind to do.'

Pillage and drunkenness, blasphemy and fornication, murder and rape. That was a brief catalogue of what was happening in Chipping Campden in the king's name. And now a threat of hanging made to himself! The steward clamped his jaw and left his eyes to speak for him as they travelled over torn tapestries, headless statues and bullet-ridden paintings: the silent victims of drunken orgies.

'You err if you think us no worthier than idle wastrels.' Sir Henry had followed his gaze. Since the steward was not intimidated, his bullying mood gave way to more boasting. 'Feast your eyes instead on the fruits of our labour this morning. Join our celebration. Be my guest in your master's house. Toast our success and you will not be hanged!'

The steward accepted a glass of his master's wine reluctantly and drank from it sparingly. He lost count of the number of times his hosts emptied theirs while they described to him the cunning of their ambush and bragged of their deeds of valour in the ensuing scuffle. Then, with the colonel unsteadily in the lead, they all descended to the cellars.

These were vast, like the house above. Subterranean alleys flanked by recesses for storing this or that ran out of sight in every direction. Here was no daylight. The party carried lanthorns and were circled by gloom until they reached a chamber lit by torches where the contents of the captured cart and other trophies seized from the enemy were piled on the stone flags, guarded by sentries.

'A fine place for a commanding officer's inspection!' grumbled Sir Henry, stumbling over a musket. 'What half-witted son of a pox-ridden whore gave orders for it to be brought here before I could look it over out of doors?'

14

There was a pause before Captain Hill answered, taking care to spread the blame. 'The sergeant and I thought it the safest course, sir,' he said, 'pilfering being rife in the ranks.' It would have been unwise to remind Sir Henry that he had been invited to inspect the booty on the forecourt but preferred to hurry indoors and slake his thirst.

'Junior officers are not paid to think. In my regiment they are paid to transmit my orders. Do you understand that, Captain Hill?'

The captain nodded, bit his lip and nursed his grudge. It was three months since he had been paid at all.

'Very well. Now what are you waiting for? Tell the men to open the barrels and be quick about it; or do you want us to stand here all day? And see that they mind where they put the torches; or we may all be blown to Kingdom Come.'

The soldiers whom Sergeant Coneybeare had selected for guard duty were the local men: Pikemen Fettiplace, Hayward and Perry, the last of whom had been a servant in the house before conscription. The barrels were sealed tight and it was hard work before the lids were prised open.

When the first flew off and clattered to the ground, everyone stepped forward to peer inside and there was a general gasp. It was not the sight of gunpowder that met their eyes, but the glint of gold. Ordering the others to stand back, Sir Henry plunged his hands in and withdrew them full of gold coins. The contents of the second barrel were the same. The garrison had intercepted a paymaster's wagon on its way to the enemy at Warwick castle!

'Beelzebub be blessed!'

After uttering this blasphemous cry of joy Sir Henry lapsed into thoughtfulness. William Harrison was thinking too—that Sir Henry was now able to offer compensation. The sentries also were thinking—of their overdue pay. The captain and the sergeant were exchanging fleeting glances unobserved.

Seeing his superior struck dumb, Major Hawkins took charge and gave orders for the barrels to be resealed and guarded with the utmost vigilance.

'There are thieves everywhere,' he warned.

15

2

Four of his men carried the garrison commander to bed that night and he snored soundly until reveille. When a trumpeter blew the summons to morning parade he buried his ears in the pillow and lay awake with his eyes closed, luxuriating in the great bed of the King's Chamber and imagining the praise being heaped on his head after his dispatch reached Oxford. At ease with himself and the world, he needed time for reflection before stirring. Major Hawkins would carry out the inspection in his absence and could be reprimanded later for not performing it to his own exacting standards.

Sir Henry was the youngest son of a rector of Staines: a living with a miserly stipend. Although schooled with the rich at nearby Eton, he had been forced to make his own way in the world, where a combination of courage, sharp wits and lack of scruple had enabled him to live as a mercenary in the style to which he believed himself entitled.

His star had risen two years earlier when he was presented to King Charles at his wartime headquarters. Prince Rupert, the king's nephew and son of the Elector Palatine, had effected the introduction and, on the strength of his service with the Elector, secured for him the command of a brigade, followed by the reward of a knighthood when he proved himself in battle.

The fortune of war had now dropped into his lap the wherewithal to provide for his old age. It was, he told himself, fair compensation for a missing arm and no more than a man deserved for a long succession of loyalties to whatever causes he had happened to be serving. He would be taking only what was his due as a pension.

It was regrettable that so many had been present at the discovery of the treasure: an uncomfortably large number of mouths would have to be stopped by bribery or other means. Sir Henry's mind worked best in the early morning (before it became fuddled by generous draughts of strong spirits at breakfast time) and a solution to the problem soon presented itself. The risk had to be offset by compromise. Both barrels must be sent to Oxford, but only one would arrive. That, together with the ambush itself, should be sufficient to win the king's gratitude and—who knows?—a much-desired peerage.

To whom could such a delicate assignment be entrusted? Again the answer sprang quickly to mind. Sergeant Coneybeare was a man who would skin his own grandmother for money if the price was right. His silence could be bought with a small portion of the loot. A body of guards would have to set out with him, but Sir Henry would find some excuse to recall most of them before they could reach their destination. Suppose one only was left—one of the sentries posted in the cellars: the little one. The sergeant could make him extravagant promises when they hid one of the barrels and then dispose of him on the homeward journey.

As his mind ran over the plan for flaws, his musing was interrupted by a knock on the door and the announcement of a messenger from Oxford. He roused himself with a curse and let loose several more when he read the dispatch. It instructed him to leave the earthly paradise of Campden House; to vacate forthwith this little realm which he ruled so agreeably. The king was on the march to challenge rebel forces in the Midlands and break the siege of Chester. He was in need of every man he could muster. Chipping Campden was to be abandoned: the garrison would not be replaced. Sir Henry's regiment was to join His Majesty's army at a rendezvous the following day.

Was his scheme thus to be strangled at birth? So it seemed. But he went on to consider how much more easily mislaying some of the gold could be contrived during a bustle of evacuation. Was he to lose his independent command? Yes; but instead there was the enticing prospect of the slaughter and pillage of battle, opening the way to promotion. He called for his orderly to dress him and was singing cheerfully when the next interruption came. This time it was his second-in-command.

Sir Henry informed him of the news from Oxford. 'Is the parade dismissed?' he asked. When informed that it was, he demanded to be told how the major dared to do so without reference to his commanding officer. He then ordered that all ranks be reassembled immediately.

Major Hawkins appeared more distracted than contrite and strangely slow to obey. 'I came to report on another matter, sir,' he said hesitantly.

'It can wait,' Sir Henry told him brusquely. He was busy grooming his moustache and beard to appear on parade at his most bristling and fierce. 'Do you hear me?' he growled when the other made no move.

But even then the major stood his ground. 'The matter is of grave concern,' he insisted.

'Not so grave as it will be for you if the men are not on parade again within the next five minutes.' The orderly had squeezed Sir Henry into his white dress coat trimmed with gold lace and was adjusting a scarlet sash round his waist. Once the broad-brimmed hat with its spray of white feathers was on his head, he would be in full fig, ready for the parade.

'The—' the major began.

'Silence!' roared Sir Henry. 'One more word from you, Hawkins, and I shall have you court-martialled. Not in all my years of service have I known such bare-faced insubordination.'

Sir Henry was in a fury, and that was indeed a daunting sight. But the major was an old soldier too. He swallowed, set his jaw and spoke out. 'Be that as it may, sir, it is my duty to inform you that the gold has disappeared.'

Sir Henry's cheeks, already at boiling point, turned from deep red to purple. Lost for words, he reached for his sword and advanced as though to run the blade through his second-in-command, who retreated anxiously towards the door.

'Stay!' he bellowed, finding his tongue. 'Disappeared, did you say? How in the Devil's name can that be? Was it not guarded as I ordered?'

'It was guarded as you ordered. All the sentries have been arrested, but Captain Hill informs me that only one was on duty in the hours before daybreak. His relief discovered him lying on the floor insensible.'

'Dead?'

'Dead drunk, sir.' The major braced himself for another storm, which was not long in breaking. The explosion came like a burst of mortar fire, but when it subsided the words which followed were as soft as the swish of steel. This was the mood in which Sir Henry was at his most dangerous.

'Listen to me carefully, major—while you still hold that rank. Those barrels are too heavy for one man to lift. Even two strong men could not carry or roll them far. There are two entrances to the cellars. Both are kept locked. Ergo, the treasure is still there. It can be recovered quickly. It must be recovered quickly. Tell Captain Hill and Sergeant Coneybeare to report its recovery to me within the hour. Otherwise I shall have them both reduced to the ranks for gross neglect of duty and then hanged for conspiracy to rob His Majesty, to whom the spoils of war belong. For it could not have been removed without their connivance—or yours perchance.'

The major improvised the hastiest of salutes and left the room at the double. The reassembled parade received its marching orders. The hour allowed for the recovery of the treasure came and went. All was confusion as the search through the labyrinth of cellars continued by torchlight while stores were being cleared and equipment packed in preparation for departure. An underground tunnel connected to the cellars was explored. It ran under a terrace and was stacked with barrels, some empty, others filled with wine. The search party was led by the captain and the sergeant who personally inspected every barrel. Finally

19

they reported failure and were placed under close arrest with the pikemen who had formed the guard and been dragged along behind them during the search.

In despair and as a last resort Sir Henry sent for Viscount Campden's steward. 'Find Master Harrison and bring him to me,' he ordered. 'By force if need be.'

The steward was out collecting rents in the neighbouring village of Paxton and having a hard time of it. Thanks to Sir Henry's depredations, the tenant farmers had no money with which to pay. William Harrison was a stern but humane man, who found their tales of misery and near-starvation almost past bearing. He had learned with relief that the garrison would be marching away on the morrow and had hoped never to set eyes on the iniquitous Sir Henry Bard again.

His response to the summons was that he would come as soon as his business was completed. But—so he was roughly told—the colonel's orders allowed for not a minute's delay. 'Are you threatening me?' he demanded of the corporal sent to fetch him. 'Yes,' came the surly answer.

Sir Henry received him with a rare veneer of courtesy. He explained the importance and urgency of his problem and begged rather than demanded assistance. But the steward, taken from his duties in such a manner, was not appeased. Before acceding to any request he required an unqualified apology; also an assurance that the corporal would be disciplined for his insolence to one in the service of a peer of the realm.

The assurance came readily enough because Sir Henry had no intention of honouring it. Apologies were not in his nature, yet he offered a mumbled one. This proved too half-hearted to content the steward, who thereupon took the offensive and proceeded to lecture the garrison commander on the suffering he had caused to an innocent community and the wanton damage to property committed by his men. He looked around him at the scarred magnificence of the mansion's entrance hall and promised that he would be taking an inventory of damaged and missing contents and making a full report to his master.

'You must do as you deem fit, Master Harrison,' Sir Henry

replied, choking back the rage rising in his throat. 'In the meantime, since you are so familiar with the house, be so kind as to guide a section of my men on a thorough exploration of the subterranean regions. There must be some hiding place which we have not discovered.'

'Management of the estate is my task,' said the steward stiffly. 'The house is in my charge when it is unoccupied, but I am not an indoor servant. You would do better to seek the assistance of Daniel Perry.'

'And you would do better to do as I bid,' warned Sir Henry, breaking into a snarl. 'Let me remind you that I command here with the king's commission and in his name. Is obedience to His Majesty's representative not what his lordship would require of you? Do my bidding, or your report will not be the only one he will receive, I promise you.'

As both knew well, the Campden family were the most ardent of royalists. The second viscount (son-in-law to the first) had succumbed to a fever while on active service with the garrison at Oxford, and his younger son died a prisoner in enemy hands. His elder son, the third viscount, had raised a regiment of Horse and a whole corps of Foot for the king's army. He led the regiment himself, holding the same rank as Sir Henry and making up in fighting spirit what he lacked in experience. Still barely thirty, he was wild and dashing, profligate and unpredictable, a braggart and a bluffer: in the opinion of the family's staid retainers, not half the man his father had been. In view of his fondness for gambling for high stakes, it was as well that the Campden estate was still held in his mother's name.

The steward recognised that he had lost the confrontation and had no choice but to obey. With a shrug and a grimace he took a proffered lanthorn, crossed the hall and descended a flight of stone steps to the darkness below. A file of soldiers carrying torches fell in behind, and he warned them sternly of the peril posed by naked flames.

Two hours later the party returned to the ground floor dusty, dishevelled and unsuccessful.

'I am satisfied that every corner, every inch of basement space, has been explored,' he reported to Sir Henry and the major, both waiting grim-faced. 'According to my calculation there are more than a hundred, perhaps as many as two hundred, barrels lying disturbed and higgledy-piggledy in the terrace vaults. But they belong to the house. That is where they have always been stored; although properly stacked. Some show signs of having been wrenched open recently—in an inspection earlier today, I am told. Part of the floor has become a lake of spilt wine, but I have searched through them once more and looked inside as many as I could reach.'

'What then do you suppose can have happened to this treasure? Has the enemy come by night and recaptured it, or has it been spirited away by witchcraft? One of my lieutenants informs me that you have a coven here, so maybe the Devil himself has been at work.' Sir Henry's sarcasm was menacing.

The steward blenched at the mention of witchcraft and offered a more mundane explanation. 'There is another entrance to the cellars,' he said: 'used for deliveries from outside the house. The gate barring it is closed, but the lock has been broken.'

'Then it has been broken in the last few hours!' exclaimed the major. 'It is regularly inspected and was in good order this morning. Or was it yesterday? I can swear to one or the other.'

Sir Henry quelled him with a glare and strode out of doors to examine the broken lock for himself. There could be no doubt that the damage was recent, and he at once ordered a thorough search of the ground outside. But neither the missing barrels nor any traces of their being dragged away towards the earthworks were found.

Grinding his teeth in frustration, he returned to the house and rampaged through the cellars with the unwilling steward in his wake, peering for missed clues in vain. The sentries had already been subjected to a none too gentle interrogation, but, sleeping or drunk, they had nothing to reveal. With all hope fading, the colonel's fraying temper snapped.

'The gold *must* be recovered,' he hissed in the steward's face, thumping him on the chest for emphasis. The two of them were standing face to face in the former splendour of the banqueting hall, now reduced to the squalor of a regimental office. The major had been dismissed and they were alone.

But the steward was no less determined. 'It is not my responsibility,' he protested vigorously. 'I have done my best to help you, although in no wise concerned. If you wish it, I shall continue the search at greater leisure after you and your men have gone. Anything found will be conveyed immediately to Oxford, I promise you. More than that I cannot say or do.'

'That will be too late.' Sir Henry was wincing at the idea of his pension receding out of reach along the Oxford road.

'The king himself may have left, but the town will still be garrisoned, will it not?'

'You mistake me, Master Harrison. It is this house which will not be here.'

The steward felt stunned. In all his years of service he could never have imagined such a threat as this; never have believed that such words could be uttered. 'What is your meaning?' he demanded.

'My orders are to fire this house before leaving. If men cannot be spared to maintain a fortification, it must be denied to the enemy. Those are the rules of war.'

'The king would never order the destruction of property belonging to the viscount's family. They have done more for His Majesty's cause than any other of his loyal supporters.'

'I serve under the command of Prince Rupert and take my orders from him.'

'Even less would the prince authorise such wanton mischief. He is his lordship's friend. I have to declare without mincing words that I give no credence to what you say. This smacks of mere revenge for the loss of your spoils. If you speak the truth, prove it. Show me the order and allow me to read it.'

'Take care, Master Harrison.' Sir Henry was smiling as he spoke, but not good-humouredly. 'Take care lest you make your wife a widow and your children orphans. The last man who ventured to doubt my word was dead before nightfall. As for your request, it is impertinent and cannot be met. You must be aware that military orders are secret in time of war. Were I to share them with you, I would be guilty of a serious offence. How can I be sure that you are not a spy in the pay of the rebels? Indeed your eagerness to take a look at my orders leads me to believe so. Rather than run my sword through you, I am tempted to hand you over to a firing squad.'

It was a measure of the steward's devotion to duty that he paid no heed to this bluster. Sir Henry was plainly accountable to no one and could have him shot out of hand if he chose, but the mansion had to be saved. 'Campden House is the pride of the West Country,' he pleaded desperately. 'It is known throughout Europe as one of the finest buildings erected anywhere in modern times. It cost his lordship's grandfather thirty thousand pounds and another fifteen to decorate. Look around you. The craftsmen were brought from Italy; the marble too. If destroyed, it can never be rebuilt.'

Warm female flesh was the only beauty Sir Henry appreciated. Naked nymphs in cold marble were good only for target practice. 'Such a cost!' he sneered, feigning wonder. 'Then the price of saving it will be but a bagatelle by comparison. What is it? you ask. It is retrieval of my treasure before dawn tomorrow.'

The steward stood bewildered. 'Do I understand you aright, Sir Henry? Are you confessing to having lied; to being under no obligation to destroy the house? Or are you telling me that you will ignore your orders should your gold coins be recovered before the garrison takes to the road?'

'Come, come, Master Steward. Fewer questions if you please. We are both men of the world. You must know that, as a serving soldier, I would never disobey the lawful command of a superior officer. My career would be at an end. Let me make my proposition plain. I want the coin; you want the house. I suspect that you must have some notion of the hiding place and intend to discover it after I have gone: to pay for the damage to the house or line your own pocket. But if you oblige me by discovering it earlier, I shall seek to return the compliment by obliging you. There is more than one method of demolishing a building. I can use my store of gunpowder, so that it is destroyed beyond repair; or I can order it to be torched, so that the flames may be extinguished as soon as the last of my column has disappeared over the hill. The choice is yours.'

3

Fifteen years had passed since Colonel Bard marched his troops away and three months since the son of Charles the Martyr was restored to his father's throne. Parliament had won the war; Oliver, the Lord Protector, had ruled and died; and now the royal fugitive from defeat at Worcester had returned from exile to assert his right to the crown and sceptre of three kingdoms. The bells were rung, the people rejoiced, and the glory of a true English summer was hailed by the re-established Church as an unmistakable sign of divine approval.

On this Thursday, in countryside far removed from the scene of these great events, the August sun shone from a cloudless sky, and a light breeze from the wolds cooled the brows of the men and women labouring in the fields. Peace and prosperity had returned to Chipping Campden. Violence and deprivation were no more than memories. It was once again a time and place to thank God for the gift of life.

The market town of a thousand souls lay in an isolated valley in the ancient hundred of Kiftsgate, a northern peninsula of Gloucestershire. Evesham in Worcestershire, Stratford in Warwickshire and outlying parishes of Oxfordshire were nearer neighbours than its own county town. Gloucester was a bustling bastion of the West Country; Chipping Campden lay hidden in the rural heart of England, more than three days' ride from London.

Yet, in earlier times, it had played a role in the life of the nation. Here, a thousand years before, the Saxon kings of the Heptarchy had met at the summons of Ina, King of Wessex, to ally themselves in war against the native Britons and Welsh. Here, before the Norman Conquest, the manor had been held by King Harold himself; and afterwards the Conqueror had granted it to his own nephew. In the ensuing centuries successive kings on progress had honoured the town with royal visits.

Outside the former almonry which served as his residence William Harrison, steward to today's lady of the manor, unbolted the gate which opened from the orchard of Campden House into a rabbit warren known as the Conygree. To his left lay the churchyard, and above it rose a tower to outshine and outsoar that of a cathedral—a monument to the wealth and piety of the townsfolk and the generosity of benefactors.

His wife followed him out of the house. 'How far will you walk in this heat?' she demanded.

Her voice was shrill and not to be denied an answer. He turned with a silent sigh, impassively. During forty years of marriage the love between them had shrivelled. Differences in religion and politics had transformed it into repugnance. At first her opinions had repelled him; then the very look of her. Once so smooth and sweet, her wrinkled face had come to resemble a weathered gargoyle on the church which had supplanted him in her affection.

'To Ebrington and Charringworth to collect her ladyship's rents,' he replied coldly.

'Will you be back before dark?'

He nodded, turned abruptly and without another word strode away through the tangled grass of the warren towards the road which bordered the park.

'Rent-collecting at harvest time!' she called after him scornfully. 'Harvesting favours from wives and daughters while the farmers are out, more likely!'

'An old man still a-whoring! Small wonder your father refuses to retire,' she added when he was out of earshot. Their son, Edward, had joined her and she squeezed his hand. Mother and son were close. For years they had been looking forward to his succession to the stewardship, but in his thirties he was still fretting at his father's beck and call.

'He has never cared for me as you do,' Edward grumbled. 'He means to spite me by living and working so long that I am passed by. But I swear to you I shall not wait much longer.'

She put her hands to his face and gazed into it. His complexion had grown sallow. Already there were grey hairs in his head. 'Be patient,' she urged. 'He must leave off soon, and there is no one else but you who is privy to her ladyship's business. I will see to it for you.'

But Edward would not be reassured. 'There is one who is learning fast,' he replied sourly, with a glance towards the orchard behind them, where a lad was splitting logs.

'That John Perry!' she spat. 'From the way your father treats him, anyone would think him kith or kin.'

'He shows more fondness for a half-witted servant than he does for his own family—and confides in him more.'

As though to confirm Edward's words, the steward waved his hand from the boundary wall, but they could see that the signal was not intended for them. It was John who at once waved back.

'Come,' she said. 'There is One Above. God will hear our prayers.' Like good Presbyterians, they went to church every day to commune with their Maker. She summoned her daughter to accompany them.

Anne came with reluctance. Tall and fair and not yet twenty, she was the fruit of her parents' last love-making and always at pains to take neither side in their quarrels. Meek and God-fearing, she was no fanatic like her mother and brother.

Within the church they found no living soul. But at rest in the peace of God lay the revered remains of two men who had acquired more earthly riches than any other in the England of their time. While the others prayed and prayed on and on, Anne's devotions were quickly done and her mind wandered in wonder at these men's achievements.

William Grevel was famed as the greatest of all wool merchants throughout medieval times, when England's wool was as precious as gold. His tomb had vanished when the church was rebuilt in its present splendour, but his memorial brass had survived and been accorded the place of honour in the chancel. By right of eminence, this lay near to the altar and therefore to God; for Grevel was the pride of the parish where he had been born and bred. At a short distance down the road stood the house which he had built of sturdy local stone. After three centuries it remained the finest building in the street.

A very different fate had been suffered by the mansion of the church's other great benefactor, erected regardless of expense not forty years before. Its charred and jagged ruins rose stark against the skyline between church and town. Like sockets without eyes, its empty windows stared blindly down at all who passed. They were dumb reminders of the troubled years of civil war: the infamous Sir Henry had fulfilled his threat.

The body and effigy of its builder, Baptist Hicks, London mercer and money-lender, lay under a marble canopy awaiting the Day of Judgment in a style befitting the wealthiest subject of the late King James. None questioned his right to the handsome private chapel which was his and his family's mausoleum in perpetuity. It had been a gift from the vicar, churchwardens and parishioners in gratitude for many favours: the repair of the chapel; the donation of a gallery, pulpit and lectern; the releading of the chancel roof; the walling of the churchyard. It was the daughter and heiress of this Croesus, the Lady Juliana, whom Anne's father now served.

Baptist Hicks had obliged his impecunious sovereign with gifts of silk and by this means became the first City merchant to be elevated to the rank of baronet. Promotion to viscount had been achieved through a loan of the princely sum of sixteen thousand pounds to His Majesty.

All the rewards were not kept to himself. The purchase of the manor of Campden by a man with the king in his pocket had brought its citizens civil benefits as well as ecclesiastical. The grant of a charter at his instigation had not only renewed the ancient liberties, franchises and immunities of Chipping Campden. It had also created a body corporate of bailiffs and burgesses endowed with appropriate legal powers to invoke and enforce these rights and privileges.

But no body corporate, bailiff or burgess had ever dared to challenge the supremacy of the lord of the manor. Thus, since the death of Baptist Hicks, first Viscount Campden, and in the absence of his daughter on her husband's estates in distant Rutland, their steward held undisputed sway in the town and surrounding villages, where his mistress owned many of the houses and all the land as far as human eye could stretch.

Anne believed her father to be a just and honest man, although stern and never to be trifled with. After a lifetime of trusty service to the Campden family, he was still full of vigour and performed his duties punctiliously. She had no wish to see him forced into retirement against his will, but chose not to take issue openly with her mother and Edward.

Their parley with God over at last, mother and son walked briskly towards the market place in search of provisions, while Anne was sent back to mind the house and prepare for their meal. On their way they passed the cottage where John Perry's family lived.

'No rents collected here,' muttered Edward, pointing towards the door accusingly.

Even as he spoke, it flew open and John's mother stood confronting them. Black looks were exchanged. Hers sprang from deep-set, staring eyes, stabbing at them like pin-points.

'It is the evil eye,' Mistress Harrison cried, lowering her head hastily. 'The woman is casting spells.'

Edward hurried her past the door. 'Our prayers will protect us; and I will speak to father about the rent,' he promised. 'He is too forbearing. Every widow does not merit sympathy, that witch least of all. Many a married man was killed in the late wars. Are all their families to be excused payment of dues for evermore? Is it not fifteen years now since Daniel Perry died? That is a mighty sum forgone.'

'Your father says he blames himself for Perry's death, but when I ask him how that can be since the man was killed in the fight at Naseby, he shakes his head and will not tell me the why and wherefore of it.'

'Just because Perry was a menial in the great house! How like father to feel responsible for a scullion! Giving employment to one of his sons is surely amends enough. John earns good wages for a simpleton. And the other son lives by theft, if reports be true. Between them, and what their mother squeezes from the credulous, they can very well afford the rent.'

'Speaking of it to your father will serve no purpose: he is more obstinate than a mule. Her ladyship must be informed. It is a sufficient reason for you to ride to Rutland, Edward, and pay your respects. Go and speak to her of this and other of your father's shortcomings. Explain how greatly her income would increase under your stewardship. Every man has his day and your father has had his and more. That is what she needs to be told.'

'But suppose she will not listen to me. Suppose she tells father. He will drive me from the house.' The more determined his mother became, the more fearful Edward grew. Silence fell between them as they reached the market place, where the stalls were heaped with vegetables and fruit and whole carcasses of meat; for here was a community blessed by a quirk of fortune.

Although nestling among the northernmost slopes of the Cotswolds, this was not prime sheep country. Campden was a centre for collection and distribution: it owed its prosperity to wool grown elsewhere. For centuries fleeces carried from the hills and valleys of Wales and the West of England had been offered for sale in this market square; and not only to local dealers and agents. London merchants made an annual pilgrimage to Chipping Campden. Every year in the selling season foreigners from Flanders and Italy came stealthily, using south coast ports to evade the exorbitant charges levied by the government monopoly at the staple in Calais.

Their purchases completed, mother and son took care to avoid the Perrys' cottage on the homeward journey, passing by on the opposite side of the street. There, sunning himself outside his premises, sat the innkeeper of The Eight Bells. He bade them a polite good-day. It was Robert Hayward, who had inherited the property on his father's death.

'That is one who could tell what there was between Daniel

31

Perry and your father,' said Mistress Harrison as soon as they were out of hearing. 'You must question him, Edward. Do you hear me?'

She had goaded him far enough. 'Lady Juliana! Master Hayward! Why should I trouble myself going hither and thither about a dead man? I will have the whole matter out with father himself this very evening when he returns from Charringworth. There! Does that satisfy you?' He spoke with the bravado of a weakling.

'Bravo!' she applauded.

'I will not take no for an answer,' he promised. 'He shall not browbeat me this time, or I will . . .'

'Or you will what?' she prompted. But he shook his head and would not reply.

4

Darkness fell but her husband had not returned, so Mistress Harrison dispatched John Perry to find him. In the morning the boy claimed to have looked in vain all night, and the search became general throughout the day. But still in vain.

When a second night had passed without sight or sign of the missing man, his son Edward, in need of a higher authority than the constable at Campden, rode the six miles to Bourton on the Hill to report to the district magistrate, Sir Thomas Overbury.

The Overburys had been landowners and Justices of the Peace in this outpost of Gloucestershire for as long as living memory stretched, but Edward travelled the dusty road with misgiving. Members of that family were not accorded the respect and confidence to which generations of wealth and office entitled them. In these parts their word was law, but their behaviour and judgments were sometimes perverse and always unpredictable.

Charitable folk kept their mouths shut when Sir Thomas's name was mentioned; others spoke little to his credit. The Overbury estates had descended to him through his grand-father, uncle and father, none of whom was cast in the common mould of country gentlefolk. Indeed his father's elder brother, after whom he was named, had won fame as a poet and notoriety as a courtier before his enemies had brought his life to an abrupt close by lacing his food with poison.

The younger Sir Thomas had not learned the lesson of his uncle's downfall. Although now past the half-way mark of his three-score years and ten—and buried in the backside of England (as he put it)—he too aspired to a role in great affairs and the giddy heights of fame and power.

Meanwhile he had become a man of the world, travelling widely overseas, and this was reflected in his manner of dress and freedom of thought. At home he wore exotic clothes of a kind never seen before on a gentleman in the shires, and he made no secret of his unorthodoxy in matters of religion. Royalist by upbringing and republican by conviction, it was as well that being sent abroad by his father had spared him from taking the side of either king or Parliament. As a proselytising free-thinker, he had been fortunate to be absent when Puritan intolerance triumphed. But even in the liberalism and licence of Restoration England there were few among his acquaintances whom Sir Thomas Overbury did not offend.

That morning Edward Harrison found him in his oak-panelled library, surrounded by cases of leather tomes and resplendent in a dark blue, ankle-length caftan. The master of Bourton on the Hill, Ilmington and Weston sub Edge was seated at a desk strewn with topical pamphlets and tracts, flanked by weightier works of philosophy and theology. Squatting on the floor beside him, at hand to fetch and carry, was his Arab servant boy, picturesque in baggy trousers. This was the quaintly named Ali John, the subject of much scandalous speculation and behind-the-hand tongue-wagging.

To Sir Thomas reading and writing were his daily occupation, but they were no substitutes for action. He willingly swept aside his papers to bring an inquiring mind to bear on a mysterious disappearance within his jurisdiction as an officer of the law. He was distantly related to the Lady Juliana and acquainted with her man of business, with whom he fell into argument twice a year at the Campden grammar school, where they sat together at meetings of the governing body.

'Are you able to assure me that your father has no private reason to absent himself without notice?' he interrupted after listening intently to Edward's first words.

'My mother and I have no reason to doubt that he intended

to go no further than Charringworth and return the same day. He told us so distinctly.' Edward was nervous and spoke stiffly.

'Have you searched the house and ascertained that nothing has been taken without your knowledge?'

'If you are referring to money, sir, the chest in my father's room contains more than a hundred pounds. I keep the accounts for him and have a key. I counted the sum again this morning and not a penny is unaccounted for. All that is missing is the money which we have learned that he collected at Charringworth and was carrying home.'

Sir Thomas rose with a frown, making the silk of his caftan swish and swirl as he crossed the room. He stood at the window locked in thought, staring down on the familiar view of his park and the herd of heavy-fleeced Cotswold Lions grazing on its slopes. After a few moments he turned to deliver judgment.

'Your father is reputed to be an honest and truthful man, Edward. If that is so'—and Sir Thomas's tone of voice suggested that it should not be taken for granted—'we must assume that he has received a confidential summons from her ladyship, and that she has bound him to secrecy. That seems the most likely explanation. Thus it behoves us not to upset her with too searching and public an investigation. Doubtless she has taken this step with good reason. We live in dangerous days. With so many of the king's followers returning from overseas bent on re-establishing the *status quo ante bellum*, who knows what measures the Lady Juliana may feel obliged to take to advance or protect the family's interests?'

Sir Thomas was longwinded because he enjoyed words and the music of his own voice. Edward responded with brevity. 'There is a strong suspicion of robbery and murder,' he said.

The magistrate affected astonishment. 'If you fear your poor father murdered, why did you not say so at once? Why have you been wasting my time by leading me to suppose that his fate was unknown?'

Edward cowered at the anger. 'It is not yet certain,' he hedged. 'No one has confessed to the crime. No witnesses have come forward. The body has not been found. Nevertheless . . .'

35

'Nevertheless you believe there has been foul play. Very well! Have you come to notify me whom you suspect? Do you imagine that I will issue an arrest warrant when you can produce no witnesses?'

Edward swallowed. 'I am here at my mother's bidding to report the matter and beg that you come to Campden and interrogate our servant, John Perry, who is both witness and suspect. He is sly and tells lies, but my mother and I are confident that Your Honour will quickly uncover the truth and commit him for trial so that justice may be done.'

In his own estimation, petty crime—always widespread in troubled times—scarcely warranted the attention of this prodigy of intellect, but here Sir Thomas scented a real challenge and his curiosity was aroused. He dismissed Edward Harrison with assurances, ordered horses to be saddled and, after dining, took the road to Chipping Campden with his Ali.

It was the custom for servants to ride at a deferential distance behind their masters, but Sir Thomas was prone to think aloud whilst on the move and required an appreciative audience for his monologues. The two therefore rode side by side, paying no heed to the stares and whispers this provoked.

'The loss of a husband and father must hard to bear,' Sir Thomas mused after rehearsing Edward's information at length.

Ali's wits were as sharp as his master's and he answered with an understanding grin. Both had noted the son's lack of grief.

At Campden they were met by Constable Fettiplace and Robert Hayward outside The Eight Bells, where the suspect was being held. Both offered to assist by attending the interrogation, but Sir Thomas refused them. Experience had taught him that informality encouraged disclosure of the truth. At this stage in the inquiry he wanted no fuss—nor the presence of former companions in arms of the boy's father.

When comfortably ensconced behind a table in an upper room with John Perry standing uncomfortably before him and Ali settled in a corner, he began without ado by asking: 'Tell me, John; how old are you?'

'Seventeen or thereabouts, I reckon,' came the reply. So he

36

was the same age as Ali: but fair and girlish; slow of speech and, as it seemed, understanding. Yet when he raised his downcast eyes, a lurking gleam of intelligence caused Sir Thomas to wonder and be on his guard against deception.

'Your mistress sent for you on Thursday evening and ordered you to go and find your master, did she not? Tell me what time that was and what happened during your search.'

John scratched his head for inspiration and then began his account of the night's adventures. He spoke hesitantly but carefully, as though ensuring that he would make no mistakes. But was he recalling from memory what actually occurred or what he had invented—or been instructed to say?

It had been between eight and nine o'clock when he set out towards Charringworth, he said. On the road he met a neighbour named William Reed returning to Campden from a day's work in the fields. He informed Reed of his errand and asked him whether he had seen his master. Reed said no, and since it was growing dark and he was frightened of going on alone on foot John decided to turn back in the man's company and fetch his young master's horse. On the way they met John Pearce, another neighbour. The three of them parted at his master's gate.

Here John fell silent, frowning with concentration, and the magistrate had to prompt him to continue. 'So you took the horse? What then?'

John shook his head. No; he did not take the horse. Instead he crept into a hen-roost and lay there—awake, not sleeping—until the church clock struck twelve. Then he rose and set off again on foot.

At this Sir Thomas banged the table and cried out a warning that deceit in a matter of such gravity could lead to his being hanged. 'What you say is not to be believed,' he thundered. 'Would you gull me with a cock-and-bull story? Do you take me, of all men, for a fool?'

The boy was trembling but not cowed. There was a determined look about him which Sir Thomas could not interpret. 'Do you desire me to lock you up until you can resume your evidence on oath?' he continued. 'Lying to me then will incur the penalty for perjury.'

'Be pleased to believe me, sir,' the boy implored.

'How can you expect me to believe that you neither went on your errand nor returned to the house, but hid yourself in a hen-roost?'

'It was sheltered and I waited there, praying for my master's return. Had I gone to the house, my mistress and the young master would have turned me out again.'

'What of the horse? Did you not say at first that you went back for it and then that you set off again on foot?'

'The stable door was locked and I dared not disturb Master Edward. That one hates me.' For the first time he stared the magistrate full in the face, and Sir Thomas could see that the hatred was returned in full measure.

'Yet you have asserted that you were too frightened to walk along the road at nine o'clock,' he sighed in exasperation. 'Now you would have me believe that you were not too frightened to make the same journey at midnight.'

John had an answer for that too: 'At midnight the moon was up. But I walked into a great mist and lost my way. So the rest of the night I spent under a hedge and did not reach Charring-worth until daybreak.'

In that village, he continued, he spoke with one Edward Plaisterer, a tenant farmer, who told him that his master had been with him the afternoon before and left with twenty-three pounds received from him, for which he held a receipt. William Curtis, another farmer, told him how he had heard that her ladyship's steward was at his house the day before but, being out of doors, he had not seen him. On the way back from Charringworth, at about seven o'clock in the morning, John had met Master Edward, and they had gone together to make inquiries in two other villages.

'Their names?' Sir Thomas demanded.

'Ebrington was the first, and there we got more news of him. Master Daniel told us that my master had called at his house the evening before on his way home from Charringworth. He could not recall the time, except that it was not yet dark. But at Paxton no one had seen hide nor hair of him.'

'So your master disappeared without warning on the evening of the day before yesterday, somewhere between Ebrington and Campden—a matter of rather less than two miles. Master Edward has informed me that there is evidence of foul play. Was it you who discovered this, John, or were you too busily engaged in exploring hen-roosts and hedges? And now that I come to reflect on it: before you set off from the hen-roost at midnight, did you not first try to go into the house?'

John shook his head and Sir Thomas pointed an accusing finger across the table at him. 'How then,' he demanded triumphantly, 'how then did you happen to know that your master had not returned home during the time when you were hiding outside? Answer me that if you can.'

The magistrate sat back in his chair with a grim smile of self-satisfaction. At last he had tripped up the young story-teller! These country folk who chose to appear dull-witted were often concealing a native cunning, but never (he flattered himself) cleverly enough to deceive the superior knowledge and reasoning powers of himself, who had been born and bred amongst them. Yet, strangely, young John Perry seemed unmoved and gave his answer without betraying the smallest sign of guilt.

'I saw the light in my master's chamber window and knew that he must still be out.'

'Come, come; that will hardly do. If the light was on, he was more likely to be within.'

'No, sir. He never worked in his chamber at that late hour. But whenever he were out and about, a lantern was lit in the window to guide him home. It was the custom in the great house before it was burned down; or so I have heard said.'

Sir Thomas remembered with a pang of disappointment. One of the features of Campden House had been a central domed cupola rising above the roof, and every night a lantern had shone from it as a beacon for travellers.

'If you do not trust my word, you may ask the mistress,' said John, wooden-faced in victory.

'That will be done, never fear,' snapped the magistrate angrily. 'Your evidence will have to be confirmed by other witnesses in every particular, and Heaven help you, Master Perry, if you are playing tricks with me. Now pray proceed.'

After another scratch of the head John took up his story again. A poor woman gleaning in the fields had accosted Master Edward and himself as they were making their way back from the fruitless journey to Paxton. She showed them a hat, comb and collar band and pointed to the place beside the highway between Ebrington and Chipping Campden where she had picked them up. The hat and comb had been hacked and cut, and the band was stained with blood. He had recognised them as his master's and hastened home with Master Edward to bring the news and raise the alarm. Men, women and even children from the town had hurried to the highway and joined in a hunt for the body. Every ditch, hedge and field was explored, and only after several hours was the search abandoned.

John Perry had reached the end of his evidence. The magistrate, who had been taking cursory notes, put pen and ink aside and addressed him severely.

'Is that the totality of what you have to tell me about this affair?' he asked. 'Do you swear to me in the name of whatever God you believe in that you have no knowledge of your master's whereabouts if he is alive, nor any of the whereabouts of his body if he is dead? You must be aware, John, that you will remain under grave suspicion until this mystery is resolved. If you are innocent of any misdoing, it is in your own interest to reveal all that you know, or have good reason to suspect. You have answered all my questions, but not, methinks, entirely truthfully. You must understand that I require from you not part of the truth but the whole of it. If you are holding back anything of which I should be made aware, you may live to regret it.'

Sir Thomas did not expect this adjuration to produce any further revelations, but suddenly, for the first time during the

40

interrogation, the suspect's face became animated, his voice eager to convince. Tears ran down his cheeks.

'I love my master, Sir Thomas,' he sobbed, sinking to his knees. 'I will swear that to you a hundred times. I owe everything to him and would die a thousand deaths before harming a single hair in his head. He is a second father to me. I am a second son to him. I have no father of my own and I love him more than I love my own mother.'

The outburst ended as abruptly as it had begun. Well, thought Sir Thomas, at least this time the words have come from the heart, not the memory. He now found himself confronted with an expression which was frank and open, pleading—begging— to be believed. Was young John, after all, a loyal and faithful servant?

Sir Thomas's own heart began to melt towards this fair, forlorn youth with those pink, wet cheeks. But then he reminded himself that the witness had sworn to something quite different from what had been asked of him. In the course of his passionate declaration of devotion, John Perry had not taken the opportunity to swear that he had no knowledge of what had become of his beloved master.

5

Two days later Sir Thomas rode under the stone arch which formed a grand entrance from the highway to the grounds of Campden House. On either side, incorporated in the supporters of the arch, were ingeniously designed lodges with decorative chimneys and finials crowning stone roofs.

All this had been erected as a fitting gateway to the finest mansion in the county, but now it was an empty promise. What lay beyond were jutting fragments and monstrous piles of fallen stone. Grouped around, like orphaned children, were the almonry; two pavilions at either end of a long terrace; a dovecote near the road; and, at a distance, the former stables, coach houses and brewhouse. Save for the almonry, all were deserted.

Sir Thomas was enjoying his own company, unattended. Ali had had the impertinence to differ from him about John Perry's evidence and been left at home as a punishment.

Reining his horse, the magistrate looked about him at the overgrown gardens once so trim and tended; at the crumbling ashlar walls and the ornamental ponds choked with weeds; at the grassy hillocks of abandoned earthworks. Ichabod! he sighed, for the glory he remembered from his boyhood had indeed departed. Yet the scene of desolation inspired him. He felt poetry coming on. What a setting for his account of this mystery, whose solution might bring him the renown and acclaim he had long craved! The first verse of a ballad to celebrate the event was already taking shape in his head:

> In Gloucestershire, as many know full well,
> At Campden Town a Gentleman did dwell,
> One Master William Harrison by name,
> A Steward to a Lady of great fame.

Humming to himself, he approached the almonry and dismounted. There Mistress Harrison greeted him with a veneer of respect which her manner made plain she did not feel. They eyed each other in hostility. Her lips were habitually pursed, and never more so than today. He knew her for a sharp-tongued harridan and unbending bigot. She knew him for an anti-Christ who would assuredly burn in Hell, and—so the look behind her words conveyed—the sooner the better.

'Where is Edward?' he demanded after returning her greeting with all the civility he could muster. 'I would speak with him too.'

'He is about his father's business,' she replied. 'Where else would he be? Whatever afflictions the good Lord has sent to try us, her ladyship's affairs are not to be neglected.'

He bit his tongue and restrained himself from inquiring how a Lord who sent afflictions could be described as good, and for what reason He needed to try us. It was the kind of disputation on which he thrived, but arguing with this narrow-minded ignoramus was beneath him. Instead he took the opportunity to pose his first question: 'If anything serious has happened to your husband, I presume that your son will expect to succeed to the stewardship.'

She glared at him as though he were trying to establish a motive for murder—as indeed he was. 'If!' she sneered. 'If! I have sent word to her ladyship that my husband has been brutally done to death in the performance of his duties. Long service to one family by another deserves recognition, and I have requested that she appoint Edward in his place. Otherwise we shall starve.'

It was on the tip of his tongue to suggest that the good Lord would provide, but this was no time for mockery. He too believed that this virago was now a widow, even if a not unduly sorrowful one. Already she was dressed in black, he noticed. Decency demanded that sympathy be expressed. 'If Master Harrison is dead, you have my heart-felt condolences,' he said. 'But let us hope that you are mistaken.'

'I assure you, Sir Thomas, that I am rarely mistaken.'

'Whom then do you suspect of killing him?' he asked, well knowing the answer.

'I *suspect* no one. I *know* the murderer. I accuse John Perry.' Her eyes were smouldering with unChristian hatred, defying him to deny it.

'His story is certainly a strange one,' Sir Thomas acknowledged. 'But yesterday I examined the men he claims to have encountered during his search—Reed, Pearce, Plaisterer and Curtis; also the old woman who found the articles belonging to your husband. They all confirmed the truth of what he says. I have inspected the place where the articles were left lying on the ground, but could detect no trace of blood.'

'Then see their condition for yourself. Do you suppose my husband treated them thus himself and discarded them to deceive us? What surer evidence can there be?' She took from a cupboard and handed to him, first, a dirty white collar band with dark stains on it, then a comb disfigured with knife marks and lastly, with a final fierce flourish, a hat which had been savagely slashed. He gazed at the grisly objects in dismay.

'Are you prepared to swear on oath to these being Master Harrison's and in his possession when you last saw him?'

She nodded brusquely.

'Then we may assume that this collar was round Master Harrison's neck, this hat on his head, at the relevant time,' he said, pocketing them and the comb. 'They constitute strong evidence, but against whom? By themselves they are not sufficient to convict John Perry. If only they had tongues and could speak! Then it would be a very different matter.'

'What more does the law require?' She turned sullen and curled her lip.

'Before young Perry or any other person can be charged, the

44

body has to be found. There can be no murder without a corpse. You must understand that only when your husband's body has been discovered is the law enabled to take its course; and even then a confession may be necessary to secure a conviction. There is also the question of a motive. Without that a confession may be deemed false. Perhaps it will surprise you to learn, Mistress Harrison, that false confessions to murder are by no means uncommon. Some wretches are driven by an unnatural compulsion to seek notoriety whatever the penalty.'

'A motive! That should present you with no difficulty, Sir Thomas. Have you not been informed that my husband was carrying rent money collected from a tenant?'

'Robbery is the most likely motive,' he conceded. 'That is already well established. But is it not an argument for John's innocence rather than his guilt? Do you in all honesty believe that he would kill his master, whom he has sworn to me that he loved dearly, for the sake of twenty-three pounds?'

Again she nodded, this time with vigour. All Mistress Harrison's beliefs were unwavering. 'To him that sum would be a fortune,' she said. 'And he has robbed his master before.'

'That was never proved,' he countered. He had investigated the crime himself and remembered it well.

One market day the previous year the Harrison family had returned from church to find their house broken open. A ladder had been placed against the window of the upper room where the steward kept the estate's accounts and money. An iron bar protecting the window had been bent with a ploughshare, and one hundred and forty pounds of the Lady Juliana's rents were missing.

'How could the thief have known where to find the money and the ladder and the ploughshare without John's help?' she demanded. 'How else could he have known that the house would be empty at that time, so that he could climb inside and steal with impunity in broad daylight?'

This tirade silenced the magistrate for a moment while he considered how far to take issue with her. Under the Puritan regime the unwilling Vicar of Chipping Campden (a disciple of the late Archbishop Laud) had been forced, under threat of eviction, to deliver an approved sermon between eleven o'clock and twelve noon on every market day. Since attendance by the parishioners was compulsory, it was widely known that many of the houses in the parish would be unoccupied during those sixty minutes, most particularly the ones belonging to prominent citizens.

'It is general knowledge that money is kept in this house,' he answered. 'And, if I recollect aright, John was with you in church at the very time.' As a strict Presbyterian, Mistress Harrison insisted on every member of her household accompanying her to divine service.

'That does not prove him innocent,' she retorted. 'That boy makes a pretence of feeble-mindedness, but he would never be so foolish as to commit the crime himself. No, no; he would have arranged for an accomplice to choose just such a time when all the parish could testify that he was somewhere else. That is what I told you then, and I tell you so again now. You would not believe me, and this is the result.'

Sir Thomas choked back his rage at the suggestion that he was the person responsible for the steward's death. He was confident that he had been right in attributing the earlier robbery to one or other of the bands of marauding vagrants who plagued the district, and no local man would have associated with them.

'I gave you the names of the guilty parties,' she continued in a scold's voice: 'his good-for-nothing brother Richard, led on by that mother of theirs, who is in league with Satan. They were not in church. No doubt the Devil forbids them to enter consecrated ground.'

'That is as may be,' Sir Thomas replied in exasperation. 'But you made the accusation not only without proof but without a sliver of evidence. You must be aware that there are dangerous outlaws at large in this county who may be responsible both for last year's theft and for your husband's murder. The two crimes may not be unconnected. Now I must bid you good-day.'

He left in a state of high dudgeon at her wild accusations and unseemly behaviour towards a gentleman and Justice of the Peace. Mistress Harrison was a professing Christian who breathed malice and bile and was no respecter of persons. Never had he encountered a woman so wrong-headed and argumentative. Had he himself suffered the misfortune of being her husband, he could very well have decided to fabricate his own death and vanish. Might that be what the wretched steward had been driven to after years of domestic misery? And if it were, might he not even have stolen the two sums of money to keep himself comfortable in his new life? Riled enough already, it riled Sir Thomas even more to think that Ali might have been right in arguing that the steward was still alive.

As he rode slowly round the empty shell of the dead mansion, peering among the fallen masonry, he brooded on the family which should have been living there and on the excessive powers and responsibilities which had devolved on Master Harrison in their absence. Matters would have turned out very differently had Baptist Hicks, first Viscount Campden, been succeeded by a son. The house would have been rebuilt, brought back to life in all its glory, and become once again a meeting place of nobility and gentry. Instead, the title had passed to his daughter's husband, Baron Noel of Ridlington, who possessed a seat and estates of his own in a distant county.

When the war ended in defeat, their son, the third Viscount Campden, took himself into exile in the Levant, where his grandfather had established trading connections among the silk merchants. Sir Thomas had met him during his travels and found him living in reckless extravagance despite the family's losses resulting from the war. Even now, with the king restored, he had not yet returned home, and management of all the family's affairs still rested with his mother, the Lady Juliana, now a Dowager Viscountess in her dotage.

Sir Thomas wondered whether he himself should write to her about this extraordinary affair and advise her to delay the appointment of Edward Harrison as her new steward until the mystery surrounding his father's disappearance was resolved. Yet it seemed that she had grown too old to care about goings-on in Campden so long as her rents were forthcoming.

He reined his horse outside what had once been the mansion's principal frontage, which looked down on a stream below and parkland beyond. Were the sallow-faced Edward and his sour-faced mother to be trusted? Even as he pondered the question, he caught sight of the man himself, emerging from a gaping opening in the ruin and walking away without noticing that he was under observation. His head was bent in deep thought.

What could the fellow be finding to occupy himself among the labyrinth of roofless walls? Were the cellars still in use for storage? Resuming his ride along the broken-down terrace, Sir Thomas remembered an underground passage which must still be there, running directly under his horse's hoofs. It connected the two pavilions with each other and the house. Perhaps Edward had been exploring beneath the ground for his father's body. Or perhaps . . .

Instead of calling to him, the magistrate rode on and out of the grounds. He and Ali were agreed on one thing: that John Perry had had no hand in the killing of William Harrison. But further thought was needed before he was ready to interrogate another suspect.

6

It was a relief to reach the highway and turn towards the bustle of the town, leaving the desolation of the mansion and its grounds behind him. There was an air of eeriness about the place, and Sir Thomas was beginning to suspect that the supposedly upright steward had been leading another, less reputable life behind those high surrounding walls.

His next call was at The Eight Bells, where he had ordered John Perry to be kept in custody. There the landlord hastened to help him dismount and usher him into a private parlour where they could confer alone.

'Take the lad away, Sir Thomas,' Robert Hayward begged. 'I was once a friend to his father and would do all I can to help him, but since his mother came to visit he has been talking so strangely that his good name has gone. Many are reluctant to come near him. We are losing custom and my wife fears his staying will bring ruin on the house. This is no fit place for a suspected murderer. I can no longer answer to you for him.'

'Pish!' responded the magistrate irritably. 'If I had believed him to be guilty of murder, I would have sent him to the lock-up. There is not enough evidence against him to hang a dog.' He had come to feel a bond of sympathy with young John Perry, and it was in his contrary nature that the louder others raised cries of 'murderer' or 'thief' against a man the more inclined he became to presume his innocence.

'He should be in the hands of the constable,' the landlord insisted.

'Why then? Has he confessed?'

'No; but I warrant you he has not revealed all he knows. Every day he had a different tale to spin. Yesterday he swore it was a wandering tinker that killed his master. Today the culprit is a gentleman's servant from the neighbourhood, but he will not say whose. When asked, he rolls his eyes and puts a finger to his lips.'

'What of the body? Has he spoken of that?'

'When I pressed him to disclose where it lay, he said at first that it would never be found and then whispered in my ear that it had been dragged from the road and hidden in a bean-rick in the field next to the Conygree.'

'Then the rick must be searched at once.'

Sir Thomas was impatient for action, but Robert held up a hand to stay him. 'That has been done,' he said. 'I told the constable and four of us were out at first light this morning. We pulled it to pieces.'

'And found nothing?'

'Nothing but rats and field mice. I came home in a fury, I can tell you, sir, and upbraided him for lying and playing games with us. I asked him whether he had a mind to be hanged, and how did the ninny answer that? He smiled as though it were a joke and told me the Devil must have carried the corpse away. So I demanded of him: "If that be the truth, who called up the Devil, pray?" "Whom do you suppose?" he answered me. That was when my wife threatened to leave the house if he were not taken away. Like others in this town, she lives in terrible fear of his mother.'

Sir Thomas uttered another pish. He sneered at Widow Perry's reputation as a witch and the dread it excited. As a man of reason, he believed in the existence of the Devil no more than he believed in the existence of God.

'Your Honour may scoff, but every man and woman in this town takes it for gospel truth that Master Harrison has been made away with by young John with the aid of his mother's witchcraft. It is being said that she had an image of him stuck with pins and then conjured up the Devil by sorcery during a Black Fast to take the dead body over land and drop it in the

50

sea, so that it will never be seen again.' The innkeeper took the precaution of crossing himself as he spoke.

Sir Thomas gave another sniff of contempt at the credulity of the townsfolk. 'If that were the case,' he said, 'a crime could never be proved and no one could be charged with murder. It would be my duty to release John forthwith.'

'If the law will not act, there are others as will.'

'Then I shall do as you ask—for his own safety. I shall have him handed over to the constable to await a formal interrogation while my investigations proceed. You may assure your wife that he will be gone from this house before sundown.'

Sir Thomas took his leave and walked across the road to Widow Perry's cottage. Belief in the occult was rife throughout the land, and he was curious to make the acquaintance of a practitioner. From his studies he knew it for a relic of pagan rites with which the population had been duped before Augustine arrived from Rome with a rival brand of nonsense. It annoyed him that a mere superstition such as witchcraft was treated seriously by the law. It was absurd that the practice of magic was a criminal offence. In Christian countries it was deemed a felony, punishable by imprisonment and confiscation of property—even, in extreme cases, by hanging. Innocent hags were brought to the gallows by the malice of neighbours.

He rapped on the door and entered without ceremony. The female within greeted him as though he were expected. She inclined her head respectfully but did not rise from her seat at a table where she was engaged in eating from a dish of vegetables. The light was dim, but he could see that she was neatly clad and the room well furnished. In looks she was dark but not ill-favoured and might once have been a beauty. She beckoned to him to sit beside her and share her meal. Her smile, as she did so, reminded him of the Great Sphinx at Giza.

So this was the infamous witch of Chipping Campden! Sir Thomas eyed her in an unconcealed appraisal and she returned his stare with an expression of amusement. The reception accorded him here was more congenial than the one he had experienced at the hands of the missing man's prim and vinegary consort. He accepted the proffered stool but declined the feast of boiled swedes and water—taking good note of it.

The power to contrive the death of another so secretly that no trace of the murder could ever be discovered was the most potent of all the black arts ascribed to witches. This, he had read, was achieved through the concentration of the witch's will-power on the victim or his image during a period of fasting. That was the Black Fast to which the landlord had alluded— and during it the witch took no meat or milk.

'I drink water and eat vegetables because a poor woman without a husband cannot afford milk or meat.' She had read his thoughts and was laughing at them.

'You have sons to support you,' he replied.

'One son,' she corrected him. 'The other is lost to me.'

'If you refer to John, I am told that he has always been thought a fine lad and one of which any mother ought to be proud. Unlike your Richard.'

'John has his charm,' she conceded, 'and boyish charms are pleasing to Your Honour, I can tell. But you are deceived. Richard is the one who has stayed at home and been good to me, not John. The two of them have never been alike. From birth and before.' She broke off, deliberately tantalising him with a riddle.

How sharp she was! Sir Thomas urged her on, but she would say no more, content to have fired his curiosity. 'Beware of trifling with me,' he said, but his tone was mild. He was enjoying the tussle of wits.

'I know you have come to ask about Master Harrison and what has become of him,' she said, 'but do not waste your breath. John is not guilty, and I am as ignorant as yourself.'

'Yet you and John are being accused, Mistress Perry,' he answered. 'Do you deny the charge? Tell me, I pray you, whether you left home that night and, if so, for what purpose. Take care to speak truthfully or it will be the worse for you.'

She stood for the first time and he could see that she was tall for a woman—and strong too, he judged.

'I confess to travelling abroad in the hours of darkness,' she told him. 'When the moon is full I ride out on my broomstick to sacrifice cocks at crossroads. You may also have heard that I can kill a man without so much as stirring from my hearth.' This time she laughed outright.

'Mistress Perry,' he addressed her solemnly, 'you have enemies enough without incriminating yourself by such utterances to a magistrate, however lightly spoken. A woman with your reputation may jest herself into a hangman's noose. Now tell me without prevarication whether you left this house at any time during the night when Master Harrison disappeared.'

'I did not,' she assured him with a look which he could not fathom. Did it mean that he was not asking the right question and she would impart her secrets when he hit upon it?

'Then tell me about John, the child of your womb, who you say is no longer a son to you. If he is innocent, why should common report judge him guilty of such a heinous crime?'

John's had been a difficult birth, she told him. The boy's unnatural entry into the world arse first had nearly killed her. As an infant he had been a skinny, puling creature, and she had never had the fondness for him which she felt for his elder brother. Yet she had done her best for him and he had repaid her with ingratitude and even hatred. He had left home as soon as he was old enough to work, and had clung to Master Harrison like ivy to a wall.

Sir Thomas expressed his amazement that, if that were the case, anyone should suppose that John would kill the master to whom he was so attached. The response was another of her sly smiles, followed by a mutter that perhaps His Honour could imagine what strong passions might be roused if an older man and a younger who stood so close should happen to fall out.

He demanded what evidence there was of a quarrel between them, thrusting to the back of his mind the very idea that she had knowledge of the quarrel between himself and Ali. She shrugged: none had reached her, but others might have heard of one. Which others, she could not or would not say. Nor would she admit to any hatred of her own towards the man who had taken her son from her.

What was it she was hiding from him, he wondered, vexed with himself at being outwitted. Something discreditable, he guessed. He knew that the steward allowed the Perrys to live in this cottage on the manorial estate rent-free. It must be gratitude or being beholden to him that was tying her tongue.

'Master Harrison and the late Master Perry were friendly, were they not?' he hazarded.

Dragging information out of her was as hard work as getting his coach up the hill at Bourton, but he flattered himself that he would succeed by importunity. No, she told him: they were well acquainted but not on friendly terms. The lord of the manor's steward was too high and mighty a dignitary for friendship with a lowly servant and tenant. They had last come together when Campden House was garrisoned. Master Harrison had been under orders from Viscount Campden to play host to the occupying force and provide for its needs whilst safeguarding the property—and a fine job he had made of that!

Her husband (she said) had been one of the local recruits assigned to assist him before the garrison left. He had been wounded at the storming of Evesham and died a hero's death at Naseby. The news had been brought to her by Constable Fettiplace and Master Hayward of The Eight Bells, who had served with him. The rent for the cottage had been remitted by the Lady Juliana herself as compensation for the sacrifice of his life in the king's service. It was not, she insisted, an act of kindness on the part of the steward.

She had seated herself close to him while speaking. Now, when he was on the point of inquiring about her other son, who worked as a thatcher but was rumoured to earn a better living from petty larceny, she produced a pack of tarot cards and signified a wish to tell his fortune. Thinking it best to humour her, he was about to consent when he became aware of two yellow eyes peering at him from a dark corner. They belonged to a grey cat, which mewed.

'Susannah is my familiar,' Mistress Perry told him gravely.

Once again he could only guess whether she was speaking what she believed to be the truth or merely teasing him. The room was airless; the atmosphere oppressive. He felt himself slipping into the thrall of this creature with her sharp mind and strange humour. He rose abruptly and made for the door, pursued by a cackling recital of a catalogue of her powers.

'Magistrates would do well to beware witches,' she called after him. 'Has Your Honour not heard that I can estrange lovers and make men impotent? That I can cause droughts and famine, fires and flood? That I can sink ships at sea and turn men and women into beasts? Interrogate the sheep, Sir Thomas. Perchance Master Harrison is amongst them, grazing happily in the fields.'

7

Outside, the sun was low over the hill which rose steeply behind the town. It made him anxious to reach home before nightfall, and he was making haste from the cottage when some instinct prompted him to look back over his shoulder.

The widow stood in her doorway with arms akimbo and nostrils flared. She was breathing heavily and gazing, not at but through him. Still smarting from his humiliation, he halted at the opportunity to recover.

'Is there more you have to tell me, pertinent to my inquiry, Mistress Perry?' he asked, but she paid no heed. It was as though she had neither seen nor heard him.

He was about to repeat the question when she slowly shook her head, appearing to waken unwillingly from a trance. 'I have been listening to the voices in the air,' she said.

'Do they tell you what befell Master Harrison and in what place or body he is to be found?'

She frowned at his sarcasm. 'My voices speak only of what is to come,' she told him. 'Today their meaning is lost in a babble of tongues. They are frantic. What I smell in the air is danger.'

He stood disturbed, his footsteps and scepticism both wavering. He wished he had not stopped, yet felt compelled to pursue his questioning. 'Danger to whom?' he asked despite himself.

'To Your Honour today and myself thereafter. From whom, I cannot say, and to know would be in vain. None of us has been granted the power to change our destinies; only to be forewarned. The spirits of the air have departed now, but there is no escaping the doom in the message they have brought.' In an instant she too had departed and the door was closed behind her.

A sorceress? A visionary? A mischievous charlatan amusing herself at his expense? Or merely a poor thing touched with insanity? Sir Thomas's mind was awhirl with uncertainty. He was no longer surprised that the townsfolk lived in fear of her. Nor that she foretold danger to herself if she was in the habit of flouting the law by making such predictions. The forecast about himself could well be deemed a threat to a Justice of the Peace whilst in the execution of his duty. If, as she asserted, there was no means of averting the impending peril, it could scarcely be interpreted as a friendly warning.

He returned to the inn to reclaim his horse and rode to the market square, where he found Constable Fettiplace on duty outside the court-house. Barrel-chested and taciturn, the constable was a reassuring representative of the law. Save for his military service, he had spent all his life in the town. He knew every man, woman and child by name—and many of their secrets, which (for the most part) he kept to himself.

Sir Thomas gave him instructions for John Perry to be taken into custody on suspicion of robbery and murder. Then, with urgency and regretting that he had deprived himself of Ali's company, he took the road southwards towards the Bourtons— on the Hill and on the Water. The journey was no more than six miles, but already darkness was gathering.

There was much to occupy his mind as he rode at a steady trot and the sun sank from the sky. So deeply were his thoughts concentrated on the events of the day that his guard was down and he was taken unawares when an attack came out of the dusk on a secluded stretch of byway bordering Northwick Park.

Two men sprang from behind the hedgerow and belaboured his horse with staves until it pulled up. One seized the reins while the other dragged the rider from the saddle. He fell bruised to the ground and his sword was snatched from him before he could rise and draw it. When he scrambled to his feet dazed, a cocked pistol was pressed against his temple and a muffled voice threatened that he would be a dead man if he attempted to escape or uttered a cry for help.

The footpads wore rough white surcoats which gave them a ghostly appearance. The lower half of their faces was covered with scarves and the brims of their hats were pulled down over their foreheads so that he could see nothing of them but eyes and noses. As they bundled him through the hedge and into the depths of a dense thicket, he cursed himself for venturing abroad alone and musing so imprudently when he should have stayed alert.

They pulled off his boots and tied him hand and foot to a tree. They gloated over the silver hilt of his sword and the gold coins which tumbled from his purse. Greedily they tore precious rings from his fingers. One had an emerald set in a circle of diamonds. The other, which he begged them to spare him, was an heirloom inherited from his famous uncle: a large oval onyx incised with the family arms. Ignoring his pleas, they also pocketed a pair of silver buckles set with rubies which had been a gift from his wife.

When they had done rifling his person and searching his saddle for hidden gold, his assailants warned him again—with oaths and obscenities—not to cry out because some of their companions would remain within earshot and one of them would assuredly return and cut his throat. His hope that they would at least leave him his horse proved vain. Soon after they had vanished in the direction of the road with their booty, he heard the familiar sound of its hoofs as it was ridden away.

In the silence that followed, his first feeling was one of indignation at the treatment to which he had been subjected. A proud man bruised in spirit as well as body and pocket, he was thankful only that no one else had witnessed the indignity. Then, as he dwelt on his fate, despair overcame him and he was not ashamed to weep. It seemed unlikely that the men had companions nearby who had not joined in the attack, but he did not dare take the risk; and even if he did call out, who else

58

would there be to hear him? What traveller would be so foolhardy as to venture on that road in the pitch darkness which had now fallen like the drop of a curtain?

He was seated on the bare earth, concealed in scrub and woodland, on the opposite side of the byway from the park, out of sight or sound of human habitation. His arms and legs were stretched in front of him straddling the trunk of a sturdy oak. They were secured by rope round his wrists and ankles. Midges and owls were his only company. And he an Overbury!

He jerked his arms desperately from side to side in an attempt to fray the rope against the bark of the tree, but the effort had no effect except to chafe his wrists beyond endurance. Consoling himself that if the villains had intended him to die they would have shot or stabbed or beaten him to death, he devised a different plan. The bonds were not tightly drawn and by tugging at them repeatedly he made sufficient play to enable his hands to slide down towards his feet, where his fingers could work on the knots at his ankles. The darkness was too impenetrable and the tree trunk too thick for him to see or guide what he was doing, but after much fumbling for an hour or two his feet were free.

Once the circulation of the blood was restored, he found himself able to stand. The relief to his back, and to his spirits, was immense. It encouraged him to renew the assault on the cords tying his wrists. Gritting his teeth against the pain, he see-sawed until they had worked loose enough for his fingers to get to work again.

He had to rest several times before, at long last, first one knot became unravelled and then a second, and the rope dropped to the ground. Staggering backwards, clutching his bleeding wrists to his chest and aching in all his tortured limbs, he collapsed like a felled log. Others would have thanked their Maker for a merciful release, but Sir Thomas lay stretched on a patch of grass blessing no one but himself.

All his strength and resolution had ebbed and were exhausted. He lay there prone throughout what seemed an endless night, reluctant to undertake the almost impossible struggle to move at all, let alone set about tracing a path back to the road without benefit of daylight.

Birdsong roused him at the first glimmer of dawn. He rose to his feet at the third attempt, stiff and dizzy, moaning and groaning, bitten during the night by innumerable insects. Lurching like a drunkard, he tripped and stumbled through the tangle of the undergrowth, taking several wrong directions before chancing on the road.

Despite the pain, he chose to scramble home on his stockinged feet without stopping in the village of Blockley to make public his plight and raise a hue and cry. The door was opened to him by his wife, who received him as though he had returned from the dead. Every servant had been dispatched to scour the countryside for news of him.

Before taking to his bed he wrote a description of his horse and the stolen jewellery and told her to get copies printed and distributed, even though entertaining little hope of their recovery. He wished for the thieves to be apprehended and hanged, but to have escaped with his life was comfort enough.

He slept the clock round undisturbed by bad dreams. When he awoke, every detail of his day of inquiries in Campden and the violence with which it ended ran through his mind, clear as the spring water which fed the Evenlode from his park. Analysis was the next step. The injuries he had suffered might confine him to bed, but his intellect was unimpaired.

Were the inquiries and the robbery connected? That was the first question, and others quickly followed. Had the men been watching for him? Forewarned by whom? Or was he the victim of an ambush by chance? Could this be what had happened to William Harrison? Had the steward been attacked in similar fashion and not succeeded in freeing himself? Might a wider search discover his body bound to a tree? But perhaps whoever instigated yesterday's attack intended him to draw that conclusion and be misled about the missing man's fate. Most puzzling of all was what part in the affair had been played by Widow Perry, who had predicted danger to him that very day.

Did she possess a genuine gift of clairvoyance or had she guilty foreknowledge of what awaited him?

His library contained several volumes on the history and practice of the black arts. He had Ali bring them to him and lay in bed reading intently of supernatural occurrences and the punishments inflicted on the wizards and witches and soothsayers held responsible. Moses had ordered them to be put to death. So had Alfred the Great. Saul had exiled them. The Emperor Augustus had forbidden his subjects to consult them. Yet everywhere down the ages they had survived persecution. Belief in their powers was too strong.

The example of Saul was the most revealing. If the Bible was to be believed, after banishing all witches from the land of Israel he had consulted one himself and learned the truth about the future from her.

Although the king went in disguise, the witch at Endor recognised him. At his request she conjured up the spirit of the prophet Samuel. He told the spirit that a host of armed Philistines was threatening to make war on Israel; that he had sought guidance from God; and that 'the Lord answered him not'. Samuel's reply, through the mouth of the witch, had been that on the morrow God would deliver the Israelites into the hands of the Philistines and that Saul himself and his three sons would be killed. And so it came to pass.

So the holy scriptures themselves confirmed the authenticity of black magic and clairvoyance! Sir Thomas was delighted and quite forgot his midge bites, torn wrists and swollen ankles while he savoured this happy conjunction of superstitions. Tossing the Bible aside, he returned eagerly to *A True Account of the Devilish Practices of Necromancy and Other Magical Arts*.

On the rise of Christianity, he read, magical rites became associated with paganism and worship of the Devil. Sabbats, the great quarterly meetings of covens, were held on the old pagan feast days of Candlemas, May Day, Lammas and Hallowtide, presided over by a Grand Master.

At initiation ceremonies converts renounced the Christian faith, swore obedience to the Devil, were baptised with new

61

names and received the pricks which were his mark. The dancing which followed was a prelude to sexual orgies, when the women had intercourse with the Devil's representative, a masked Man in Black known as The Chief, who wore horns and an animal's skin. The Chief's lieutenant, the leading woman, was called The Maiden—a far from accurate description, it seemed.

Esbats, the regular weekly coven meetings, at which celebrants signified their submission by kissing the Devil's arse, were held at night by candlelight. When there were enemies to be punished, they were ceremonially cursed, limb by limb, from the crown of their heads to the soles of their feet. The candles were then extinguished, as the victim would be.

Ideas tumbled through Sir Thomas's head as he turned the pages. His mind focused on The Maiden. That must be Widow Perry's role in the coven which was rumoured to meet on Kingcombe Plain, the high ground between Chipping Campden and his own estate at Weston sub Edge, which lay under its other lip. Was William Harrison the coven's victim, snuffed out like a candle at the command of a mysterious Man in Black? Or—the thought struck him like a blow on the head—might Master Harrison himself be the Man in Black, suddenly and secretly summoned to the presence of the Grand Master of all covens?

8

Two prominent members of the community assaulted within days! The gravity of the situation called for a conference of the great in the land, and it assembled a few days later in Sir Thomas's chamber where he was still confined to bed. The visitors, as they made plain, had responded to his appeal out of a sense of duty and self-interest, not from any tie of friendship. Their expressions of sympathy were formal.

A baronet of mature years, Sir John Keyte of Ebrington, was the senior in rank and age. Local magistrates were small fry to him. He had refused the appointment before it was offered to Sir Thomas. There were more important calls on his time in London, where he was a man of affairs. Now he was angry with himself for neglecting to ensure that the office went to one who was worthy of it. Keytes and Overburys had ruled here side by side for generations, but seldom in harmony; and this Overbury he could not but regard as the worst of a bad lot.

John Dover was of an age with Sir Thomas. He was a lawyer who had taken up arms for the king during the Great Rebellion and was now the Captain of Militia for the district. Married to the heiress to a modest estate at Barton on the Heath which adjoined manorial land belonging to the Overbury estates, he resented Sir Thomas both as an awkward neighbour and for the knighthood bestowed on one who had preserved his property and position in society despite skulking abroad when duty called. He thought it a sad sign of the times that the restored king's government should choose to buy the loyalty of deserters with honours whilst disregarding those who had risked their lives for his cause in battle.

Illness had prevented Master Bartholomew, the vicar of Chipping Campden, from attending the gathering. In his absence the Church was represented by the Reverend Giles Oldisworth, who held the living of St Lawrence, Bourton on the Hill. His compassion for unrepentant sinners did not extend to militant non-believers, and he had been driven to dispute his squire's godless dialectics in a pamphlet war. Sir Thomas, for his part, had made strenuous efforts to be rid of what he contemptuously referred to as 'that sanctimonious gadfly', but the patronage of the living was not his. That privilege belonged to the dean and chapter of Westminster, and those distant dignitaries were deaf to his demands that their incumbent be removed for disrespect to the lord of the manor.

This unctuous cleric was now begging his forgiveness for being the last to arrive. 'I grieve for your injuries and pray to the Lord that your recovery will be swift,' he assured Sir Thomas. 'Who would have imagined that riding from Campden to Bourton would be as dangerous as going down from Jerusalem to Jericho? And your dear lady, how is she? I trust that her ladyship is in good health despite her condition.'

In Sir Thomas's ears the parson's solicitude on the second count sounded the more sincere. Lady Overbury was given to piety, and the two of them were conspiring to guide him back to their notion of the true faith, as his suspicious nature had made him angrily aware.

'My wife keeps to her own quarters and craves your pardon for not greeting you in person, gentlemen,' he replied. 'She is six months gone and—I thank you kindly, Master Oldisworth— in as good spirits as I am informed can be expected.'

It had better be a boy this time, he thought fiercely. He had not married the creature for love; for she was not a beauty. Nor for her dowry; although a portion of her father's ill-gotten wealth was not to be despised. Certainly not for companionship; for she was an ignorant, empty-headed chit little more than half his age. Nor even for the sake of his reputation; for he rather relished the whisperings of the world about the unnatural life of a bachelor approaching forty. No; the single attraction of his Euphemia was the breadth of her hips. She came of good breeding stock and he was in desperate need of a son to inherit the family estates and prevent their passing to a cousin with whom he was at loggerheads and bent on frustrating.

The visitors welcomed the news of his wife's condition without meeting his eye. They all knew of the foreign habits he was reputed to have formed during his sojourn in Egypt and the Levant. Indeed he made no secret of his belief that in affairs of the heart between one human being and another gender was irrelevant. It pleased him to scandalise loyalists by citing the example of His Majesty's grandfather, King James, who flaunted male favourites yet fathered six children.

In his cups he would sometimes enthuse over the pale-skinned, barely ripe Circassian girls on offer in the brothels of Damascus. Yet the trophy he had brought home with him was Ali John, whose looks he described as irresistible when he purchased him in the slave market in Alexandria. Others among the gentry in England possessed curly-headed Jamaican blacka-moors, but Ali was unique. Bursting upon Gloucestershire like the vision of a sunburnt cherub, he had set tongues wagging the length and breadth of the county.

At that moment he was offering cups of posset and glasses of malmsey wine to his master's guests, kneeling to each in turn. His master sat cross-legged under the canopy of a tester with its silk curtains drawn back. Arrayed in an embroidered gown and cap and buttressed by a heap of gaudily-coloured pillows, he was playing the role of an oriental potentate holding court from his divan. His wounds were healing and he was beginning to enjoy the comforts of convalescence.

When the serving was done, he shocked the others by ordering Ali to remain in the room during their deliberations. Enduring the company of a servant they suspected of being his catamite would be a test of their Christian forbearance, he thought with glee. As soon as his cherub had settled himself on his haunches beside the door, he opened proceedings with a long account of what he had learned from the missing man's son and wife, his interrogation of John Perry, his visit to the boy's mother and the attack he had suffered.

After questions discussion turned on the two topics of immediate concern: the continuing search for William Harrison's body and the hunt for the men who had waylaid Sir Thomas.

Alerted by a message from the magistrate, Sir John had led a posse of horsemen who scoured the vicinity of Ebrington, Charringworth and Chipping Campden itself. They had travelled as far as Mickleton to the north, Paxton and Broad Campden to the south, and then west beyond Aston sub Edge, Weston sub Edge and Saintbury to the Worcestershire border. Every copse and hedgerow had been beaten; every villager and farmer encountered had been questioned. All without success.

Captain Dover, similarly alerted, also reported failure. His troop of militiamen had swept vainly along the Warwickshire border, then turned to pass through Moreton and on to Blockley and Broadway before returning home via Longborough and Stow.

The vicar described how he had called door to door at every house in his parish to make inquiries. He had spread the word that no one making even the shortest journey could feel safe from robbery or mortal injury until the perpetrators of these crimes were brought to justice, but he had stumbled on no clue to their whereabouts.

'The villains would have moved on,' growled the captain. 'They were allowed time enough to show us a clean pair of heels, and I warrant you they were quickly away. There will be richer pickings for them around Evesham or Stratford, and no hue and cry in that quarter.'

'I raised the alarm immediately I reached home,' protested Sir Thomas, rising to the charge of tardiness.

'It was two days before you enlisted our aid,' insisted the captain. 'The first news I had of the attack came from my groom. In incidents of this kind the promptest action is essential. Hot pursuit is the sole remedy if law and order are to be maintained.' He concluded with a hard stare at their host lolling on his pillows.

Sir John intervened. 'Your sentiments match my own, Captain Dover,' he said, 'but this is no time for falling out. It is the future we must consider, not the past. Maintenance of law and order is the duty of us all. Sir Thomas has begged for assistance and he shall have it from me with a whole heart.'

'If we are to act with due diligence, the lessons of the past cannot be ignored. Let Sir Thomas remain in bed nursing his wounds while you and I take this matter in hand.' Old grievances rankled, and the captain was not to be appeased.

His reference to Sir Thomas's wartime record was as pointed as Sir John's to his cry for help, and the vicar made haste to restore peace. 'Judgments are not for us to make,' he pronounced. 'That is the prerogative of God, without whose aid all human endeavours are in vain. I pray you, gentlemen—'

He spoke to mollify their host, who had shot upright in his bed and was preparing to deliver an impassioned response to the reflections on his competence and honour. But this mention of God was a provocation which could not be allowed to pass unchallenged.

'Pish and likewise tush, Master Oldisworth!' he exclaimed. 'If you subscribe to that dogma, pray be so good as to explain how society can be held together without obedience to the law, and how the law can be enforced except by judges and magistrates like myself passing judgments on our fellow men. Would you leave Master Harrison's murder and my assailants to the tender mercy of your Christian God? In accordance with the doctrine of His Church, would He not forgive them if they were penitent and send them away with His blessing, trusting them not to sin again? But sin again they would, as you and I know full well, and what salvation would He then provide for law-abiding folk, eh? I speak of this world, not the next.'

'My words referred to moral judgments, Sir Thomas, as you will surely have surmised. It is beyond question that the law must be upheld and the guilty punished until the coming of

God's own Day of Judgment. There is no disagreement between us about that.'

'So you would have me believe that the law and morality are distinct—that criminals are not immoral? Is that your contention? If it is not, logic dictates that you are preaching a subversive gospel to the effect that judges are presumptuously arrogating to themselves a prerogative that the Deity has reserved for Himself. Let me enlighten you on the superior teaching of Islam on that point.'

'Stop!' commanded Sir John. 'I will not listen to blasphemy nor hear what morals your lad here and his fellow infidels are taught. You are feverish, sir. Pray calm yourself.'

After a week in pain without company or argument, Sir Thomas was enjoying himself. He winked at Ali and chose not to take offence at this rebuke. Instead he insisted that the captain withdraw his innuendo and the insulting proposal to relieve him of the duties of a magistrate which he was bound in law to exercise. When that was reluctantly conceded, he agreed to adjourn the theological debate and lock antlers with his parish priest on another occasion.

'I think we may take two facts for granted and—I trust—beyond dispute,' said Sir John, returning to the business in hand. 'First, that it is your assailants who also waylaid Lady Juliana's steward and killed him when he resisted or recognised them. It would be far-fetched to suppose that two separate gangs of desperadoes making similar attacks are at large in this district at the same time. Secondly, it is plain that they have eluded us; our search came too late, and there is nothing more to be done until they attempt to sell what they have stolen or attract suspicion by the money and goods in their possession. Only then may we expect to catch them.'

Captain Dover concurred. 'I cannot deny the strength of Sir John's conclusions,' he said. 'But what we have heard from Sir Thomas leads me to the supposition that the Perrys may not be without some measure of guilt.'

'We must indeed not overlook the possibility that they acted as informers for the culprits,' Sir John agreed. 'It is a suspicious circumstance that they knew in advance where and at what time both the victims would be vulnerable to attack.'

'Permit me to disagree,' Sir Thomas interrupted, shaking his head vigorously. 'Mistress Perry would have had no time to warn my assailants of my approach. I rode home directly after taking my leave of her.'

'She could have informed on you earlier in the day,' argued the captain. 'It would be a reasonable assumption that you would be returning home later, and you were seen to be alone.'

'She warned me of danger,' Sir Thomas replied. 'That suggests innocence, not guilt. Had I paid heed, the robbers would have lost their prey. If any in Campden are in league with the marauders, it would rather be Mistress Harrison and her son. There is bad blood between them and Master Harrison.'

This suggestion outraged the others—as Sir Thomas had intended. A fresh altercation broke out, and more harsh words were exchanged until they were interrupted by a knock on the door. Ali went outside to answer it and returned to whisper in his master's ear.

'It seems that we are favoured with the presence of another man of God,' Sir Thomas announced. 'Master Bartholomew has come from Chipping Campden after all, bringing with him what he declares to be important news about Master Harrison's fate.'

9

No one could have guessed that the figure who stumbled into the room was a renowned hero. He was gaunt and grey-faced and bore the stamp of death upon him. Stooping in pain, he paused to gather breath before paying his respects to the company of gentry assembled in the bedchamber. William Bartholomew, vicar of Campden, was (as they all knew) mortally afflicted with a stone in the bladder. He would not be cut and lived in daily expectation of meeting his Maker, when—so he fervently prayed and believed—all suffering would cease.

'Learning that you were confined to your bed, Sir Thomas, I have risen from mine. By the grace of God, I have accomplished the journey unscathed.'

'Unscathed' was a description scarcely fitting his appearance. What the company beheld was the pitiful ghost of a formerly doughty protagonist of the High Church militant. Appointed to his living by Edward, Viscount Campden, the Lady Juliana's long-dead husband, the Reverend Bartholomew had remained as staunch and fearless a royalist as his patron. Under the Commonwealth his sermons and lectures on Sundays and market days were defiant. They had provoked charges designed to lead to his ejection, but he had mounted a sturdy defence and finally triumphed over his prosecutors—at the prodigious cost of two hundred pounds in fines and fees. On the day the restored king was proclaimed in London, he had celebrated the occasion with a jubilant sermon which was printed and circulated throughout the kingdom. That had been a mere three months ago. 'The Strong Man ejected by Stronger than He' had proved to be the vicar of Campden's swan-song before his affliction laid him low.

The baronet and the captain rose together to assist the dying martyr to a chair. 'You are foolish to have ventured abroad in your condition, Master Bartholomew,' Sir John chided him. 'Our host would have been fit to visit you within a day or two.'

'I live by the hour, not the day,' the old man replied, 'and a younger life is at stake—the life of a young Christian, for I baptised John Perry myself. I have told the constable that he must be released forthwith.'

'You have ordered his release!' Sir Thomas bridled. His dignity was offended, his prerogative usurped. 'Whatever the circumstances,' he said, 'there can be no excuse for interference with the due processes of the law.'

'Incontrovertible evidence of John's innocence has reached me, and I knew that you, Sir Thomas, with your insistence on uncovering the truth in all matters, would not wish to see an injustice prolonged. Had I felt certain that God would grant me the strength to make this journey, you may rest assured that I would have acted less hastily, so that the order could have come from you yourself.'

The length of this speech exhausted the vicar, and Sir Thomas's indignation, though by no means assuaged, turned to alarm lest he should find himself with another death on his hands. If it happened here, he would never be able to sleep in his favourite room again.

'Hold fast, Master Bartholomew!' he cried. 'Rest and refresh yourself with a glass of wine while I send for my steward. He will take a statement from you in proper form.'

'Do not so trouble yourself, I pray you, for I have nothing more to add,' gasped the old man.

At this Sir Thomas's indignation returned. In the name of the law he demanded to be told the nature and source of any information allegedly exonerating the prisoner.

'A message has been conveyed to me, and I am bound to secrecy,' was all the answer he received.

'You and your popish practices!' sniffed Sir Thomas, barely

restraining an outburst of fury. 'Have you begun hearing confessions again? Is that it? The secrecy of the confessional places you above the law. Is that what you would maintain?'

The old man's chin had been resting on his chest, appearing to signify that he was done with speech in this world. But a sip of wine proffered by Ali roused him to a last display of spirit and vigour. His eyes found Sir Thomas's and clamped them as though in a vice.

'You are in error,' he rasped. 'There is no question of a confession in this case. Understand, moreover, that I accuse no man of murdering our dear friend, William Harrison. I assert only, with all the strength left in my poor body, that John Perry did not kill him. I will most willingly sign an affidavit to that effect, but that is all.'

He lay back with eyes and lips now both closed. The battle of wills was over, and he had scored his last victory. Sir Thomas continued to press him, but the only response was a twitch of the body as a spasm of pain ran through it. His breathing grew uneven, and the other visitors rallied to his side to prevent him from falling to the floor.

'Fetch a physician,' demanded Captain Dover, but the sick man shook his head.

'Obstinate to the very end!' muttered Sir Thomas, who did not relish obstinacy in others.

'Let him be carried to my parsonage,' pleaded his fellow clergyman. 'I will see that he is cared for until he is sufficiently recovered to return home.'

'There are beds here,' remonstrated Sir Thomas, perceiving a slight on his hospitality. 'Let the poor fellow stay.'

'My house will be more fitting,' the vicar of Bourton insisted. 'With your permission, Sir Thomas, I shall ask your servants to help remove him, and myself withdraw to accompany them and make the necessary arrangements.'

'Every comfort is available to him in this house,' Sir Thomas protested.

'Not spiritual comfort, I think.'

The magistrate was silenced, and no one spoke until the two

vicars had left the room, the one borne away unconscious by Ali and a footman, the other giving further offence to their host by praying aloud for the good man's soul.

The sound of the procession descending the stairs could still be heard when the arrival of Master Fettiplace, the Campden constable, was announced. He hovered in the doorway, over-awed by the company, twisting his hat in his hands while he bowed to each in turn.

Here stood a suitably humble target for the magistrate's pent-up wrath. 'So you have come hotfoot to confess your dis-obedience!' he cried. 'But know that I will accept no excuses. A constable who is persuaded that a parson has the authority to countermand the order of a magistrate is not fit to hold office. Do you fancy a taste of your own cell, sirrah?'

'As Your Honour knows, the vicar is not a gentleman to be gainsaid,' pleaded the constable. 'Therefore I felt it right to come at once to report the matter to Your Honour and inquire what is to be done.'

'What is to be done, Master Fettiplace, is to recapture without delay a prisoner suspected of murder. If he is guilty he may kill again and you will be held as an accessory. If he is innocent others who think him guilty may take the law into their own hands, and in that event you will be accounted responsible for his death or injury. Go immediately and seek him at home or as far and wide as he may have fled. And before you depart allow me to remind you again that, although he may be blessed in Heaven, the Reverend Bartholomew is empowered with no jurisdiction over bodies here on earth. His business is with souls—assuming that such things exist.'

'The prisoner is safe, sir,' replied the constable.

Sir Thomas was lost for an explanation. 'Why then are you standing there like a guilty man?' he demanded.

'It did not seem right to disturb you on your sick-bed and intrude on your company. For that I ask your pardon, sir.'

Before Sir Thomas could respond, Sir John Keyte held up a hand to stop him and addressed the constable himself. 'Do I understand correctly that the prisoner has not been released, and that you have come all the way from Campden for the purpose of asking Sir Thomas whether or not to pay heed to your vicar's words? Is that the case? Then, Master Fettiplace, your conduct has been exemplary, and I commend you on it.'

'So John Perry is still under lock and key?' Sir Thomas asked the constable in a milder voice, chastened by his mistake and the rebuff.

'No, sir; I am truly sorry if I did wrong, but I could not bring myself to upset the vicar in his state of health.'

'First the prisoner is safe, and then he is not!' The magistrate trembled between bewilderment and exasperation. 'The Devil take you, constable, where is the lad?'

'He is below stairs, Sir Thomas. I left him in the kitchen with your servants.'

'Are you telling me that you have brought him with you, and he is now being fed in this house at my expense?'

'He is docile and makes no trouble. He was hungry after our journey, and your servants offered to refresh him while I spoke with Your Honour about questioning him again.'

'How kind of them! I would have you know that my servants are the most inquisitive gossip-mongers in the world. All they want is to take a look at the notorious Master Perry and hear what he has to say, while plying him with my bread and ale. Very well! Go and join them, Master Fettiplace. Help loosen the prisoner's tongue and bring him to me as soon as I send word.'

Mention of food had made Sir Thomas conscious of his own hunger. He invited his remaining guests to stay for the interrogation and share dinner with him first. He looked forward to recovering from his humiliation by demonstrating how a man of intellect applied himself to unravelling a mystery and laying bare a truth which would remain hidden but for him. He congratulated himself on the confirmation of his belief in John Perry's innocence. Now the boy must reveal all he knew.

10

'Prisoner, state your name and the place where you reside.'

'John Perry, of Calf Lane, Chipping Campden, sir.'

For the purposes of the interrogation the steward of the Bourton estate had been summoned from his normal duties to perform the function of magistrate's clerk. He sat with paper, pen and a horn of ink at the dressing table, which had been cleared for his use.

The magistrate himself was conducting the court proceedings from his bed, still clad in gown and cap. He maintained the dignity of the law by raising himself stiffly upright and assuming the fierce expression which he customarily adopted to intimidate defendants when he sat on the bench.

As if in the body of the court, Sir John Keyte and Captain Dover were seated side by side in front of an open window which overlooked a herb garden and a wide expanse of park beyond. Although disapproving of the irregularity of proceedings, they were keen spectators—and ready participants if need be. At the far end of the room the constable and Ali stood on either side of the door to foil any attempt by the prisoner to escape.

'Come now, John,' coaxed the magistrate, relaxing his sternness and striking an avuncular note. 'Information has reached my ears which leads me to the conclusion that you are guiltless in the matter of your master's murder. You have been kept in custody because you are guilty of telling lies and concealing what you know. I cannot conceive what reason you may have for such foolish behaviour, but I assure you that it is both unlawful and misguided. Consult your conscience now and speak the truth. Then you will be released and free to go home. You have my word upon it.'

'Are you aware that protecting others who have committed a crime is itself a crime?' put in the captain when the prisoner continued to stand mute. 'In withholding information in this case you may well be judged an accessory to murder.'

'What in truth occurred between Charringworth and Campden that night? You were there. Confess what you know, young man, or worse will befall you,' urged Sir John.

The boy trembled before them. He was frail, dishevelled and barefoot. His breeches were torn and dirty; his shoes had been deemed unfit to tread on the lord of the manor's precious carpets. But although browbeaten, he did not appear abashed—alert, rather, and wary-eyed. There was a long pause while they waited on his words. It was plain that he was pondering on what to say to satisfy his inquisitors.

'It is true that my master was murdered—brutally done to death, good sirs; but never by me. Were I a murderer, which (God be my witness) I am not, his would be the last blood in all the world that I would shed.' The words came with a sudden gush and he almost choked on them.

Now we are coming to it, thought Sir Thomas, rubbing his hands in anticipation. 'If you have certain knowledge that Master Harrison was murdered, then you must know, or at least suspect, the identity of the murderers. Speak out, and do not fear the consequences. The law will ensure your safety. The culprits will be quickly arrested and brought to justice.'

'Between two and three weeks ago, when I was alone outside my master's house, I was attacked by two men with swords. They threatened to kill me if I did not reveal where his money was hidden. I was in fear of my life but would not tell them. They were cut-throats who would stop at nothing. They must have returned and killed him for the money he was carrying.'

'Why was I not notified of this incident before?' demanded Sir Thomas suspiciously. 'To whom did you report it?'

'To my master, sir, after they had gone. The robbery was

thwarted, and he had no loss to report to you. I fought them off with a sheep-pick and made an outcry. They took fright and ran off empty-handed.'

'Describe the appearance of these men. Were they young or old? Tall or short? Clean-shaven or bearded? How did they speak? Were they from these parts or foreigners?'

'I was too hard at work defending myself to take notice of their looks. It was dark and they fell on me without warning. Like wild beasts they were. I feared afterwards they would come back and waylay my master himself if they had the chance. I cannot be sure, but I doubt they were natives from hereabouts.'

'How then, I pray you tell me, do you account for strangers discovering on what day and at what time your master would be walking abroad alone with money in his purse?'

'They would be lurking and watching, as outlaws do.'

'Have you anyone to vouch for their lurking, or anyone to verify your tale besides Master Harrison? Would you have a search made for men of no description?'

'They were wearing white coats. That I do remember.'

The three gentlemen exchanged glances. 'The lad speaks truly then,' said Captain Dover. Sir John nodded his agreement. Sir Thomas was sceptical.

'Master Fettiplace,' he called out, 'have you been gossiping to the prisoner about the villains who wounded me? Have you told him of their wearing white coats?'

'We talked of the assault when we passed the place this morning,' the constable admitted, red-faced. 'We spoke of what Your Honour suffered, and I may have mentioned your description of the assailants. I meant no wrong.'

'May have! May have! If you have lost the memory of what was said but an hour or two ago, you are no longer fit to hold the office of constable. Answer me straight. Did you or did you not make mention of those men and their coats?'

'I did, sir,' confessed the constable.

'As soon as Master Fettiplace spoke of them,' said John, 'it sprang to my mind that those would be the very same men.'

'Or are you fastened upon a false tale to tell.' The magistrate pointed an accusing finger at him. 'This assault upon you is an invention, is it not? You have no witnesses, no wounds to display, no evidence of any kind.'

'I can show you the sheep-pick, Sir Thomas, and you will see the marks of their sword thrusts on the handle.'

'That is no evidence. Such marks could have been made by any blade at any time. How dare you try to deceive me with this absurd story of a lad with a sheep-pick putting to flight two desperadoes with naked swords.'

'They fled because I cried out so loudly for help. That is the truth. I swear it.'

'Then it is strange that no one seems to have heard these cries of yours, despite their being loud enough to frighten your attackers away. Now hearken to me, Master Perry. A few minutes ago you gave me to understand that you knew—let me repeat the word, *knew*—that Master Harrison had been brutally murdered. If you are now saying that all the evidence you have for that assertion is an unwitnessed, unreported assault upon yourself, one of his servants, by two rogues some days earlier, it ought not to surprise you that I am coming to disbelieve every word you utter, however much you swear to the truth of it. Do you take me for a fool?'

'Your Honour will not have forgotten my master's hat and band found stained with his blood. Is that not proof enough?'

After this John Perry was forced to hang his head while Sir Thomas harangued him in measured tones. The judicial crust was thin. Below the surface the magistrate's temper was rising to the boil. An Overbury was not to be duped and then defied.

'I have not forgotten the hat and band,' he said, 'but a witness who makes a confident and unqualified assertion that a man has been killed is, in my experience, one who has seen the victim's dead body. I put it to you, John Perry, that you have looked on Master Harrison's corpse with your own eyes and can tell me where it lies concealed if you so choose. Now look me in the eye and favour me with a straight answer, sirrah!'

The prisoner's head remaining stubbornly bowed, Sir Thomas

leaped from his bed in a fever of wrath and frustration. He seized the boy by the hair and jerked his head upwards so that they stood nose to nose. It was a performance to relieve his spleen and impress his visitors.

'Would you toy with me, you wretch?' he shouted as though they were half a mile apart. 'Answer me, damn you, or you will spend the rest of your worthless life in prison for contempt.' He tugged the offending head from side to side to shake the guilty knowledge out of it.

The prisoner made no attempt to defend himself, nor did he utter except for a squeak of pain. Instead he wept. To Sir Thomas's dismay, large tear-drops fell from the youngster's cheeks and splashed one by one on the carpet purchased in the souk at Kairouan which was its owner's pride and joy.

'Leave off blubbing and find your tongue this instant,' he ordered. 'Otherwise I shall have you dispatched in chains to Gloucester gaol to be arraigned for murder at the next Quarter Sessions. Your silence will be no protection then. It will condemn you.' At this the boy was so pathetic in his distress that Sir Thomas's heart was melted. This was an innocent, he thought, who must be rescued from his own folly.

John Perry stood swaying, like a sapling in a passing storm. Gradually the sobbing ceased. He steadied himself, wiped his eyes with his sleeve and raised them to the ceiling as though for inspiration. Then he cleared his throat and began to whisper.

'Speak up!' Sir Thomas commanded as he climbed back into bed.

The words which followed were to echo in the listeners' ears for months. They were softly spoken but distinct. 'It was my mother and my brother Richard who murdered my master.'

The room fell silent save for the urgent scratching of the clerk's quill.

'Take good care that what you now affirm is the truth at last,' Sir Thomas urged. 'If this charge be false, you will be drawing innocent blood upon your head—the innocent blood of your nearest kin. Have you considered that your words may send your own mother to the gallows?'

'In this I speak nothing but the truth. So help me, God.'

'He is lying! The lad does not mean what he says!' It was the constable who cried out, and Sir Thomas called him to order with an imperious gesture.

The boy sank to his knees. The blood had fled from his face. His eyes were staring unfocused. On being bidden to rise and repeat the accusation, he could not summon the strength to regain his feet. It seemed that every bone and muscle in his body had turned to jelly.

Ali brought a flask of water and poured it down his throat and over his face and wrists. Constable and clerk dragged his limp body on to a stool, where he crouched quivering and whimpering, head in hands.

Sir John Keyte advised that a physician be sent for: 'the boy is ill,' he insisted. But Sir Thomas, hot on the trail of truth, would pay no heed. To him physicians were charlatans of the body and as little to be consulted and relied upon as clergymen, those charlatans of the soul.

'Declare to me without further prevarication where the murder was committed and when; and how it was committed and why,' he demanded after what he judged a sufficient respite. 'Take your time and omit no detail. Speak clearly and slowly so that your statement can be faithfully recorded by the clerk as you make it. Have done with lies, John. Understand that if now you deviate from the truth by so much as a hair's breadth, you will be punished for perjury.'

'Have pity on the wretch,' intervened Captain Dover, incensed by Sir Thomas's bullying. 'He is in no fit condition to make any formal statement, let alone one condemning his own mother and brother. In common humanity, allow him an hour or two to rest and reflect that this is a matter of life and death. You can see that he is presently not in his right mind. He is saying whatever he thinks you want to hear. He will be talking under duress and may even incriminate himself to oblige you.'

'There is no question of self-incrimination. Have I not already assured the prisoner that I hold him guiltless?' With that Sir Thomas waved aside the objection. He was not to be taught his job by a country lawyer—a member of the worst class of charlatans of all—or deflected from such a triumphant demonstration of his skill as an interrogator. How could he stop when on the point of solving a mystery which would have baffled lesser mortals for evermore?

'Proceed,' he commanded, and John Perry, now recovered and evidently eager to unburden himself of the truth at last, gave an account of the events of that fatal Thursday night which was very different from the tale he had told at The Eight Bells.

11

Speaking without hesitation, the young prisoner now stated that, ever since he had entered the service of the Lady Juliana's steward, his mother and brother Richard had pestered him for money. His father had been dead for many years and although Richard followed the trade of a thatcher few in the town would employ him, because of his bad reputation. So they looked to John to relieve their poverty. He was told to give them notice whenever money would be lying unguarded in the steward's house and on what days the rents were collected from the villages, so that Richard might then force an entry into the house or lay an ambush.

'That accounts for the break-in when the family was in church,' noted Sir Thomas grimly. 'You scoundrel!'

John acknowledged the reproof with a blush, but did not allow it to interrupt his narrative. His gaze remained steadfastly on the wall in front of him.

On the morning of the day when the steward took himself to Charringworth, he had, he said, met Richard in the street while on an errand in the town. His brother had forced him to reveal his master's business and destination.

In the evening, when his mistress had sent him out to look for his master and he had turned back and parted from the two men he met on the way, his brother was waiting for him in the shadows beside the road. He had dragged him into the church-yard and told him of his plans for the robbery. Under threat, John agreed to act as a look-out—no more.

As a precaution against being seen together, John had then

taken the footpath which ran across the churchyard and led directly to the Conygree, while his brother walked the long way round along the highway towards Charringworth. They met again in secret near the gate in the wall which enclosed the Conygree. This was kept locked, but the steward had a key and always used that entrance to take a short cut across the warren. There they took up their positions.

'The witness may not be confessing to murder, but he is accusing himself of being a party to robbery with violence,' Captain Dover informed the magistrate.

'But not of committing the crime of his own free will, I think,' Sir Thomas replied, cursing this know-all lawyer under his breath. 'That will be the defence open to him.'

'That is God's truth,' said John. 'You must believe me, sirs. My brother threatened me with a beating if I did not obey him. He will kill me when he learns I have betrayed him.'

'He will not be granted the opportunity,' Sir Thomas assured him. 'Now describe how the robbery occurred.'

'That I cannot do, Your Honour. I refused to be there when they laid hands on my beloved master. When he approached along the highway it was too dark to see him, but I knew his tread. As soon as he came through the gate my brother held me fast with a hand over my mouth. Then he thrust me to the ground and sprang at my master, and I ran away.'

'Without uttering a warning or raising the alarm?'

'I wanted to but dared not, and when I returned to find out what had happened it was too late. My master was lying on the ground with my brother on top of him and my mother standing by. Believe me, I am not guilty of killing or robbing him, only of being too frightened to come to his rescue.'

'So you did nothing for the man you swear you loved?'

'My brother is too strong for me.'

'Was your master already dead when you came back?'

'I believed so, but suddenly he called out from the ground— from the grave, as it seemed: "Ah, rogues, would you kill me?"'

'And it was then that he was murdered?'

'Richard had promised me not to harm him. There was no

need. We would not be recognised in the darkness. That is what he said beforehand. But when my master cried out, Richard thought he knew who we were. I begged him to honour his promise, but he called me a fool and bade me hold my peace.'

'Well, what happened next? Finish your evidence,' Sir Thomas urged as sobs broke out again.

The tears were brushed away. The words came low and trembling, but distinct: 'And then he strangled him.'

No one chose to break the silence which descended until the boy resumed his tale unbidden. He described how he saw his brother snatch the bag of coins from the dead man's pocket and throw it to his mother, and how she at once ran off with it.

'What part had Mistress Perry played in the killing?' Sir Thomas wanted to know.

'She helped hold my master down.' John had hesitated before replying and Sir Thomas detected yet another lie. That woman was no murderess. He remembered her during his visit; but also the furnishings in her cottage. These could not have been come by honestly if the family was as poor as her son had implied.

'The body!' exclaimed Sir John Keyte, seeing the magistrate lost in thought. 'Come now; who disposed of it?'

In this John confessed to helping his brother. Reluctantly, he swore. Between them they had hoisted the body from the grass and carried it into the grounds of the great house. There they rested their load on a fallen pillar while they consulted what to do with it. John wanted to bury it in a corner of the graveyard, but Richard's decision had been to throw it into the cesspool which lay just beyond them, outside the garden wall.

'Do I understand you to refer to the Great Sink beside Wallington's mill?' demanded Sir Thomas aghast. 'Are we truly to find a good man's corpse immersed in that filth?'

Hesitant again, John replied that he had not agreed to it and was sent instead to hearken whether anyone was stirring nearby. His mother it was who had returned and helped his brother move the body. If it were not in the sink, he knew not where else it might be. That was where Richard said he would put it because no one would want to search for it there. John himself, finding all quiet, had stolen away and not seen his brother since.

'Where did you go?' inquired Sir Thomas. 'To your mistress, who was expecting you?'

'She had told me not to return without my master. I knew she would scold me if she saw me, and what was I to say if she questioned me? So I crept into the hen-roost and hid myself there until midnight. When the moon was up I took to the road again, as I told Your Honour before.'

'To look for a man you knew to be dead and lying at the bottom of a cess-pool! Your journey was nothing but an excuse for your next piece of mischief, was it not?'

'It was my brother's idea, not mine. When I refused to lift the body a second time, he said I must do something else for him and handed me my master's hat and band and comb. He told me to leave them by the roadside where they would be seen in daylight. First I slashed them with my knife in the hen-roost, as he told me to.'

'A barefaced attempt to deceive me! But you will find I am not so easily outwitted.' Sir Thomas scowled. 'I am satisfied, John Perry, that you are more deeply involved in this crime than you would have me suppose. I cannot believe you are in truth such a coward that your brother must take all the blame for this outrage. Now answer me this. If your master was strangled, as you allege, whose is the blood on his hat and band, pray? Did you cut yourself on purpose in the hen-roost? If so, show me the wound.'

'The blood is not mine,' answered John, flustered and stammering. 'My master must have been stabbed at first, when he was brought to the ground. I can say no more.'

The boy would not open his mouth again. The interrogation was at an end, and the magistrate gave the constable his orders. 'Take the prisoner away and lock him up securely—whatever Master Bartholomew may say. Arrest Mistress Perry and Richard Perry on suspicion of murder and have the Great Sink trawled at day-break tomorrow. The body must be recovered.'

'Never before have I met such a devious, snivelling wretch,' declared Sir John Keyte as the door closed behind them.

'Nor such a shameless attempt to put the blame on others,' added Captain Dover.

They rose to leave. Sir Thomas snapped his fingers and signalled to Ali to escort them out.

'*Ala raasi, ya bey*,' Ali replied gravely. Brought up in Sir Thomas's household in Egypt, he could speak English perfectly, but it amused Sir Thomas to tease visitors by having him pretend ignorance of the language.

When he returned, Sir Thomas beckoned to him to sit on the bed beside him while he reflected on what they had heard.

'So you were in error in thinking Master Harrison still alive, and we were both in error in believing young John innocent. He is like a chameleon. His look changes from half-witted one moment to crafty the next. Sometimes one has to wait an age while he thinks what to say next; at other times he gallops along like a Demosthenes, but mixing lies with the truth so that one can hardly tell the one from the other. Yet he met his match in me.'

'As you say, O master.'

Sir Thomas glanced at his favourite suspiciously. 'Does that mean you agree with me or disagree?'

'Suppose Master Harrison's body is not found in the cesspool?'

'Where else would it be? Every other place has been searched and searched again. The constable should not have overlooked the sink.'

'Would you venture a sovereign upon it?'

'Two,' answered Sir Thomas boldly. 'Now straighten my pillows and put me to rest. If I feel well enough tomorrow, we will go in the coach to Chipping Campden and I shall steel myself to view the wretched fellow's stinking remains.'

12

Mistress Harrison looked up from stitching a kneeler for the church. Through the parlour window she spied two figures dismounting from a coach. 'Go warn your brother and hide yourself,' she called to Anne, who was at work in the kitchen. 'The godless and the heathen approach.'

Edward was upstairs bent over the manor rent books. He closed them hastily and locked them in the chest which protected them from prying eyes.

By the time Sir Thomas reached the almonry mother and son were awaiting him at the door. His mood was fretful and he came prepared for their customary surliness. It was the morning after the interrogation in his bedchamber. His wife had judged him not yet fit to rise from his sick-bed; so he had risen to spite her. But now he was forced to admit to himself that she had been right. Jolting over rough roads had been damnably painful, and all his bruises were aching.

'Pray enter and take bread with us while we hear your news.' The sweetness of the termagant's greeting took him by surprise and filled him with suspicion.

He declined the invitation: his business was unfinished and he had food more to his taste at home. 'Forgive me,' he excused himself. 'I have ridden from Bourton urgently on this sorry matter of your husband's death and may require Master Edward's assistance, but I must not delay.'

'You can rely upon him, as others do,' she answered with a mother's pride. 'Since your last visit letters have reached us from Rutland. Her ladyship has confirmed his appointment as steward in his father's place. My Edward has grown to become the chief person in Chipping Campden—after your good self, of course. He has ever been a strong upholder of the law and you will find that he will oblige you in every respect.'

She was wearing widow's black but showing no other sign of mourning her husband. Sir Thomas brooded on this, and on an eagerness to please which ran clean contrary to her shrewish nature. He marvelled, too, at the new Sultan of Campden who stood silent before him, ruled by a maternal Grand Vizier.

Edward nodded his assent to his mother's words and looked to her before opening his mouth. 'We have heard that the Perrys are arrested. The sooner the three of them are hanged, the better for the town,' he said.

'Did I not inform you that young John Perry was the culprit?' his mother added. 'Did I not say that his mother and brother were his accomplices? I beg you pay no heed to their denials. Edward speaks truly. Campden will be well rid of that whole family of Devil-worshippers. It is God's will. I have prayed to Him and He has spoken in my ear.'

Sir Thomas smiled grimly to himself. 'Were Master Harrison's feelings about them the same as your own?' he inquired, hoping to catch the self-righteous hussy in a lie.

She disappointed him. 'My husband was too trusting,' she said. 'If only he had done as I constantly implored him and taken Edward with him when he went rent-collecting, he would be alive today. But he had his reasons for going alone.' She sounded more angry at his behaviour than regretful at his fate.

Rumours of Master Harrison's philandering with tenants' wives and daughters and of furious quarrels between himself and his wife sprang to the magistrate's mind. How he must have fought against her and her God to be master in his own house! How contented she must be now that she could rule the roost! Through her precious son she would even rule the manor too. What these two stood to gain from his death was worth far more than the sum of stolen money. And if she was making a false accusation to put him off the scent, might jealousy be at the bottom of it? He remembered Widow Perry's charms. What a contrast to the repulsiveness of the hag confronting him!

'What was the nature of your husband's relationship with Mistress Perry?' he asked.

The unexpected question unbalanced her, as he had intended. 'What are you suggesting, sir?' she demanded indignantly.

But they were interrupted before he could reply. Constable Fettiplace had arrived at the door. He paid his respects to the lady of the house and the new steward and then turned to Sir Thomas. 'I was told Your Honour was here,' he said.

'You have news for me? You have found the body?'

The constable reported that he had come directly from the Great Sink, where a team of men whom he had recruited for the purpose had waded unwillingly into the evil-smelling pool and swept it from end to end, watched by most of the women and children of the town.

'I had to promise them payment and even then urge them in with threats and stand over them,' he said, wrinkling his nose at the recollection. 'But all the bodies they fished out were dogs and cats. I can assure Your Honour there is nothing else in that pool but the filth one would expect.'

Sir Thomas cursed the lying John Perry.

'The witch and her son must be put to the torture until they confess the truth,' declared Mistress Harrison. 'They must suffer for their crime and their lies. May their black souls burn in Hell for all eternity! For is it not written in the holy scriptures, in the Epistle of St Paul the Apostle to the Romans, chapter twelve, verse nineteen: "Vengeance is mine; I will repay, saith the Lord"?'

Sir Thomas refrained with difficulty from delivering one of his homilies on the unmerciful character of the Christian God, in the course of which he was wont to make unfavourable comparisons between the teachings of the Old Testament and St Paul and those of the spiritual sages of the Orient: Mahavira and the Lord Buddha. 'Trawl the fish-pools a second time in case the boy has made a mistake,' he ordered.

'That has already been done,' the constable replied.

'Then the ruins here must be searched. Reassemble the men who have been dragging the Great Sink and conduct a thorough exploration underground. That is the only remaining hiding place. I shall delay my departure and accompany the party myself.'

Edward's lips tightened. He glanced at his mother. 'My father's body is not to be found among the ruins,' he said. 'We have already hunted there in vain.'

'It must be done again,' Sir Thomas insisted. 'They are too extensive for a single person to poke into every hiding place. The cellars could house half the town, could they not?'

'With respect, Sir Thomas, what you propose cannot be permitted without the Lady Juliana's personal consent. I am under strict instructions that the area is not to be entered. It is too dangerous.'

So this self-important weakling was flexing his puny muscles! Sir Thomas was not to be deterred by such opposition. 'I will answer for it to her ladyship,' he promised, brushing the objection aside.

'I am so charged, and the responsibility is mine,' Edward insisted, chewing his lips and scowling defiantly at the ground. He had become as stubborn as a mule.

'The law demands it,' the magistrate responded sharply. 'That responsibility is mine, and it overrides yours, Master Steward. You must surely be aware that without a body there can be no trial; so we have to find it wherever it may be. The fields and the hedgerows, the ricks and every stretch of water have been explored. Where else is there to look? Or do you desire me to release the Perrys for want of evidence against them? For how, do you fancy, would a judge rule when asked to preside over a charge of murder with no proof of death? Raise your eyes, look me in the face and answer those questions.'

At this Mistress Harrison intervened. 'It would be wrong to hinder a Justice of the Peace in the execution of his duties, Edward,' she scolded him. 'Her ladyship will understand.'

'Then he and I shall go, but no other. Those men cannot be

90

trusted: they may pilfer what is stored below. And I shall be held accountable if they are kept from the fields a full day at harvest time.' He spoke sulkily, but when his eyes met the magistrate's at last, they were pleading.

'Very well,' Sir Thomas conceded. 'It shall be you and I alone—with my footboy.' He stepped round the corner of the house to fetch Ali and caught him exchanging banter with Anne, who was leaning out of an upstairs window laughing. 'Leave the girl alone and attend to your duties,' he called angrily.

Ali was not put out by the reprimand. He flashed a set of pure white teeth in one of his winning smiles, first at Anne as a farewell and then at his master. 'I heard what the constable said,' he grinned and held out a hand until Sir Thomas reluctantly produced the promised sovereigns—relieving his feelings by cuffing him over the ear at the same time.

While Ali went with the new steward to fetch lanthorns and Mistress Harrison hurried upstairs to punish her daughter for flirting with a servant, and a dark-skinned one at that, Sir Thomas strolled towards the ruins in contemplative mood. His expectation was high. Excitement had banished his aches and desire for bed.

Ever since the destruction of Campden House fifteen years before, the ruins had been the closely guarded preserve of the Harrisons. Their house, known as the almonry, had been built as estate offices with a dovecote above. It stood just inside the boundary wall, facing almshouses across the road, and had long been the only occupied building on the whole vast site. The lodges were empty; the pavilions at either end of the long terrace were derelict; and the distant Court House, roughly converted from stables and brewhouse into lodgings, had been scorned by the Lady Juliana.

The lady of the manor had, indeed, not been seen on her Campden estates since before the war. The heavy fines levied after Parliament's victory had deprived her of the means to rebuild the house, and the sight of its humbled pride was too painful for her own. Even now, when the monarchy had been restored, no funds were available to recompense the family for the cost of its loyalty. In her old age she herself lived comfortably enough on the estate of her dead husband, Baron Noel of Ridlington in the county of Rutland. But her surviving son, the madcap Baptist, third Viscount Campden, was reported to have gambled away the last of his grandfather's fortune and be skulking, an impoverished exile, in distant disgrace.

Sir Thomas picked his way gingerly through the wilderness that had, in happier times, been tended by a dozen gardeners. Ahead of him sprawled charred fragments of once stout limestone walls. Amongst them was a forlorn forest of fallen pillars with, here and there, a broken arch. A few of the pillars were still upright, leaning like drunken guardians of the past. He mused on what undiscovered secrets might lie beneath their feet; on the tragedy of the house's destruction by fellow Royalists; on the wretched fate of a famous family.

The grandson of the richest man in England a pauper! How indeed were the mighty fallen! What a blow the goddess Nemesis had struck! As a boy, Sir Thomas had twice been taken to meet Baptist Hicks, the upstart London merchant who had descended on this part of the West Country to buy the manor and all the land within sight and become an overpowering neighbour of all the Keytes and the Overburys and the other established gentry to whom supremacy in the area rightfully belonged.

The first meeting had been in London; the second, a few weeks later, here in Campden. By that date the Mammon of Cheapside had been elevated to the dignity of Baron Hicks of Ilmington and Viscount Campden of Campden. He had gained notoriety as the first and only peer of the realm to defy convention and carry on with his business as a tradesman, buying and selling silks and lending money at prodigious rates of interest. His fellow peers despised him; other tradesmen distrusted him; but he had captured the hearts of the citizens of Chipping Campden by the munificence of his benefactions. The almshouses, the grammar school, the charter of liberties, above all the splendification of the church—these were investments in the hereafter, his passport to Heaven.

His place of business was at the sign of the White Bear in the busiest shopping street in the city of London. He also built himself an inn, named The Baptist's Head, nearby and a second Campden House in Kensington. But his main residence was Hicks Hall, a palace to proclaim his wealth erected beside the Session House in Clerkenwell. It was there that the young Tom Overbury had been brought by his father to pay his respects. This he had done with a much-practised bow from the waist and the nervous shake of a gnarled and clammy hand. All too vividly he remembered the greasy feel of it and how he had wiped his own surreptitiously behind him afterwards.

How well he remembered, too, the old man's fierce eyes, smouldering with rage at senility and the approach of death! It was said that he had not forgiven the Almighty for the loss of his three sons; which had left him with a female heir and only a son-in-law to inherit his titles by the special remainder which he had cajoled, bullied and bribed the Crown into granting. In his mind's eye Sir Thomas could still see the untrimmed white hair straggling from beneath an old-fashioned periwig and the hard, wrinkled mouth drooling saliva.

His memory of their second meeting was not of the man, but only the house: not the shell of greatness in its dotage, but the magnificence of his gift to posterity. Campden House was then a bright new jewel on the fair face of what young Tom's father informed him was the fairest county of the fairest country in all the world. To an eight-year-old, the house in its pristine glory was a wonder never to be forgotten.

Sir Thomas leaned on one of the pieces of broken-down ashlar wall which had once divided sections of the formal garden with mathematical precision. He shut his eyes and indulged his romantic nature; for was he not, like his well-known uncle and namesake, an aspiring poet as well as a man of affairs?

Through closed eyelids he recalled the vision of an Italianate palazzo, a French château, a Spanish alcazar all blended into

93

one shimmering miracle of symmetry under an extravaganza of towers and pinnacles clustered round a central dome. The parapets were surmounted by exotically carved pediments. The chimneys rose in twisted spirals to be crowned triumphantly—against all expectation—with Corinthian capitals.

The enormous building was so cunningly designed and perfectly proportioned that it appeared to float weightless above its man-made and natural settings. It was surrounded by orderly beds of flowers planted within rows of box hedges; by gravel paths running straight as arrows; and by water gardens with ornamental ponds and fountains playing. Standing four-square, it disdained a back or sides. There was not one frontage but four, each a mason's masterpiece boasting as much glass as stone. There were three storeys of long, close-set windows, the lower two jutting and curving into bows at each corner. Marking the principal entrance stood a grand portico supported by fluted pillars of the five orders.

This entrance faced south, away from the town and highway, over meadows and pasture land towards a far horizon of gentle wolds. Immediately to its front, along the whole length of the house, stretched a broad, stone-balustraded terrace running between twin pavilions. Steps from the terrace led to the gardens below, where the ground ran down to coppices and a stream which separated garden from park.

Of the interior Sir Thomas's memory was dim. There was a long gallery lined with marble statues of naked Greek heroes and stately Roman emperors in togas; and another hung with full-length portraits—freshly painted ancestors, he now sup-posed. Otherwise he could recall nothing but his amazement at the number of rooms, the grandeur of the furnishings and the ornate extravagance of the plasterwork ceilings.

The sound of footsteps broke in on his daydream. The whey-faced Edward was approaching. It was time to discover why the new steward was so anxious to keep the cellars to himself.

13

Before exploring below, the three of them picked their way to and fro, forwards, backwards and sideways, across the whole area of ground on which the great house had stood. After so many years it was a wilderness: much of the debris lay hidden in a flourishing undergrowth of weeds and wild flowers. But there were tracks to be followed, winding between scattered fragments of the noble mercer's pride.

Sir Thomas kept to the paths, head down, his eyes darting from side to side. Ali, more adventurous, leaped from stone to stone through the wreckage of collapsed walls and floors, peering down for any sign of human presence, dead or alive. Agile as a monkey, he even scrambled up a crumbling wall to the first floor of a perilously standing wing, until Sir Thomas, heart in mouth, ordered him down. Edward lagged in their rear, morose and unhelpful, complaining that it was hot work in the noon sun and all to no avail.

'My mother and I trod here for many hours last week,' he sighed reproachfully when they eventually came to halt. 'With respect, Sir Thomas, you waste your time and mine.'

'Then we will continue below.' The magistrate's head was swimming, but he was determined not to give up.

'Under ground is no fit place for a gentleman in your present condition, sir. You had better return to my house and lie down.' Edward paused hopefully for a change of mind.

But although desiring nothing more than a rest, Sir Thomas was not to be deterred. Taking advice from another was foreign to his nature. 'Would you have me shirk my duty?' he demanded.

Edward shrugged. Moving a few paces into the undergrowth, he kicked aside some stones holding a makeshift wooden platform in place. Then he lifted the boarding itself to reveal a flight of steps. After lighting the lanthorns and taking one for himself, he descended and disappeared into the black hole beneath.

Sir Thomas followed gingerly, holding a flickering light in front of him. The steps were broken and uneven, and half-way down he stumbled and fell, unable to save himself with his one free hand. The others helped him to his feet and offered to carry him back up the stairs, but he refused and brushed Ali's solicitous hands aside, more humiliated than hurt.

The air as he crept forward was so dank and musty that mere breathing was as painful as his grazes. The darkness ahead was Stygian and filled with unseen hazards. The floor was littered with broken objects which he tripped over when holding his relit lanthorn high. Cobwebs trailed across his face like dead men's fingers when he lowered it and directed the light towards his feet. Worse still were the eerie squeaks and scuffles which broke the silence. Furious at the invasion of their territory, rats ran over his boots and between his legs, while bats circled blindly around his head and flew into his face.

Ali appealed to him again to turn back. The whites of his eyes, caught in the candlelight, were rolling in alarm. Another flame illuminated a ghostly face that was Edward's. This wore a mutinous expression. 'Lead on,' commanded Sir Thomas, unyielding.

Each room opened into another in this labyrinth of cellars. If they had once had doors, these had either been burned in the conflagration or already used for firewood during the military occupation. One room contained rotting barrels; another smashed crockery; a third tattered fragments of what might once have been army uniforms; in others the rubbish was unrecognisable. The remainder were empty, doubtless stripped bare by the departing garrison before the fire.

'Where are we?' Sir Thomas demanded, limping to a halt at

last. They were standing in front of an iron gate which barred further progress. Beyond was a patch of darkness in which they could glimpse nothing through the bars.

Edward explained that they had reached the centre of the southern range: the main entrance was directly overhead. The gate gave access to an underground corridor which ran left and right under the terrace, connecting the house with the two pavilions which had served as banqueting houses and summer belvederes. By this route furniture and provisions could be carried to and from them under cover, protected from the weather and out of sight of family and guests.

To the magistrate's demand that he open the gate, Edward answered that the key was missing and the lock had rusted. It had never been opened, to his knowledge, since the house was destroyed.

'Then it must be broken down, if there is no other means of entry.' Sir Thomas shook the bars impatiently.

'Formerly there were entrances through the pavilions, but they are blocked.'

'Take me to them,' the magistrate ordered.

They retraced their steps and thankfully breathed fresh air again. Edward went to fetch keys and they met once more at the west pavilion.

Before entering, Sir Thomas ran an appreciative eye over this small gem of the mason's craft. Built of matching stone from nearby quarries, it was surmounted by carved pinnacles and finials which had echoed those of the mansion itself. It and its twin survivor of the conflagration stood like a pair of redundant sentinels, inspiring the poet in him. 'Shabby with neglect. But proudly still erect,' he murmured to himself, struck by the vision which came to him of two faithful pygmies mounting guard over the body of a dead Colossus.

What beauty and ingenuity! They were so designed that the only entrance from outside was on the same level as the ground floor of the house. There one entered the middle of the three storeys. The lowest stood at the foot of the long terrace, to whose sweeping steps and balustrades these follies added a final flourish at either end. On that level there was no means of entry save through the tunnel.

Edward had to wrestle with the lock, and when the door was pushed open it surrendered with a loud, protesting creak. Inside all was dirt, dust and desolation. The room was empty, but, as he had warned, the stairs leading downwards from it were blocked with a pile of huge stones.

By way of contrast, the view through the broken windows was an enchantment still. It led the eye across a placid, lazy stream, through a decaying arch, to the sun-soaked fields beyond. How transitory are the works of man, mused Sir Thomas, and how timeless the majesty of nature!

Turning back to the business in hand, he scowled at the topmost boulder and kicked at it like a thwarted child. 'Whose work is this? For what purpose was it done, and on what occasion, pray?'

'It dates from the war,' Edward told him. 'The regiment stationed here left the pavilions in this condition when they burned the house. My father told me they had done it to protect the house from spies and backstairs intruders creeping in through the cellars. When the war ended he asked her ladyship whether these pavilions should be cleared and cleaned and made habitable, but she refused to have strangers on the premises. So nothing was done, as you see.'

'All left untouched for fifteen years?'

'In obedience to her ladyship's wishes and against my father's. He argued with her that they could be used as dwellings and fetch a good rent.'

Sir Thomas climbed to the room above. It was in the same state as the other: nought but the view cheered the eye. Framed in one gaping window was the church tower, but even that sublime sight failed to raise his spirits. Had he dragged himself from a sick-bed on a fool's errand? So it seemed; and he left the pavilion downcast.

'Let us inspect the other,' he demanded as a parting shot and proceeded along the ruined terrace with Edward and Ali lagging at his heels.

'That is no different, I do assure you,' Edward pleaded, hastening to dissuade him. 'It was the very first place I searched when my poor father vanished.'

'I shall examine it for myself nonetheless. Then I shall trouble you no longer.' Although undeterred, Sir Thomas was now reconciled to failure and yearning for home and bed. A quick look and he would be away, duty done.

No more than a faint flicker of hope remained. The east pavilion overlooked the field known as the Conygree, from its use as a warren in times when a dish of rabbit was a delicacy. There, if John Perry was speaking the truth, the murder had been committed, and here was the readiest hiding place for the old steward's body.

When Edward set his hand upon the door, it yielded before the key was in the lock. As one, they all peered down at it: force had been used to splinter the surrounding woodwork.

'How many days ago did you conduct your search?' Sir Thomas rounded accusingly on the new steward, whose eyes had widened in surprise.

'Ten it was; the morrow of my father's murder. As God is my witness, the lock was secure and undamaged then.'

The windows here had been roughly boarded, but shafts of light penetrated the cracks and when they crossed the threshold the scene was familiar. Dried bird and bat droppings carpeted the floor. Sir Thomas trod warily and then uttered a cry of triumph, for several of the heavy stones which barred the passage down the stairs had been dragged to one side and a narrow gap created. He signed to Ali to squeeze through.

'Stay, Sir Thomas,' Edward begged him. 'The intruders may be below. Would you risk your servant's life?'

Silently, the magistrate agreed that he would not; but he insisted on an immediate search. Ali was accordingly dispatched to the town with orders for Constable Fettiplace to come immediately with a body of men, armed and prepared to enter the tunnel.

Sir Thomas was persuaded to accept hospitality at the almonry while waiting. There the mistress of the house sustained him, against his better judgment, with pease porridge and sour ale until the constable arrived, accompanied by four stalwarts bearing axes, staves and torches.

Spurred by a rare excitement, the townsmen set to work with a will, widening the opening until one after another clambered down and vanished from view. Unable to restrain his curiosity, Sir Thomas brought up the rear with Ali, while Edward—despite his protests—was required to remain above and raise the alarm at the first shout for help from below.

The unlit passageway which had been dug beneath the terrace was chilly and airless, and the explorers found themselves all but entombed in a fetid vault. Sir Thomas sweated and shuddered at a premonition of death and clung tightly to Ali. Ahead, as if it were an omen, two of the party's torches guttered and died.

The tunnel was lined with empty barrels and little else, but when a light was shone between two of them in a corner it illuminated a rumpled heap of straw which appeared to have been laid as a bed. That was the only trace of recent occupation until those in the lead had almost reached the central gate. There one of them threw aside a piece of cloth draped over the top of a barrel and something glittered in the torchlight. Thrusting his hand down, he brought out a sword.

'A gentleman's, and newly polished!' he exclaimed, and the weapon was handed back for the magistrate to inspect.

Sir Thomas's scrutiny was brief. He stared at the sword in wonder. 'It is my own,' he cried, 'the one that was stolen from me last week. Guard yourselves well, men, lest we have surprised the desperadoes in their den.'

Tremors ran through the party like a gust of wind through a field of wheat. Staves and axes were raised and poised for instant defence. The leaders shuffled cautiously forward, while those behind hung back. Sir Thomas comforted himself that he was now armed, sword in hand.

To the relief of all, the blocked entrance to the second pavilion was reached without any further discovery. Unless the villains had crammed themselves inside the barrels, there was no other place for concealment. The brave band about-turned, eager to be out and away, slaking their thirst at the nearest hostelry and spreading news of the adventure.

'Less haste,' called Sir Thomas. 'Every barrel must be searched before we leave.' He was anxious to recover more of his possessions.

It was Ali, leaping nimbly from barrel to barrel, who found the one which was not empty. It had been pushed on its side behind the others and was sealed. The whole party clustered around. The constable raised his axe and shattered the lid. Sir Thomas peered inside and recoiled in horror. Inside was something which had once been a human being.

14

'Death is a process, not an event.' So spake the surgeon.

'The cells of some tissues may continue to live after others have died,' he went on. 'Moreover, the rate of a body's decomposition can vary, dependent on the state of the body and the temperature and other conditions in the place where it lies or the nature of the soil in which it is buried.'

Two days had passed since the discovery, when Sir Thomas had decided to leave the corpse *in situ* and send to Oxford for this learned doctor, known to him from his student days.

Nightmares had followed that first glimpse of the corpse. Even Sir Thomas's fertile mind could not imagine what savage ill-treatment the hapless steward must have suffered during his last moments. He could not rid his mind of the grotesque distortions of once familiar features. The face was white as chalk, drained of blood, and bloated beyond recognition. A spasm had forced the nostrils open, making the nose flatter and wider than a negro's. The mouth was frozen into a hideous grimace of agony. The tongue and the globes of the eyes protruded in a charade of defiance or amazement.

Also locked in his memory was the pungent odour of over-ripe cheese which the body exuded. This had made his stomach heave like a ship in a storm, and after a futile attempt to quell the flood its entire contents had splashed on the ground at his feet, hastening the party's departure.

As soon as they all emerged into the open air, he had given orders to close the exit behind them. The constable and his band of helpers he had dismissed with coin in the hand to buy themselves recuperative draughts of ale. Then, overcome by faintness, he had seated himself on a fallen pillar to breathe the sweet scents of a tranquil summer day.

Deductions were not difficult to make, for the implications of this new evidence were plain. The presence of the sword was decisive in confirming his belief in John Perry's innocence: the Perry family was exonerated, whatever young John might allege. His own and John's assailants had been using the tunnel as a refuge. They were lurking close to the spot where William Harrison had been attacked and brutally murdered. It would have been easy and natural for them to conceal the body in their lair. Afterwards they must have taken to their heels, leaving the sword behind in their haste or discarding it because it could not be hidden about their persons and would cast suspicion upon them if worn openly. With his own valuables and the steward's money they would have made away with loot enough.

But when he announced these findings to Edward, standing fretting beside him, they had been hotly disputed. 'How then do you account for John Perry's behaviour?' he had wanted to know. 'What reason could the wretch have for confessing to a crime he did not commit?'

John's motive in willing his own hanging and that of his own mother and brother was certainly an unsolved puzzle. Mistress Perry had made no secret of her dislike for her younger offspring, and this appeared to be reciprocated. But was it credible that grudges between mother and son could be carried to such extremes?

Were there other instances except among madmen? Sir Thomas had wondered. To run so against nature argued a sickness of the mind; yet in all other respects John Perry's behaviour was as sane as any man's. The unfortunate youth needed, not a noose around his neck, but guidance and affection. Edward was scarcely likely to take him back into employment. Sir Thomas had felt his sympathies aroused, and he had pondered whether to take the boy into his own service. Would Ali be jealous or would they embrace as brothers?

Before returning home he had stopped the coach in the town and ordered the Perrys' release.

The constable had shaken his head. 'You and I may believe them innocent, Sir Thomas,' he had said, 'but we are the only ones in Campden so minded. If I set them free they will not reach the end of the street alive. There's many a one with a score to settle against Mistress Perry. Few doubt the steward fell victim to her spells. They are sure she is in league with the Devil and has evil spirits at her beck and call.'

'Spells and evil spirits!' Sir Thomas had sneered. 'How can creatures endowed with reason believe in a Devil, and one who walks abroad here in Chipping Campden? As you know better than I, Master Fettiplace, Mistress Perry is a widow who lost her husband fighting for the king. She pretends to powers of divination to get money to keep herself alive.'

'With respect, she foretold the attack upon your good self,' the constable had answered. 'If that was not black magic, it was guilty knowledge. I pity the poor soul but would keep her in custody, all things considered.'

'She merely foretold some misfortune, such as we all suffer from time to time. Now do as I bid you. If you fear for their safety, wait until after dark; and if they come to harm then, I shall hold you responsible. Law and order must be maintained. I will have no mob rule within my jurisdiction.'

The next day he had spent at home in bed, but on the following morning, when he returned for his meeting with the celebrated Professor Arbuthnot, he learned that the Perrys were again in custody. Threats that their house would be burned about their ears had driven them back to seek sanctuary in the lock-up.

Now he was once more crouching in the dank, dark tunnel, handkerchief to nose. The surgeon had refused to have the corpse moved before inspecting it. As soon as the barrel was reopened he had become absorbed in a rare case. Revelling in the macabre sight and treating Sir Thomas like one of his pupils, he proceeded to deliver a lecture on some relevant aspects of what he termed pathophysiology.

'It is not uncommon for corpses in airtight coffins to be mummied and preserved for many years. In an atmosphere that is warm and dry the skin may acquire the texture of leather. Here we have a notable example of total putrefaction arrested by want of air, but the result is very different owing to the coldness and moisture in the environment. I have encountered a similar post-mortem condition in wet graves and damp vaults, but never so remarkable a specimen as you have here. This, I deduce, was a young person in good health.'

'To the best of my knowledge his health was excellent, but he was far from young,' Sir Thomas replied.

The professor was unaccustomed to contradiction. He straightened himself and looked Sir Thomas coldly in the eye. 'Indeed!' he murmured. 'Let us say then that age cannot be reliably determined at this stage of the examination. As to gender, you have used the possessive "his". On what grounds do you postulate a male person, pray?'

'Because his identity is known to me. It is the body of William Harrison, our lady's steward, as I mentioned in my letter to you.'

'Yet you concede that the state of the body has made recognition impossible. Verification of sex, however, should not prove difficult. Hold the lanthorn lower, I beg you.'

Together they bent over the barrel once more, and the light revealed the lower half of the corpse. The knees had been bent tight when it was thrust down, and some rags of clothing still clung to the thighs and groin. The surgeon brushed them gently to one side to uncover the organ of generation. Astonishingly, it had swollen to the size of an elephant's, and the scrotum below resembled an inflated balloon about to burst.

Sir Thomas muttered an involuntary 'Sweet Jesus!' and covered his face. He was aware that hanging caused an erection in the victim and facial features were distorted by strangulation, but he had entertained no notion of a monstrosity such as this.

'Most interesting and significant,' mused the professor. 'The cause is not strangulation. Nor is strangulation responsible for the protruding eyes and tongue as you may have conjectured. Both have occurred after death.'

'I have information that Master Harrison was strangled. Is it proved false? Are there no marks on the neck?'

The great man was too busy with his thoughts and explorations and did not leave off to answer. Instead, after a short delay, he asked a question of his own: 'On or about what date do you contend that this Master Harrison met his end?'

'He has been missing, presumed dead, since the sixteenth day of this month—two Thursdays ago. My interrogations have extracted a confession that he was strangled to death and his body hidden on the night of his disapppearance, but the perpetrators may be other than I had been led to believe. We were deceived about the hiding place and have searched in and out, high and low. The hunt was all but abandoned when I insisted on these ruins being combed for a second time. I was guided by reason and instinct and am pleased to say that I myself led the party which made the discovery. That was but two days ago, when I dispatched my messenger to you.'

'So I take it that you are asserting, as an undoubted fact, that this steward was alive less than two weeks ago, seen and recognised beyond peradventure by those who knew him well?'

Sir Thomas's stomach sank as he gave his assent. The question pointed to only one conclusion. He felt the qualms of one whose pride was about to be punctured by pedantry, and his fears were immediately confirmed by the professor's first words, which were not framed to spare his feelings.

'In that event I must inform you of another undoubted fact: that your search has not met with the success that you imagine, for this is not Master Harrison's body. I regret the necessity of disappointing you, but the scientific evidence is indisputable. The action of the chemical processes on this cadaver must have occurred over a period of many months at least; more probably many years. Do you doubt my finding? Then pray observe this.'

The professor prodded and probed the waxed skin covering the corpse's chest. It was fragile and paper-thin. The flesh underneath had disappeared, creating a hollow between skin and skeleton. The hole made by the finger exposed a rib.

'If it is not Master Harrison, who the deuce can it be?' Sir Thomas was dumbfounded by the demonstration.

'That is a conundrum for you to answer, not me. But, if I may presume to offer you some guidance, these are the remains of a young man and some of these tatters suggest a military uniform, do they not?'

'No soldiers have been stationed in this neighbourhood since the late king's defeat. Unless the body was carried here from a distance—'

'There is no need for that hypothesis, my good sir,' the professor interrupted. 'We have here a body which could well have been preserved in this state for that length of time. And for much longer if undisturbed. But take care when you have it brought to the surface, for the skin will not be resistant to fresh air. Should you be set on attempting identification, I would not advise moving it lest you destroy the evidence.'

'But the features are unrecognisable already, and it is my duty to report the death and arrange for an inquest.' Sir Thomas's customary clear-headedness had deserted him. His mind was in a whirl of humiliation. On the journey home two days ago he had called Ali an imbecile for not sharing his certainty that the body was the missing steward's. And now he was being lectured on his error and told what to do.

'A few more days will make no difference to the coroner, nor to the body if you seal the barrel tight again. I surmise that your inquiries will not take long, for if he was a member of the Campden House garrison during the recent wars he could have come from any part of the country and your task will be hopeless. However, for what it may be worth, I would advocate summoning your local surgeon to take a note of his measurements and any distinguishing marks which may have survived. At the very least that might serve to eliminate others who were lost without trace during the campaigning.'

'I will take your advice,' Sir Thomas promised, contrite. 'But before you go tell me, I pray you, what was the cause of death if it was not strangulation?'

After further examination the professor tore away a strip of shirt and pointed to the corpse's chest again. 'Those were not made by my finger,' he said. 'If your surgeon undertakes a full post-mortem, I would expect him to find portions of the rib cage shattered.'

Sir Thomas found himself staring at holes in the skin made, it seemed evident, by bullets fired at close quarters. There were six of them, still gaping.

'I think we may safely conclude that young Homo Campde-nensis was not killed in battle,' said the professor drily.

15

It was past noon when the two men emerged into the daylight, the one in high spirits, the other gloomy. The professor was still relishing the treat of such a fine specimen of embalmment, while Sir Thomas was vowing never to venture into Campden House's subterranean labyrinth again.

Deaths which were violent and unnatural, unexpected or unexplained, had to be investigated by the county's senior Justice of the Peace. He it was who held the office of coroner. Normally, Sir Thomas resented this requirement to surrender his most interesting inquiries, but not on this occasion. When passing on the professor's report he would stress that the body was too fragile to be moved before an inquest. To hold it, the coroner would be obliged to travel the twenty miles from Gloucester and climb down into the grime of the tunnel in all his finery followed by twelve or more Campden jurymen, who must somehow find room to stand around the body and establish the who, how, when and why of its demise under his supervision. It was an assignment which would lie well beyond all their thick wits.

Before leaving, one clue to the dead man's identity had come to light, and Sir Thomas had it in his pocket. It was a coarsely engraved metal ring which he had not been able to restrain himself from pulling from the corpse's finger despite a warning cry from the professor. To his dismay, the skin had come away with the ring, leaving a single finger bone exposed on the left hand until he had hurriedly covered it again with its waxy scabbard.

Ali was waiting beside the coach to take him home, but he decided to clear his head by walking into town for refreshment. With his guest he repaired to The Eight Bells, where they washed away the taste of death with a dinner of beef pasty and rabbit pies accompanied by generous draughts of mum, the heavy ale for which the hostelry was renowned. 'There is nothing like a corpse for giving a man an appetite,' observed the learned doctor. 'Let us eat and drink our fill and enjoy ourselves while we may.'

To satisfy Sir Thomas's curiosity, he discoursed on the state of the university following the Restoration. He was pleased to relate how Puritan heads imposed on colleges under the Commonwealth were being expelled and the Royalist and High Church fellows who had been evicted were returning. When Michaelmas term began after the long vacation, Oxford would be in a fair way towards reverting to the *status quo ante bellum*.

'Here some things are past restitution,' said Sir Thomas. They were in the upstairs room where John Perry had been held, and he gestured out of the window towards the remains of the great house. The professor followed his gaze gloomily.

'A country which cuts off the head of its king cuts off its past from its future, and neither can ever be put together again. For all the talk we hear about a Restoration, nothing will be as it was, mark my words. The fate of Campden House mirrors the state of England.'

'Yet, if I mistake not, you have a moment ago asserted that you are hopeful of Oxford returning to its old ways.' Sir Thomas quickly seized the opportunity for argument.

'Seats of learning form an exception to the general rule. Scholarship is universal. Its threads cannot be severed.'

'Except simultaneously throughout the world? Is that your contention?'

An encounter with another superior mind was a joy to a man who had to make do with the likes of Sir John Keyte and Captain Dover for company, but Sir Thomas's expectation of an afternoon of assertion and counter-assertion under the pleasurable influence of mum was cut off as abruptly as the king's head. As soon as the meal was over, the professor pocketed his fee, begged to be excused and, without more ado, rose and rode unsteadily away along the Oxford road.

The magistrate summoned his Ali and strolled with him the short distance along the street to the court-house, where he ordered the Perrys to be brought before him. But when he took his seat on the bench he found himself at a loss how to conduct what, earlier in the day, had presented itself as a simple summary dismissal of the charges. Shaken by the morning's revelation, his self-confidence was playing truant.

The discovery of his sword and a body in the same hiding place had appeared to solve the mystery, but instead it had turned one mystery into two. One dead man was still unaccounted for, another unaccountably stumbled upon by chance. His prepared reprimand to John for the fabrication of malicious lies had now to be abandoned. At least it was a blessing that his foresight in consulting an expert witness in privacy had rescued him from the public humiliation of a mistaken identity.

The constable coughed to attract his attention. The prisoners were all present. Proceedings could commence.

Widow Perry and Richard stood apart from John and would not so much as glance at him as he gave his evidence, accusing them to their faces. His eyes were red and ringed with dark circles from weeping and lack of sleep. Yet he remained dogged in repeating word for word the gruesome tale which he had unfolded at the magistrate's house.

'There stand the murderers of the best master a man could ever hope to have,' he ended, jabbing his finger in their direction across the room. 'They killed him for his money. May God have mercy on their souls!'

'He lies! He lies!' screeched his mother with such venom that the constable cowered and Sir Thomas himself became frightened. No wonder she struck terror in even the stoutest breasts among the townsfolk! This was not the woman he remembered admiring in her cottage.

'I speak nothing but the truth, Your Honour,' John shouted back undaunted. 'She knows full well how they were always begging me to help them get their hands on Master Harrison's money; how Richard kept following me demanding that I give him notice what day my master would be collecting his lady's rents; how he twisted my arm and threatened to choke the breath out of me if I would not tell him.'

Richard was a dark, uncomely youth with a sharp-featured, untrustworthy appearance. He answered the charge with a pitying smile. 'My brother is daft,' he said and tapped his own forehead. 'He has invented tales like this since childhood. It is his fondness for making mischief. Do not believe one word he utters.'

'I have my wits about me, and what I say is true,' John insisted. 'Would you deny questioning me on the morning that my master went to Charringworth—and that I told you whither he had gone and on what errand?'

Richard pursed his lips and shrugged his shoulders.

'Answer the question,' Sir Thomas ordered. 'Do you or do you not deny your brother's allegation?'

'It is another of his tricks,' Richard complained. 'Yes; I spoke with him in the market that morning. Folks will have seen us together. But nothing of that sort passed between us.'

'Look me in the eye, John,' his mother intervened.

'That I will not,' he replied trembling, his eyes fixed on the ground. 'You shall not practise your craft on me. Stop her, Your Honour. Stop her, I beseech you, or she will get the Devil to twist my tongue.' He buried his face in his arms.

Sir Thomas held up his hand to halt the hearing while he whispered to the constable. News of the discovery of the body must have been the talk of the town, and he needed to know whether the accused had learned of it or whether it had been kept from them. The constable whispered back that assuredly they knew: they had had the news hurled in their faces when they were released. It was what had inflamed the feeling against them.

'Which of you hid the body in the passage beneath the terrace of the great house?' he demanded. The secret that it was not the steward's body was his alone.

'Not my mother and I. We were at home that night and can vouch for each other,' answered Richard sullenly. 'How often do we have to swear that neither of us ventured abroad after darkness fell? Had we done so, we would not have trespassed on the grounds of the House. We know nothing of all this. We have told the constable so time and again.'

'Yet you poach rabbits from the Conygree, I'm told. Do you expect me to believe that you have never sneaked through the ruins with an eye to what might be filched?'

Richard did not choose to answer this question; he merely scoffed at the suggestion. 'Whatever was of value was taken long ago. I was still a child then. Now there is nothing left worth stealing. I do but wonder that Mistress Harrison bothers to keep such a sharp eye open for scavengers.'

'That is the one who slanders us worst,' said his mother. 'Some folks' tongues are soaked in vinegar. None of them would dare to say these wicked things were my husband alive, but he died for the king and they are Commonwealth curs and bitches,' she spat.

Sinister and bitter the pair of them, judged Sir Thomas as he turned to the third member of the family, so different in looks: a comely lad tortured by shame or guilt or guilty knowledge.

'And what have you to say about the body, John? Do you too plead ignorance? Remember that you have described how your master was killed at a short distance from the place where it was found. Confess that you assisted your mother and brother in the arduous work of carrying it underground and concealing it in an old barrel. Come now; have you lost your tongue?'

The magistrate took pleasure in setting this trap, repaying deceit with deceit to unlock the truth.

John was unsettled by it; there could be no doubt about that. He stood brooding dumbly, his brow knitted, uncertain how to respond. 'Is it indeed my master's body?' he asked at last in a voice of puzzlement or disbelief.

'Why should you question it?' Sir Thomas spoke gently so as not to frighten his quarry. John had grown as nervous as a deer scenting a huntsman on his trail.

'Because they were going to throw it into the Great Sink.'

'But the Great Sink has been searched and it was not there.'

'Then I know not what to think.' The words were barely audible and he would say no more.

Sir Thomas pleaded with him to unburden himself, tempted him with promises, offered to order his mother and Richard from the room while he spoke. But John's jaws were clamped tight. Nor would they open when the magistrate began to shout at him and rattle the windows with a hurricane of threats.

To be defeated by a dumb peasant boy was intolerable, and Sir Thomas's patience had snapped. He decided to let fly with the last arrow in his quiver and share his knowledge of the truth about the body. A wiser instinct warned him to keep the information to himself, but he could see no other way forward.

'Let me inform you then that, in the opinion of a learned medical friend whom I have consulted, the body in the tunnel is not your master's. What have you to say to that?'

All the accused looked as startled as he had expected; the constable more so. 'Whose body might it be, sir?' he asked.

'I cannot say until a fuller examination has been conducted. We must await the coroner's report. The identification of the corpse will be his responsibility, not mine.'

Sir Thomas read relief on the prisoners' faces. He resumed his interrogation hopefully, but it proved fruitless. They clung to their stories like storm-tossed sailors to a mast. One or two or all three must be lying, but he came no closer towards discovering which.

While he was hesitating whether to release them a new voice was raised. Edward Harrison had entered the court-room unnoticed and was requesting to be permitted to speak with him in private. Not displeased at the timeliness of the interruption, Sir Thomas gave orders for the court to be cleared and the prisoners returned to their cells.

'Your Honour will see that we are fairly treated,' Mistress Perry implored with a wheedling glance.

'Justice will be done,' he promised, and she was led away.

Edward could hardly wait for the room to be emptied. 'Can

it be true what I heard you saying when I opened the door a minute ago—that the body is not my father's? I could not believe my ears. With all respect to your friend, Sir Thomas, the gentleman must be in error. How can there be a second body?'

'That is a question that I was about to put to you, Master Edward. Professor Arbuthnot is the most respected pathologist in England. There is none whose reputation stands higher. His opinion cannot be gainsaid. You and your mother will need to satisfy me and the coroner that you had no knowledge of an unreported death or disappearance—or of any possible connection between it and your father's.'

Edward was quick to take offence. 'If any of my family had suspected a crime it would have been reported in due form,' he answered stiffly. 'As her ladyship's representatives, we uphold the law in Campden as she would herself were she in residence. That is the very reason why my mother has sent me here. She insists that the witch and her brood be indicted for the murder to which they have confessed. Every night she is troubled by visions of my father's spirit walking abroad, denied a Christian burial. She cannot rest or sleep until his killers are brought to justice.'

'Doubtless Mistress Harrison sent you to me in the belief that the body discovered was her husband's, as I myself believed until this morning. But since it is not so, the circumstances are different.'

'There remains the confession.'

'One confession and two denials, allow me to remind you. That is slim evidence for a conviction. Would you have the Perrys tried and acquitted for want of a body?'

'With their reputations no jury would acquit them.'

'No Campden jury perhaps, but they would not be tried here, as you must be aware. Charges of murder are heard at the Gloucester assizes.'

'On behalf of my widowed mother and myself, I beg you to dispatch them thither without delay. And pray do not overlook the robbery last year when our house was broken open while we were at church and Richard stole seven score pounds on information regarding its whereabouts given to him by John. Two indictments will make conviction sure.'

'That other is an unsolved crime to which no one has confessed. But you may tell your mother that I will give serious consideration to her request.' Sir Thomas rose to signify that the interview was ended.

Edward left and Ali emerged from the floor behind his master where he had been squatting unobserved.

'Did you notice John's surprise at being told the body was the steward's?' asked Sir Thomas while Ali was helping him with his cloak. 'I am wondering whether you have been right and Master Harrison is not dead at all, and John knows it.'

'Did you notice the look on the constable's face?' Ali responded. 'I am wondering whether he knows whose body it is you have found.'

16

A week had passed, and with it August. The afternoon sun peering through the library window was already low in the sky. It was the day of the inquest and Ali had been sent to Campden to keep an eye on proceedings and bring back news of the findings.

His doublet discarded, Sir Thomas sprawled at ease on a chaise-longue, resplendent in an Indian undress gown embroidered with purple peacocks. The door was locked. Safe from domestic interruption, he was basking in what he had described in one of his favourite couplets as 'The blessed peace that comes, men say, With wife and daughter far away'—or, at any rate, out of earshot.

Relaxed but not idle, he was reading attentively. The latest news-sheet from London told of an unending scramble for the power and privilege which he longed for but did not deign to solicit for fear of rebuff. Veterans of the war who had not made their peace with the Lord Protector were clamouring to be rewarded for their loyalty to the Crown. Most had been condemned to disappointment by the settlement forced upon the king at Breda as the price of his Restoration. With all except the signatories to Charles the Martyr's death warrant protected from retribution, the former Commonwealth ministers and functionaries were clinging tenaciously to their offices and dubiously acquired estates.

He turned the page to study the report of an Act of Parliament which had received the royal assent the previous week after three months of furious debate in both Houses. It was a second

117

Act of Indemnity and Oblivion, relating to all offences committed during what was designated 'the recent troubles'. The Declaration of Breda had promised a general pardon, but not the validation of legal proceedings during the interregnum. The new Act stipulated that all treasons, felonies, crimes and misdemeanours committed between the first day of January 1637 and the twenty-third day of June 1660 be pardoned, released, discharged and put into utter oblivion.

Sir Thomas whistled aloud at the implications of what he read. Did it mean that if William Harrison had been killed two months earlier his murderers would have escaped justice? That would be unconscionable; yet it might prevent a miscarriage of justice. But no! He read on and discovered that an offence as heinous as murder was excepted under the provisions of Section 10. The Act would have provided no loophole for the Perrys.

Because of the importunity of the missing man's family they had been transferred to Gloucester and lay there in gaol awaiting trial, despite Constable Fettiplace's protests and his own misgivings. Now, for one moment, he had fondly imagined that this Act would set the poor wretches free.

Since the confrontation in the court-room he had interrogated John once more, this time alone. It had been a new John who stood before him, no longer emotional and tearful. Instead he appeared calm and withdrawn. Yet his story was unchanged. He had held fast to that, outwardly heedless of the terrible consequences, until the magistrate was convinced that the steward had indeed been murdered as stated, although John himself and probably his mother too were innocent of the intent. Richard Perry was the villain.

'You do understand that as an accomplice you will be liable to suffer the same fate as your brother?' Sir Thomas had pressed him. 'A plea for mercy will avail you nought. You are aware of that? Then tell me, I beg you, why you have made this confession. Is it your wish to be hanged? Do you imagine yourself to be suffering from a mortal sickness so dreadful that you have decided to cut off your life before you succumb? Shall I send for a physician to examine you and confound your fears?'

The reply was a stubborn shake of the head and a mumble about 'my master'.

'So you see no prospect in life without Master Harrison, is that it—and you a young lad of parts and promise? Answer me this: if you were freed, would you enter my service? There! I have made you an offer. Admit to a fabrication and you shall have a livery, good wages and enough to eat and drink. You shall accompany me on my visits to Gloucester and London and see the world. No person of your birth could hope for more. What do you say to that?'

The blunt response had festered in the magistrate's mind ever since. He had been thanked with due deference, but then came the fatal, softly spoken words: 'I would die for my master.' Madness was the only explanation. It was inconceivable that any sane person would choose to be hanged rather than enter the service of an Overbury.

He had spent the succeeding days wrestling with his doubts, and the longer he considered John Perry's behaviour the more convinced of his innocence he became. Perhaps he was intending to retract his confession at the trial. If so, he was playing a game more dangerous than he realised, for by that time it would be on the record, duly attested by witnesses.

How to save a foolish innocent who would not or could not save himself: that was the challenge. Had he dismissed the denials of the mother and brother too readily? Should he be looking for the real culprits elsewhere?

Two sets of suspects sprang to mind. Sir Thomas's distrust of the Harrisons, mother and son, ran deep. Most murders were family affairs. Might it be that the Harrisons' determination to see the Perrys hanged for the crime was caused by a more sinister motive than thirst for vengeance? They were said to be jealous of the steward's affection for his pretty young servant and alarmed lest the boy was being groomed to supplant Edward Harrison in the succession to the stewardship. But were they heartless enough to rid themselves of a hated husband and father so cruelly?

Upon consideration Sir Thomas judged Mistress Harrison's

119

religious fervour to be no deterrent. Her bloodthirsty Old Testament God could be relied upon to whisper in her ear whatever she felt inclined to hear. As for Edward, it was no secret that he had grown embittered from waiting over-long to step into his father's shoes.

No less under suspicion lay the mysterious villains who had had the temerity to ambush a Justice of the Peace and were still eluding capture. That they had been using the undercroft of the great house as a hiding place was proved by the finding of his stolen sword. They might well have ambushed the steward in a similar manner and left him not tied up but dead. In that case, though, where was the body?

Or what of a conspiracy? Might a member of the family living in the almonry have become aware of their presence? Suppose Edward Harrison had stumbled upon them and been threatened. They would have demanded money and he might have saved his own skin by informing them when and where to come across his father carrying the rent money collected from the farms at Charringworth and Ebrington. If the killing of the steward during the ambush was part of the bargain, who would ever know or believe it?

Sir Thomas frowned at the ceiling. He had a personal score to settle with those men, but would they ever be caught? They were but two among hundreds. He felt few regrets for the now loudly lamented Charles the Martyr, but his reign before 'the recent troubles' had been a time when outlaws hung from gibbets where they belonged and a man of property could sit at home or ride abroad confident in the protection of the law. Malefactors then were quickly brought to justice, for they were local men and known. Now, uprooted by war and revolution, idle, nameless vagrants from distant regions roamed the county in search of easy pickings at the expense of honest folk.

Such men could not be lightly eliminated from his inquiry. These two had also attacked John Perry—or so he claimed, and why should he have invented that story? If true, it was evidence that they had been prowling the neighbourhood for several weeks; and, if weeks, why not months? They could well have been responsible, not only for William Harrison's murder, but also for the unusual number of thefts of animals reported by farmers during the winter.

Then there was the incident of the robbery from the steward's house the previous autumn. That crime too could be attributed to them. Yet here again account had to be taken of a statement by young John. It had come at the end of their meeting a few days earlier. Although maintaining his denial of his own involvement, he had again pointed the finger at his brother.

'He guessed where the money was kept without my telling him.'

'Where did he hide it afterwards?'

John had hesitated at this and scratched his head. 'In the garden behind my mother's cottage,' he said at last.

Richard, interrogated by the constable, had ridiculed the story as yet another instance of his brother's malice towards him. 'Search the garden,' he had scoffed, 'and you will learn which of us is the liar.'

The garden was not large, and it had been dug from side to side and end to end to the destruction of Widow Perry's precious vegetables but without a single coin being unearthed.

'What did John say when you told him?' Sir Thomas had asked the constable when he came to report the failure of the search.

'Richard must have moved it to waste ground behind the garden, he said; but we had done digging enough.' The constable had wearied of John as a source of misinformation.

Sir Thomas was brooding on this when Ali's head appeared round the door. 'Come and sit beside me,' he ordered, 'and enlighten me with the news from subterranean Campden.'

Ali was in buoyant mood, bubbling with all he had to report. Curiosity to view the grisly sight below ground in the ruined mansion was so great that almost every man in the town had been a volunteer for jury service. The constable had had to lay about him with his staff to control the crowd while he selected twelve who were known to him, with Robert Hayward of The Eight Bells as their foreman.

121

'And their verdict?' Sir Thomas demanded impatiently.

'First I handed the coroner the Oxford professor's report as you instructed me. He read it out to the jury and explained it to them before they went below. I was not allowed down, but when they came up I told Master Hayward that you had sent me and he must tell me everything. He obliged, but was not his usual self. Nor, come to think of it, were the rest of them when they clambered out. The gentleman from Gloucester was in the worst shape. He was so fat he could hardly get down and up again at all.' Ali laughed at the memory and his little joke.

Sir Thomas tugged at his hair. 'The verdict, you imp!'

Ali pulled himself away, stood up and delivered it in a solemn, deep voice as though in court. 'Murder of person unknown, by persons unknown,' he intoned.

The coroner, he said, had instructed the jury that the professor's evidence allowed for no doubt that this was a case of execution by firing squad, dating from the occupation of Campden House during the war.

'Then the man is an ass,' declared Sir Thomas. 'An execution ordered by a garrison commander appointed by the king would not amount to murder. Did the coroner consider that point in law?'

'According to Master Hayward he took the view that hiding the body in a barrel was evidence of a killing without authority.'

'Did he rule out the possibility of establishing the victim's identity?'

This question was prompted by a twinge of conscience. Sir Thomas had suddenly remembered the ring he had taken from one of the corpse's waxen fingers. It was of base metal, roughly made and of no value, suggesting only that it had belonged to someone of low rank. Nonetheless it was evidence which should have been handed to the coroner.

Ali nodded. 'But Constable Fettiplace and Master Hayward both served with the garrison, did they not? They were whispering together when I left. I think they can tell you more than they told the coroner—if they so wish.'

122

'Very well. And the body? Is that still to be seen in case the features can be recognised?'

This time Ali shook his head. 'I followed it straightway to the churchyard. A grave was dug to rebury it there and then. Everyone was in a hurry to see the last of it.'

'But the parson is lying sick. Here in this village. Who conducted the service? Did they send to Ebrington?'

'There was no minister, no ceremony. With the parson away the coroner took it upon himself to order the burial. Because the body was so fragile it was left in the barrel. No one could bear to touch it.'

'A barrel for a coffin!' The impropriety tickled Sir Thomas's fancy. 'But at least this Unknown Solider lies in consecrated ground. He will be able to jump out and plead his case before the Almighty on the Day of Judgment.'

'Not Unknown to some,' said Ali.

17

Sir Thomas did not believe in coincidence, but detecting a connection between the two Campden House murders was a puzzle which taxed even his superior intellect. The following morning he spent on business in Ilmington, but his mind was preoccupied. On his return he excused himself from dining *en famille* and ate instead with Ali in the library.

Ali's table manners were fastidious and he never spoke to interrupt his master's thoughts. He had brought to the house a blessing for which Sir Thomas daily thanked whatever gods might or might not be: the oriental gift of silent service.

The immediate challenge was how to save the Perrys, for after veering this way and that the magistrate's intuition had settled firmly on their innocence. His nature had always inclined him to favour the friendless and the doomed, those reviled and deserted by others.

The best—perhaps the last—hope for these unfortunates rested on his bludgeoning the dying vicar of Chipping Campden into unburdening himself of the proof of their innocence which he claimed to possess but would not disclose. Success would not be easy. The two of them had been locked in several hard-fought tussles, and that bigoted man of God had proved himself unyielding when his mind was set.

'You must go now to the parsonage, master.' Ali guessed his thoughts and broke the rule of silence.

The vicar of Bourton had called the previous evening with the news that his fellow clergyman was sinking fast and wished to be removed from Bourton to his own parish, where he might die in his own bed within sight of his own church. Before leaving, he desired to converse with the magistrate in private.

Sir Thomas had graciously offered the use of his coach to convey his dying foe home the next day and promised to visit him beforehand in the afternoon.

'God is beckoning his faithful servant towards eternal bliss. The physician opines that he may breathe his last at any moment. I pray you come sooner,' the Reverend Oldisworth had pleaded.

'That cannot be.' Sir Thomas's graciousness was already fully stretched. 'These days I am ordered to bed early after my rough handling, and in the morning I have an engagement which cannot be broken. Tomorrow afternoon is the earliest time I can come. God must stay His hand till then.'

Even now he was not to be hurried. 'Pray allow your master to finish his meal in peace,' he grumbled at Ali.

As soon as it was over Ali helped him doff his undress gown and don his slashed doublet, his light summer cloak and his high-crowned felt hat with golden cords glistening around the brim. He had a silver-hilted dress sword buckled to his waist and, with gloves in hand, stepped out like a lord, fittingly clad to strike underlings with awe during a promenade through the hamlet which formed the seat of his domain.

Bourton on the Hill sat on a steep slope overlooking Moreton in Marsh and the gentle countryside of Warwickshire and Oxfordshire beyond. Thatched cottages perched on either side of a road which climbed westwards towards the height of Broadway Hill before winding down through Broadway itself to the next valley, where Evesham and the gaunt ruins of Pershore Abbey stood among the orchards of Worcestershire.

To Sir Thomas, whose travels had taken him through distant lands vaunted as cradles of civilisation, this part of Gloucestershire and its surrounding counties was the finest country in the world. In this he was at one with his father. The rainfall was high, but it brought prosperity, watering lush grass which fattened the sheep and had made their wool the most prized in Europe. With the warmth of the sun and the coolness of a breeze making merry together on his face, all thought of lawlessness was banished from his mind. Instead he mused how those who had spent their lives in this paradise on earth must find Heaven a disappointment.

His manor house commanded the crest of the hill. Relishing the prospect of the Reverend Bartholomew's frustrated expectations of the next world, he strolled out of the gates and down the street in a glow of self-satisfaction. In his wake marched his footboy, Ali, resplendent in the Overbury livery, incongruously crowned with a turban. He too was armed: with a half-sword in a brightly polished scabbard. Their destination stood beside the parish church of St Lawrence at a short distance below.

Sir Thomas had needed a period of cerebration to prepare himself for this encounter with the hammer of sectaries and unbelievers. If anyone knew the secrets of Chipping Campden, it would certainly be that parish's long-serving incumbent. His request for a private meeting was a hopeful sign, but how much of what he had learned would he freely divulge? Most likely the truth would have to be squeezed from him, but squeezed it would be.

Approaching the door, Sir Thomas braced himself for the battle of wills, but to his dismay it was opened by the Reverend Oldisworth wearing a long face and crying 'Too late' at the sight of him. He was led inside, and there on a bed lay the mortal remains of the old man, already gone to his Maker.

Unable to accept that his adversary had thus outwitted him, Sir Thomas slapped the pallid grey cheeks vigorously in an effort to recall him to consciousness. The Reverend Oldisworth interposed himself to shield the corpse. 'Desist!' he cried aghast. 'You ought to have come sooner.'

The justice of the reproach touched Sir Thomas on the raw and redoubled his rage. 'How long has he been dead?' he demanded.

'He passed a peaceful night, slept through the morning and joined the heavenly host no more than an hour since. You will be glad to know that he felt little pain. I stayed at hand to comfort him, knowing that his time was come. All his suffering is over now.'

Sir Thomas ground his teeth. 'A plague on all parsons, dead or alive!' he muttered under his breath, adding aloud: 'You were remiss in not sending me a second warning, Master Oldisworth. No; do not plead that you were ignorant of the importance of my business with him. You knew it as well as I. Now, unless I am much mistaken, you will have innocent blood on your Christian conscience.'

The vicar of Bourton knew better than to defend himself against this unjust tirade. He met it with silence. A dispute in the presence of the dead would be unseemly, and there could be no doubting where the blame really lay.

Deprived of argument, Sir Thomas turned on his heel. 'I shall order my coach to carry the body to Campden,' he called over his shoulder. 'Kindly send to inform me of the time appointed for the funeral.' Paying his last respects to one he did not respect would be his penance.

'You will join me in prayer for the good man's soul before you go.' The call was more of a statement than a question. Sir Thomas responded with a snort, leaving his parish priest kneeling alone as he banged the door behind him.

Outside, he threw his arm around the waiting Ali's shoulder and walked back up the hill leaning on him for support. He was overpowered by feelings of frustration and guilt and self-pity. He was the victim of his own misjudgment and an enemy who had slipped away unfairly. Tricked and provoked by fate, he had behaved badly. Yes; he admitted that to himself. Why, oh why, had he been so foolish as to delay his visit for the sake of some trifling disagreement with a tenant over payment of a paltry rent?

The sun had disappeared behind a cloud, the breeze was strengthening, and the climb made him sweat like a labourer. Heavenly bliss, he thought miserably, might be preferable to life in Gloucestershire after all—and if the place existed outside the Church's imagination William Bartholomew was already there enjoying it! Ali was murmuring words of comfort, but he refused to be consoled.

Back in his library, he lost no time in penning an urgent appeal addressed to the Lady Juliana, Dowager Viscountess Campden, at Brooke, her home in Rutlandshire. In it he explained the circumstances of the charge of murder against the three Perrys and begged her to write to him with any other explanation for the disappearance of her steward which might have occurred to her. He was at pains to emphasise the attachment of John Perry to his master, and how this cast doubt on the genuineness of his confession, which—mere suspicion apart—stood alone as evidence of the guilt of the accused.

If the vicar of Campden's information had not reached him by way of the confessional, then the most likely source of a confidential communication was Brooke. It would be natural for the lady of the manor—and patron of the living—to choose the parish priest as her correspondent. That was Sir Thomas's conclusion, and he waited on tenterhooks for the reply, which took a full week to arrive.

Her ladyship was confined to bed with a fever, her steward wrote, and was therefore unable to answer Sir Thomas's letter herself; for which she begged his forgiveness. Edward Harrison had kept her informed of events at Campden. He had assured her that the accused were the guilty parties, but she would gladly lend her support to any move which Sir Thomas might deem necessary to avert a miscarriage of justice. She knew of Mistress Perry and her elder son only by name, but Master Harrison had told her that the husband and father was a servant below stairs at Campden House who had heeded the call to arms when war broke out, and laid down his life in battle for the king. She therefore felt some obligation towards his widow. As for John, her steward at Campden had expressed nothing but praise for his work in helping to manage the estate.

The letter ended with a reminder that, although the Campden property was hers under her father's will, she was now some years past her allotted span of threescore years and ten and had long ago stated her intention to hand responsibility for it to her son, who would inherit it on her death. She was daily expecting his return from abroad, when he would come to Campden and assist Sir Thomas in arriving at the truth: in the event of a trial he would attend and give evidence on her behalf.

On reading the last sentence Sir Thomas curled his lip in a sneer at the prospect of such a devious witness. He knew Baptist Noel, third Viscount Campden, for a stranger to the truth and a feather-brained scapegrace incapable of unravelling a ball of wool, let alone a mystery as deep as this. Swagger and low cunning were the prime ingredients of this nobleman's own pernicious character, as Sir Thomas had learned to his cost.

They had met in Damascus, where his impoverished lordship was living on his wits and what his mother could afford to send him. As a gambler he had not looked back since the occasion of his marriage when his bride had received a gift of £3000 from the king and he had promptly lost £2500 of it at tennis in a single day. In Damascus he was rumoured to be inextricably in debt to Levantine money-lenders. He had tempted Sir Thomas to a game of cards for high stakes and cheated outrageously. The cards were marked, although he had sworn it was a new pack. When Sir Thomas remonstrated, he had first laughed in his face and then demanded satisfaction for the slur on his honour.

The humiliation of leaving Damascus in a hurry to avoid being killed in a duel with a card-sharp rankled with Sir Thomas still. The ne'er-do-well viscount was the last person he wanted interfering with his inquiry. No doubt he would be coming home, with creditors on his heels, to see what the king would do for him. Nothing, Sir Thomas expected and hoped. His Majesty possessed no largesse to scatter except what he could wheedle out of Parliament, and that was quickly spent on his mistresses and other royal pleasures.

After the disappointment of the Reverend Bartholomew's untimely departure from this world and the missive from the Lady Juliana's steward came a third blow. Later that same day a summons was delivered requiring the presence of Sir Thomas Overbury, Justice of the Peace, at the county court to testify at the trial of Joan, Richard and John Perry, of the parish of Chipping Campden.

The date was set for the following week; which allowed him little time to explore ways of harnessing her ladyship's good will to a case for the prisoners' defence. What could be the secret she had imparted to the parson but not to him? Could he extract it from her in seven days? Should he ride to Brooke? Or would her son reach Gloucester in time to reveal whatever it might be in court?

He rang for Ali and they put their heads together.

18

Although Ali urged it, Sir Thomas did not ride to Brooke. It was too far. Instead he wrote giving the date of the trial, but no reply had been received when the time came for him to leave.

He was accustomed to travel to the county town in his coach, displaying the Overbury arms so that his importance should not be overlooked. The disadvantage of this means of transport lay in the need to persuade his wife not to accompany him, since he preferred to spend his time there in exclusively male company. Political news and scandalous gossip were not for female ears; still less the bawdy tales and songs of his less respectable acquaintance. Nowadays every visit provoked an argument. Their annual sojourns in London were proving insufficient to slake Lady Overbury's thirst for a wider social world than the rustic hundred of Kiftsgate.

'If your heart was set on the follies of town life,' he told her testily, 'you should have married a money-grubbing merchant or an attorney like your father who profits from bending the law in the courts. A mere knight of the shire has nothing to offer but such trifles as comfort, position and a title.'

Merchants he held in scarcely lesser contempt than lawyers, priests and physicians. All stood almost as low in his esteem as women in general and wives in particular. What infuriated him most about his own wife was not so much her lack of intellectual curiosity as her stubborn refusal to answer him back. Whenever they quarrelled and he was whetting his appetite to rout her in a battle of words, in quodlibets of pure reason, the sorry creature chose to sulk in silence.

On this occasion he expressed concern for her condition and reminded her of the brutal assault he had suffered: footpads were rendering the highways unsafe, and there could be no question of endangering the life of his unborn son and heir. He told her he would go on horseback and be escorted by Ali and a groom, all three of them well armed with pistols. She looked away to hide her disappointment and said not a word to plead that a well-armed escort could protect her too and in Gloucester she would be glad to lodge with her parents during her pregnancy.

He made the journey without incident on the day before the assizes were due to open. The approach to Gloucester was enriched by a view of the cathedral's soaring central tower which was Chipping Campden's magnified. It rose into the sky above the houses and ruined fragments of the buildings of the Greyfriars and the Blackfriars and Llanthony priory. Good riddance to those temples of Error and Unreason, he thought.

With Ali at his side he rode through the North Gate and turned into the courtyard of the New Inn. Someone was in occupation of his favourite room on the upper storey looking down on the market cross, and he had to remonstrate with the landlord and kick his heels in the parlour while the interloper and his effects were moved. While passing the time, he wrote and dispatched a message to Sir Christopher Turnor, the circuit judge, requesting an audience on the subject of Rex versus Perry, Perry and Perry.

The reply was prompt and civil: it would be convenient and give Sir Christopher much pleasure if Sir Thomas would do him the honour of calling after supper to discuss the case and assist him in broaching some bottles of canary wine which he had been resigned to drinking alone in his lodgings.

The day was fine. It invited a perambulation, and the magistrate was not above inspecting the cathedral out of historical interest. Every man of education must be conscious of the relevance of the past in the life of the nation, he believed. Inside lay the remains of Edward II, another royal martyr, formerly revered like the unworthy Charles. His tomb found a sympathetic visitor in Sir Thomas: Edward too had spurned his wife for male company.

Then he stumbled upon Duke Robert, William the Conqueror's eldest son, who should have been King of England but had to be content with Normandy thanks to the perfidy of the Church. An archbishop had crowned a younger brother, who (Sir Thomas was pleased to remember) had turned out to be a pagan. No more fortunate in death than in life, Duke Robert was commemorated by a battered wooden effigy which rested in disgrace in the gloom of a dusty side-aisle, broken to pieces by the musket butts of Puritan soldiers.

Moving to the quiet of the deserted cloisters, Sir Thomas collected his thoughts in preparation for the meeting with Sir Christopher. It proved as well he did so, because in the evening he found himself subjected to a stringent examination.

At first the judge listened attentively to his long account of the circumstances of the case, including the attack on himself and the coincidence of chancing upon the corpse of another man. Their glasses were regularly replenished; which became an aid to eloquence. Sir Christopher then responded with a veritable cannonade of questions. It took an hour and more before he was satisfied. By that time there were four empty bottles on the floor and Sir Thomas was arguing ever more loudly and vehemently for the prisoners' lives.

When his submission on behalf of the defence was exhausted, he said that he trusted he might sleep easy that night confident that the judge's address to the jury on the morrow would instruct them to return a verdict of not guilty.

'I do assure you I shall do no such thing.'

Sir Thomas was overcome, first by astonishment and then by wrath. All his masterful advocacy had counted for nothing! He had been enticed by an offer of hospitality, only to be grossly insulted by a pig-headed dotard who had deceived him with a pretence of conferring as colleagues. He was affronted. The fellow was even smirking.

Fortunately, before he could give utterance to his thoughts, the judge spoke again. 'What we have here, Sir Thomas, is a disappearance, not a death, as you yourself have acknowledged. Until death is proved there can be no question of murder, and I am not persuaded by the evidence you have put before me—so cogently, if I may say so—that this William Harrison is dead. This is not a question of guilty or not guilty. In such circumstances there can be no trial.'

Sir Thomas was amply appeased. 'That has been my own conclusion precisely: no body, no murder. But those accused of the crime have now been indicted.'

'I shall strike out the indictment, and gladly. The list before me this session is so long that the end of it will scarcely be in view when I have to depart. You live in a county where crime is burgeoning, Sir Thomas, and justice must not be dispensed in haste. Some less pressing cases will needs be held over, but I shall make good use of the time saved.'

They celebrated their accord with another bottle apiece, after which Sir Thomas gratefully accepted the offer of a footman to guide his footsteps round the corner of the street to the inn, where Ali was waiting patiently to put him to bed. To his boy, who listened impassively whilst undressing him, he gravely recited the judge's parting peroration, repeating the words aloud to fasten them in his own memory:

'While recognising the impossibility of proving that Master Harrison is dead, let us at the same time not forget that we have no evidence, or reason to suppose, that he is still alive. After a greater length of time his death may be presumed, but the laws of England and the demands of justice look to you, the examining magistrate, to anticipate that eventuality by uncovering the truth. In my judgment no Justice of the Peace in the entire country is better equipped for the task than your good self, Sir Thomas.'

In the morning, as he entered the court-room, he was still glowing with gratification and pride at the trust reposed in his intellectual powers by one so highly placed. It was a trust which he was determined to justify.

He ran his eye over the assembled company. Edward Harrison was in attendance as a witness; doubtless with the intention of ensuring that the accused were condemned to death. Sir

Thomas was pleased to think that he was about to suffer disappointment.

The Perrys were the first prisoners to be called. They shuffled into the court, manacled and pitiful. Two indictments had been found against them: first, breaking into the house of William Harrison between eleven and twelve o'clock noon one market day in Chipping Campden in the month of October during the year of Our Lord 1659 and robbing him of the sum of one hundred and forty pounds; secondly, robbing and murdering the said William Harrison on the sixteenth day of August 1660. They were allowed no lawyer to present their defence and stood bewildered by the proceedings.

When the legal jargon was interpreted and they understood that the second charge had been struck from the record on the judge's order, Richard broke into tears of relief and embraced his mother. John displayed no emotion. He stared about him indifferently as though the words meant nothing to him. The judge then beckoned to Sir Thomas, who approached the bench for a whispered consultation.

'I rejoice to see you in good spirits after that little Bacchanalian revel last evening. Our colloquy gave me much pleasure as well as enlightenment. Now that the more important issue which we discussed is settled, would you be agreeable to obliging the court in the matter of the remaining count against these prisoners? You are, of course, aware of the terms of the recent Act of Oblivion?'

Charmed by Sir Christopher's affability and ashamed at his own momentary spasm of anger the previous evening, Sir Thomas at once signified his willingness and awareness.

'Very well. The alleged robbery was committed last year, within the period covered by the provisions of the Act. The accused will therefore be set free at the conclusion of the trial whether found innocent or guilty. Hearing the case will take up the court's time unnecessarily, but I am, of course, bound to proceed with it if they plead not guilty.'

'You wish me to persuade them to enter pleas of guilty on the assurance of a pardon, as decreed by Parliament?'

'I do. The new law is unequivocal. Robbery is not among the crimes excepted. They can come to no harm by doing as we ask.'

'But suppose they are innocent? Although the younger brother at first confessed, nothing he says can be relied upon and the others are insistent that he was lying. They have been unswerving in their denials.'

'But can their word be relied upon either? You have informed me that neither enjoys a savoury reputation. I would be vexed to spend the day trying them and rise at the end of it with a finding of guilty, when the very same verdict could have been reached within five minutes.'

Sir Thomas approached the unfortunate prisoners reluctantly. If there was insufficient evidence to convict, the law ought surely to require a clear verdict of 'not guilty'.

When they heard his proposal, the prisoners became indignant. John had changed his story as expected and joined the others in protesting that he too knew nothing whatever about the robbery. 'How can I be guilty if I was in church at the time,' he snivelled. 'Half the town was in the congregation and can vouch for me. And I never blabbed to my brother.'

Anxious not to disoblige Sir Christopher, Sir Thomas rounded on them fiercely: the judge had saved them from the gallows; they were ingrates not to trust him; did they not wish to be set free? Struck dumb by his vehemence, the sons shuffled their feet in indecision. The black pupils of their mother's eyes looked straight through him. She was wearing an expression he could not read.

Disconcerted by her gaze, he nonetheless pressed on: 'I cannot believe that you all mean to disobey His Honour. How can you think of being so wicked and foolish?'

At this rebuke the sons inclined their heads, which Sir Thomas chose to interpret as a sign of submission to the judge's will. At his nod Sir Christopher entered a plea of guilty, instructed the jury to return a verdict accordingly and pronounced the promised pardon. The trial was over.

Outside the court Sir Thomas's demand for the release of the prisoners was respectfully refused by the keeper of the gaol, who had them in his charge: 'They remain in custody until I receive orders to set them free. That is the rule, sir.'

Edward Harrison then emerged from the court and burst between them, shaking his fist in the prisoners' faces and vowing that they would never be released. They had not been acquitted of his father's murder, he shouted, and he intended to produce new evidence and press further charges. To free these robbers and murderers would be a travesty of justice.

Not to free them would be the travesty of justice, the magistrate riposted, and while the argument raged the prisoners were led away. Sir Thomas returned to his inn bruised by this setback. The Perrys' last reproachful looks haunted him throughout the long ride home. He presumed the order of release would come, but could not hold back a surge of foreboding. Where, O where was the promised viscount who could have produced evidence of John Perry's innocence and put the impudent new steward in his place?

19

The winter months passed uneventfully. Frost lay thick on the hillside above Chipping Campden and sprinkled the fields below. The harsh weather induced inactivity. Sir Thomas stayed within doors busying himself with another treatise, while above stairs his wife gave birth to another daughter. Even this misfortune failed to distract him from his self-appointed task of hammering the faithful in *Queries Proposed to the Serious Consideration of those who Impose upon Others in Things of Divine and Supernatural Revelation and Persecute any upon the Account of Religion.*

His investigation into the fate of the missing steward and the whereabouts of his body was suspended. Defeat was hard to swallow and he strove to erase it from his consciousness, but guilt haunted him. Night after night he lay awake thinking of the Perrys held in custody despite his promise.

They were still in Gloucester gaol, with Edward Harrison still hounding them towards the gallows. He was assisted by John himself, who clung to the story that his mother and brother had killed his master for the money he was carrying. John was even refusing to eat or drink with them because he believed they were intent on poisoning him to suppress his evidence.

Edward had conducted a search of Widow Perry's cottage. On the strength of some clay fragments found there, he was preparing to bring a charge of invultuation against her. This was for making an image of his father for the purpose of witchcraft. He was now accusing her of having caused the body to vanish by sorcery.

Sir Thomas learned this from a lengthy document addressed to him by Edward. It contained a copy of a petition sent to Sir Robert Hyde, the judge appointed to preside over the spring assizes. Preoccupied with his writing, the magistrate had tossed it aside until it demanded his attention during the first week of March, when he was once more summoned to appear as a witness.

The character and views of this new judge were very different from those of Sir Christopher Turnor. This time the indictment of the Perrys was allowed to proceed to trial, body or no body. Sir Robert was related to the Lord Chancellor and owed his elevation to his cousin's patronage. His knowledge of the law was frail. On the bench he was noted for curt manners, erratic judgments and severe sentences. On reading his name Sir Thomas's foreboding in the autumn returned redoubled.

On arrival in Gloucester his fears were confirmed. So far from eliciting an invitation to partake of wine, his request for a meeting before the trial met with a brusque refusal.

'His Honour is fully informed of the facts of this case,' wrote Sir Robert's clerk, 'and will brook no further delay over the trial of the accused, which he believes to be overdue. A discussion with an interested party before the hearing would, in his view, be prejudicial and improper.'

Interested party! Prejudicial and improper! A letter in the third person! The blood of the Overburys rose in Sir Thomas's gorge. Who was this jumped-up metropolitan placeman to descend on the county and insult a prominent member of its gentry?

Also summoned as witnesses were Sir John Keyte and Captain Dover. Together with Sir Thomas, they were required to prove John Perry's confession by giving evidence that he had made it in their presence. Three witnesses of such high station were bound to impress the jury, some of whom seemed to suppose that swearing proof of evidence meant endorsing the truth of it. The judge refrained from ensuring that they were not misled.

At the beginning of proceedings all the accused had pleaded

not guilty. That John should enter this plea came as no surprise to Sir Thomas: he had made a similar retraction at the previous trial. But why had he not withdrawn his confession earlier while he was still in Campden, where Sir Thomas might have saved him? It must be that he had never expected to be brought to trial. And after his escape through Sir Christopher Turnor's ruling he had evidently reckoned without the likes of Sir Robert Hyde who, as soon as the evidence of the confession contradicted his plea, turned on him like a stoat on a rabbit.

'John Perry, you have heard what has now been said. Do you admit to having confessed to this abominable crime, or would you have the court believe that all these distinguished gentlemen are lying on oath and thereby endangering their good names and liberty by committing perjury? Come now, do not imagine that the demands of justice will be frustrated by the spectacle of tears. Dry your eyes. Speak up like a man. Above all, speak the truth. Which is it to be: the confession or the plea? No more prevarication! I tell you, the law will not be trifled with by blubbing country urchins.'

Sir Thomas gnashed his teeth at the bullying and condescension. So the law could only be trifled with by dry-eyed townsmen! Was that it? The tears were gushing from this country urchin as though they would never stop, but not a fleck of pity was softening the expression on the judge's ugly mug.

'In God's name, I am innocent.' John spoke through his tears, brushing them away with his sleeve as they fell.

'Then you must tell the court why you thought fit to deceive these gentlemen with so many lies.'

For a moment it appeared that John was going to blurt out a long-suppressed truth and lift a heavy weight from his conscience. The tears ceased to flow. His eyes lost their dullness. He moistened his lips and swallowed hard. But then his head dropped. 'It was madness,' he muttered. 'A fit of madness. I knew not what I said.'

Sir Thomas moaned beneath his breath. He felt certain that John had been on the brink of naming the real perpetrator of the

140

crime and could not fathom why he had held back. The judge, though, interpreted the hesitation as a struggle to produce a more plausible fabrication than a sudden bout of lunacy. He recalled Sir Thomas and the two other gentlemen to testify to John's condition and behaviour at the time when he swore to his account of the crime. All were forced to admit that, although the accused was labouring under some strain, they had detected no symptom of insanity.

Next it was Richard Perry's turn to swear that he was wholly innocent of the crime of which he was accused. 'I know nothing of Master Harrison's death, nor what became of him,' he cried, trembling and choking. Like his brother, he was a broken man.

Their mother, by contrast, exhibited no fear. She stood erect, calm, iron-willed, as though knowing her fate and accepting it. Such a show of self-possession in the shadow of a sentence of death cast a spell over the officers of the court and the throng of spectators. In the silence which fell whilst awaiting her words, it was the jurymen who felt fear. The witch was defying them to find her guilty: they would risk retribution from the Evil One.

Even Sir Robert on the bench seemed momentarily affected, but he quickly recovered himself. 'Speak, woman, if you have anything at all to plead in your defence.'

In a clear, strong voice she repeated Richard's denials and attributed their plight to the malice and mischief-making of her younger son. 'John was his father's boy,' she said. 'Ever since my husband left to fight for the king and never returned, the boy's mind has been disordered and he cannot tell truth from falsehood. He became a stranger to his own family. Master Harrison was a new-found father to him. Never would John have allowed a single hair of his head to be harmed.'

'Yet he agreed to his being robbed, did he not? Murder may not have been in his mind at first, but the one crime followed the other because Master Harrison recognised you. That is the truth of what occurred, is it not?' It was the judge again, assuming the prosecutor's role.

'The truth,' she scoffed. 'There is not a word of it in what you say. I am neither a murderess nor a thief.' She answered him undaunted and returned glare for glare.

'Beware how you address one of His Majesty's judges, Mistress Perry,' Sir Robert thundered. 'Treat the court with respect or I will have you removed and tried *in absentia*. How dare you assert that you are no thief when you pleaded guilty to just such a crime at the last assizes?'

At this Sir Thomas felt obliged to intervene and explain the circumstances. He rose to his feet and cleared his throat, but Sir Robert cut him short.

'Pray resume your seat, Sir Thomas,' he demanded. 'You have twice been called to give your evidence. That is opportunity enough. I cannot consent to hear you a third time. That would be inordinate.'

He turned his back on the magistrate and began his address to the jury with a further snub by taking pains to emphasise that these defendants who stood accused of robbery and murder were already self-confessed and convicted thieves. The jury might well find that a relevant consideration, he suggested. The absence of a body in a case of murder was, he conceded, unusual. But when a man had vanished without trace—and that despite the most diligent searches and inquiries extending for more than six months—what other explanation could there be? He put the question to them as reasonable men.

So, he continued, if murder it was, they must ask themselves who were more likely to have committed this terrible deed than the prisoners in the dock. The youngest defendant's confession had not been made lightly. It had been repeated on several occasions over a period of weeks. When taken together with what might be thought strong circumstantial evidence, it would enable the jury (if they thought fit) to bring in a verdict of guilty with clear consciences. The eyes of their fellow citizens and countrymen were upon them. This was a case of wide notoriety; it had attracted notice even in London. A finding based on sentiment and not on the facts would be a matter of reproach for the rest of their lives.

After this summing-up the verdict was not in doubt. It was reached without the jury retiring, and they were rewarded by the judge's congratulations upon a duty well done. He thereupon pronounced sentence: 'Joan Perry, Richard Perry and John Perry, you have been found guilty of the most heinous crime known to man and must answer for it in accordance with the law. You will be taken hence to a place of execution and there hanged by the neck until you are dead.'

He had barely concluded with the formal request to God to have mercy on their souls, when two altercations broke out. Richard struggled free from his warder and set about his brother, belabouring him savagely over the head, fists flailing in a frenzy, until they were pulled apart. On the other side of the court-room Edward Harrison and his mother were locked in argument. She was waving a sheet of paper and trying to force her way to where Sir Robert sat glowering and bellowing at the ushers to restore order. Edward was restraining her and snatching at the paper.

Everyone was standing, talking excitedly, caught up in a general mêlée of exhilaration at the fate awaiting the prisoners. Only Widow Perry appeared unmoved. Every eye was on her. What powers had she, what spirits could she command, to save herself now? Clad in black, the attire of widowhood and death, she stood like a queen of the night surveying the disturbance around her with frozen dignity.

That was the last, admiring memory Sir Thomas took away with him. He left the court hurriedly in deep disgust. Anxious to be gone, he paid no heed to the Harrisons, who had been ejected and were now engaged in argument in the street. If she had been endeavouring to present a petition for mercy, he supposed he must revise his opinion of her and her fiery brand of Christianity. But when she ran after him to draw him into the dispute he brushed her aside and strode on. She had come too late and her cause was hopeless. Between her and any prospect of mercy stood her son and the judge, both of them as merciful as blocks of stone.

At home that evening he vowed not to attend the hanging

and drank himself insensible over a bowl of punch. But when the appointed day came he could not keep away.

The gallows had been erected on Broadway Hill. Riding there with Ali in attendance, he overtook clusters of men and women, some with children, walking along the roadside in holiday mood. At the summit, looking down, he could see similar groups approaching from every direction and hear them chattering like magpies. The air was a-buzz with excitement. Hangings were rare, and this was a free show not to be missed. They had Edward Harrison to thank for it. He had petitioned for the place of execution to be moved from Gloucester, so that every citizen of Chipping Campden could witness and enjoy the sight.

Near to the foot of the gallows, stalls had sprung up for the sale of food and drink, knick-knacks and mementoes. It was still early in the day, but vast quantities of ale had been consumed by the time the cart bearing the prisoners creaked up the hill from Gloucester to be greeted with jeers and boos.

Because it was believed that her sons would not confess while under her spell, it had been decided that Mistress Perry should die first. The cart was halted and the first noose fastened round her neck. She stood in chains, bound hand and foot, assaulted by cries of 'Go to the Devil!' and 'Confess!'

She was in a trance, and when she took no notice of the taunts they turned into appeals to 'Speak! Speak!' Her last words were what most had come to hear, and the mob were behaving like children deprived of a treat. If she would not confess, they willed her at least to say something, even words of defiance so that they could launch her on the downward path to Hell with a final volley of execrations and insults.

Sir Thomas was sickened. He would never forget the look she swept over the sea of faces. As so often with her, it was mysterious, enigmatic. What did it signify? Not menace. Not even contempt. Mere indifference, he judged. She was at peace with herself. Perhaps she was expecting to find Hell more agreeable than earth.

Suddenly, without waiting to be pushed, she struggled off the back of the cart and her feet were beating the air. It took

nestled below on one side and his village of Weston sub Edge on the other. It was Mother Nature's gift to man: a playground in the sky to rival that at Delphi. Here too stood the ancient Kiftsgate Stone, the moot place of the hundred in Saxon times.

Sir Thomas reined in his grey mare and drew in his breath at the first view of the Malvern hills and the distant outline of the Olympian mountains in Wales. The thrill of magic was in the air, and a surge of exhilaration ran through him at the thought of past revels and orgies, and what he was to perform and witness that day.

It was exactly fifty years since the traditional rustic sports at Whitsuntide had been taken in hand by the present Captain Dover's father. Captain Robert Dover had been a staunch papist, and his Games were held in defiance of local Puritan sentiment. The Puritans of the Commonwealth had responded by suppressing them, and they had not been held for the past twenty years. But now, on this auspicious anniversary, the celebrations were to be resumed. To Sir Thomas there was little to be said in favour of either of the opposing factions (save for their dislike of each other), but on this occasion his heart was Catholic. Let joy be unconfined, it sang.

All was to be as before the interregnum. The portable wooden fortification, dubbed Dover Castle, was already assembled and in place, bristling with imitation heavy ordnance and real light guns which would be fired to open proceedings and signal announcements of the various events. As the mock-royal Master of Ceremonies, Robert Dover had arrayed himself in King James's cast-off clothes, which he had obtained by courtesy of His Majesty's Groom of the Bedchamber, who lived nearby. When the king published his anti-Puritan Book of Sports, the captain had seized upon it as a mark of royal approval of his venture. He had taken to reciting a passage from it, which Sir Thomas had been to some trouble to discover and memorise for today's opening ceremony.

'And as for our good people's recreation', (it ran) 'our pleasure is that after the end of Divine Service our good people be not disturbed or discouraged from any lawful recreation, such as dancing, archery, leaping, vaulting or other harmless recreations; nor from having May games, Whitsun ales and Morris dances.'

Sir Thomas was regally attired for his role. He wore his grandfather's doublet, hose and ruff, surmounted by a red cloak and crowned with a feathered hat in a style made familiar by portraits of King James. His subjects for the day now awaited him. The numbers were larger even than for the hanging of the Perrys, and growing by the minute. Word of the pre-war fame of the Cotswold Olympics had brought competitors and sight-seers from far and wide.

How fitting, thought Sir Thomas, that an Overbury should preside over this historic event! He was preening himself and about to order the firing of the castle's guns when another horseman, similarly attired and also mounted on a white horse, approached at the gallop. It was John Dover and the two men stared at each other in dismay.

'I have been delayed on the road,' he explained breathlessly. 'But happily I am here in time to perform the opening in my father's name. As he most surely would have wished.'

Sir Thomas dismissed the claim tersely, without hesitation: 'It was distinctly understood that the honour should be mine, by virtue of the seniority of my position and office.'

The captain was not so easily put down. 'It may have been so understood by you, Sir Thomas, but not so by me,' he answered. 'As I recollect, the question was never so much as discussed between us. It scarcely seemed necessary. These are the *Dover* Games, permit me to remind you.'

'First and foremost they are the *Cotswold* Games,' Sir Thomas riposted. 'Permit *me* to remind *you* that they date from long before your father settled in this district. His inspiration entitled him to the personal honour of Master of Ceremonies, but a Norfolk family resident in Warwickshire can by no means lay claim to precedence in Gloucestershire.'

Captain Dover's response was a furious rattling of his sword in its scabbard. He was lost for words, but appeared about to inaugurate the day's events with a duel on horseback. Sir

Thomas stifled his alarm and hastened to offer a compromise in a show of magnanimity.

'We are under observation. Let us rather share the honour than mar the day with unseemly dissension in public. I shall make the opening proclamation and present the winners with their prizes. You shall be accorded the privilege of conducting all other proceedings.'

The argument could not be prolonged: the crowds were growing impatient, whistling and stamping. Captain Dover indicated a disgruntled acceptance, and Sir Thomas congratulated himself on achieving the lion's share of the honour while freeing himself from some tiresome duties. He raised his hand. The guns roared. The mob cheered.

At another signal a more or less respectful hush fell and he made his prepared speech declaring the 1662 Olympic Games open. The traditional proclamation was in English, but he added lines in Latin from Ovid and Horace and some sentences in Greek culled from a speech by Demosthenes. Although heard by few and understood by fewer, the oration was destined for immortality when embellished, printed and bound in morocco covers. How infinitely superior to the vacuous nothings which would have fallen from the lips of a bone-headed captain of militia!

The Games were soon in full swing and he sauntered amongst the throng in a healthy glow of self-satisfaction, little suspecting how the day would end. On his way to the sporting arenas and running tracks he paused to kiss a buxom wench scantily clad as Venus, Goddess of Love, and to throw a few pennies at the feet of an old man with a white beard who was playing the harp with his eyes shut, representing the blind Homer. Here, as celebrated in verse by England's finest poets in *Annalia Dubrensia*, were the immortals of Greece and Rome come amongst the rural swains and nymphs of Gloucestershire on this enchanted hill of sport and merriment.

The competing swains were rough Cotswold men, famed for their strength and courage. They were grappling fiercely with each other in wrestling bouts and setting about each other without mercy with singlesticks, backswords or bare knuckles. Admiring womenfolk formed raucous audiences. Not many of them, alas, were slender and beauteous nymphs.

For the fleet of foot of both sexes there were long races and short races. For the agile, leaping high and leaping long. Others were competing at throwing the sledge-hammer or pitching the bar or pike-handling. The nimblest and most resourceful were engaged in the painful sport of shin-kicking, as practised in local alehouses and traditionally the special event of the Cotswold Games.

More innocent amusement was provided by clowns and tumblers and games of leapfrog. Tom Fools attended groups of ribboned Morris dancers making music with viols and bells. Quack doctors were selling dubious nostrums, and innkeepers who had abandoned their premises for the day and carried their wares uphill were being well rewarded. A maypole was the centre of attraction for dancing, and round it were jigging the fairest nymphs, wearing flowers in their hair in honour of the goddess of spring. Watching them with Ali wide-eyed at his side, Sir Thomas felt a rush of poetry to the head:

> Above the earth, beneath the clouds,
> The cynosure of thronging crowds,
> Here the young men and maidens meet
> To exercise their dancing feet,
> Tripping the comely country round
> With daffodils and daisies crowned.

This would form a graceful appendage to his printed oration. He was reciting the verses aloud for Ali's benefit when a disturbance at a distance distracted his attention and he broke through a circle of jeering spectators to investigate.

In the eye of this human storm a sour-featured Puritan divine was standing on a platform declaiming like Stentor. He was preaching against the sin of dancing, warning of the pernicious effects of Whitsun ale, and generally denouncing all the debauchery associated with these heathen frolics. His strictures on swearing were being greeted with oaths. Finally, to Sir Thomas's delight, he was reduced to silence by some drunken merrymakers who invented the new game of Pelting the Puritan with Sheep's Dung.

The gentry were out in full force, congregating apart from the common folk. They were clad in their most expensive finery, buttoned and plumed; their horses groomed and shining; their carriages as polished as Sir Thomas's prose. They had come to see and be seen, and even to take part. For the gentlemen there was horse-racing, hare-hunting, coursing with greyhounds. In tents chessboards were set out and card-tables at which the ladies could play ombre and loo. Among the rich and the reckless betting on the outcome of the contests was the order of the day.

Sir Thomas joined his acquaintances for an exchange of pleasantries and gossip. His wife had come in the coach too late to hear his speech, but Sir John Keyte's wife was full of praise for his eloquence and rose in his esteem by declaring that he was more fitted to be in Parliament than any of those who sat there. It was rare to meet a woman of such mature judgment.

In the afternoon he made another speech, commending all the competitors on their prowess. He handed the champions their prizes, dispensing feathered hats, gold rings, stout belts, doe-skin gloves and laced shoes, all of the best quality. There were silver tokens too, and a silver salt modelled on the castle. This, the most valued of the trophies, was awarded to the winner of the marathon and claimed by Robert Hayward, landlord of The Eight Bells, amid applause and calls for free drinks.

The Games had been a triumph. With the light fading, the no less eagerly awaited debauchery was about to begin. No day could have been more perfect. The sun had shone in splendour and Sir Thomas was standing, lost in wonder at the giant golden ball sinking behind the Welsh peaks, when a commotion broke out. People were rushing, babbling, towards a copse where the lane from Weston sub Edge breasted the rise to the summit.

A solitary rider on horseback had appeared and drew to a halt at the onset of the mob. His figure and bearing were familiar, and when he was close enough for a better view Sir Thomas was seized with one of his violent spasms of anger. Some ill-natured prankster had got himself up to represent Master William Harrison. Everyone was clustering round, gaping at him, overawed. Alarmed mutterings about Widow Perry and the witch's powers reached Sir Thomas's ears as he elbowed through the throng to remonstrate with the man.

On his approach the horseman looked up and stared around him. There was no mistaking the face. For the first time in his life the magistrate was rendered speechless: his mouth open, his tongue tied.

'I wish you a good day, Sir Thomas,' the man said. 'And the same to all you good people.' Without another word he urged his horse forward and disappeared down the hill towards the town.

The hubbub was hushed. Some of the crowd stood as though bound to the spot. Others sank to their knees and crossed themselves.

Sir Thomas's face was contorted in amazement while he struggled for words. Ali was unperturbed. He was smiling. What they had seen was the speaking image of the murdered steward. 'It *is* the murdered steward,' gasped Sir Thomas when he recovered his voice.

After nearly two years William Harrison had risen from the dead.

For days folk could talk of little but the old steward's resurrection. The pious marvelled at it as a miracle wrought by Almighty God, but most believed that witchcraft could be the only explanation. Rumour spread that Master Harrison was none other than the mysterious Man in Black who presided over the pagan rites practised on moonlit nights on Kingcombe Plain; that he had been spirited away and back again through the magical arts of Joan Perry, his partner in sorcery. Despite her death the Devil was still at work in Kiftsgate hundred, and some in terror expected her resurrection too.

Sir Thomas brushed aside such nonsense and raged against a cruel deception. He wanted it known that he, and he alone, had not been hoodwinked. He, and he alone, had argued that the Perrys were innocent. The truly guilty parties now stood revealed: a judge ignorant of the law, and Master Harrison who had allowed the wretches to suffer for a crime that never was.

In a full flood of indignation the magistrate paced up and down the precious carpet in his library haranguing Ali while his wife kept thankfully out of his way in her own chamber.

What had the disappearing and reappearing steward to say for himself? Not a syllable! As taciturn as ever, he had simply resumed his old life as though absent for no more than a single day. There was no rejoicing in his family. He had taken back the duties of stewardship from his son as though of right, and Edward's sullenness was plain for all to see. Mistress Harrison's face as she scurried to and from church was a veritable thundercloud.

After three days waiting impatiently for an explanation Sir Thomas issued a peremptory summons and the two men met in Chipping Campden's court-room. The magistrate was accompanied by Ali, and they were joined by Constable Fettiplace. The steward came alone, striding impassively down the street, impervious to the stares of the curious who gaped at him and the superstitious who shrank away.

He greeted Sir Thomas deferentially. 'No one can regret the misfortune of Joan Perry and her sons more than I,' he said.

'Except for them, myself and all lovers of justice.'

The steward was breathing heavily, stifling some emotion. 'I would speak with you in private,' he said with a glance at the others. 'What I would disclose are the names of the persons responsible for this tragedy, but it is a matter of the utmost confidence.'

'Your request is rejected. Your extraordinary conduct has astonished a nation, and now you have the effrontery to ask me to keep it secret. The whole world is entitled to learn the truth.' The magistrate was abrupt, incensed.

'You misjudge me, Sir Thomas. Secrecy about my absence is not my intention. The whole world shall learn where I have been and why I was unable to save a family who have always enjoyed my favour. I have prepared a statement for you.'

The steward had aged little. His complexion was tanned and there was strength left in his bulky frame. He bore the air of a man whose conscience was clear, but Sir Thomas looked him over with distrust. All tricksters appear honest, he told himself: this is one whose tale will have been well prepared.

Instead of speaking, the steward handed a paper across the table between them. It was formally addressed 'For Sir Thomas Overbury, Knight' and began 'Honoured Sir'. Sir Thomas fingered it suspiciously. 'Is this written in your own hand?' he demanded.

The response was a slight inclination of the head. Did that signify an affirmative or was it to avoid a meeting of eyes? Sir Thomas's suspicions mounted. He was conscious of Ali craning over his shoulders to catch a glimpse of the words.

minutes for her to die, and while she was swaying and jerking the crowd found its voice again and took its revenge, hurling mud and stones and obscenities until the target was no longer a woman but a body whose soul had fled.

Richard showed no such courage. He was sobbing and had to be held upright while he swore yet again that he had had no hand in Master Harrison's death and knew nothing of what had become of him. He then addressed John, who was awaiting his turn, propped against the side of the cart like a trussed fowl.

'I earnestly beseech my brother—to satisfy the world and his own conscience—by revealing the truth.' He was stammering and spluttering. 'I beg you, John. Before we both go to our Maker. I beg you. Do you hear me?'

John made no response and Richard was pushed from the cart. He was more fortunate than his mother. A bone in his neck snapped like a pistol shot and he hung limp and lifeless within a few seconds. Much to the disappointment of the crowd.

John too was quivering with fear, his voice reduced to a hoarse whisper. But he spoke doggedly. Amid a deep hush every ear was bent to catch the words: 'My confession was false. That is God's truth. I am ignorant of my master's fate. But you may learn something hereafter.'

With a wild stare over the heads of the crowd and a desperate cry of 'Save me, father' he threw himself off the cart. The noose half-tightened at his throat. He struggled in the air panic-stricken, kicking and gurgling in agony, until Sir Thomas could bear it no longer and ran forward to tug at his legs and break his neck.

That was the end of the Perrys. Sir Thomas went home to brood over man's inhumanity and puzzle over John's last words and get drunk again. Ali, waiting to undress him, thought he knew what the words meant, but he said nothing. It would be important for his master to believe that he had made the discovery for himself.

The words were in both their minds in the morning. 'Why do you suppose John appealed to his father to save him? Was it God the Father that he meant?' Sir Thomas was musing gloomily over the horror of the previous day as Ali helped him rise.

Ali ducked the questions. 'At the trial Mistress Perry called him his father's boy,' he hinted.

'But Master Perry is long since dead. Unless the report that he was killed at Naseby is false.'

'He was not killed at Naseby,' Ali replied.

'Then where is he now? Tell me that if you are so sure.'

Ali's response this time was a roll of the eyes. Sir Thomas searched his own mind for an answer until roused from his reverie by Ali asking whether he had noticed Anne Harrison.

'I have noticed you noticing her,' Sir Thomas answered sharply, irritated by the change of subject. 'A fair beauty, but not for you, you rascal.' Marriage into the Harrison family was not what he planned for his favourite: although he would relish the sight of Mistress Harrison's face if it were proposed.

The plaguesome Harrisons! He turned his thoughts to them. It was now a full nine months since the old steward's disappearance, and with every day that passed it seemed more and more certain that he had indeed been killed. Sir Thomas entertained no doubt that what he had witnessed the day before was a monstrous miscarriage of justice; so who was the real murderer?

His suspicion of Edward Harrison had festered and grown. It was Edward's influence which had kept the Perrys in gaol after the first judge dismissed the charge of murder against them. It was Edward who had pressed the prosecution on another judge. Who but Edward had been responsible for the macabre scene on Broadway Hill? Was it not at his insistence that the condemned wretches had been transported twenty miles to suffer within the sight of their home and neighbours? At the foot of the gallows he had stood shaking his fist in the face of his victims as they were dragged to their death. 'Vengeance is mine,' he had shouted at each: 'Go suffer the vengeance of eternal fire.' Quotations from the Good Book of the Christian religion!

All this clamour for retribution from one who had hated his father—was it not strange? In his determination to fasten a lasting guilt on others Edward had even succeeded in having John Perry denied burial. The body was sentenced to hang in chains beside the highway as a dreadful warning to all who passed by that servants who killed their masters would never lie at rest.

His mind made up, Sir Thomas wasted no time in riding to Chipping Campden for a confrontation—only to be rebuffed. 'The affair is over and done with. Now my father's soul can rest in peace,' Edward said and would say no more.

From his mother Sir Thomas sought to learn the cause of their quarrel in the court-room, but she was no more forthcoming. 'Such questions bruise my memory. They bring back nightmares. And to what purpose? Justice has been done. Your inquiry has ended.' She was nervous, frightened of him, not at all her old self; which heightened his suspicion.

On a second visit he found a new confidence and arrogance in Edward, now comfortable in his father's shoes. The viscount, he reported, was still overseas, and his stewardship was secure in the dowager viscountess's favour.

'You would greatly oblige us, Sir Thomas,' he said, 'if you would refrain from calling again on this business. Your importunity distresses my mother, who naturally desires to be left alone with her grief. Pray spare us these intrusions or the Lady Juliana must be informed of the nuisance.'

Sir Thomas had left choking with rage. At home he at once wrote to the Lady Juliana himself. His letter was, he flattered himself, a clear exposition of events and concerns penned in a flowing hand and polished prose. It demanded a reply and he was mortified to receive none.

Was her ladyship past caring? She had been born long enough ago to remember the year of the Spanish Armada, as she had once told him. After waiting in vain for a month he began to doubt whether the old woman could still be *compos mentis*. Perhaps she had not even known of the letter her steward at Brooke had written to him in her name.

With the investigation at a dead end, the neglected business of his estate claimed his attention. That and his *Queries* about religion. And then came the arrangements for his momentous enterprise. More than a year had passed since the hangings when the great day he had spent so long preparing for arrived. On the way to its scene he made a detour up Broadway Hill to see what had become of John Perry's mortal remains.

The corpse was still there, imprisoned in its chains. Crows and rooks had long since picked the flesh from the bones. Only the bare skeleton was left to swing in the breeze while the soul (if it existed) burned in Hell (if that existed). Sir Thomas doffed his hat and bowed his head to all that was left of the fair young country boy for whom his heart had once beat faster.

Escorted by Ali and a groom in their Sunday best, he turned his horse's head towards the bridle path which wound across the high ground to the plateau overlooking Chipping Campden. He had made his last salute to the innocent dead and now cast murder and hangings from his thoughts. For this was a day to be savoured, a day of festivity to celebrate the triumph of paganism over bigotry, a day to be recorded in the annals of the county. Thanks to his own efforts and those of Captain Dover, the Cotswold Olympic Games, which had brought manly sports and revelry to Chipping Campden in former times, were now to be revived.

Kingcombe Plain ran for a full mile and a half from north to south and half a mile from east to west. Chipping Campden nestled below on one side and his village of Weston sub Edge on the other. It was Mother Nature's gift to man: a playground in the sky to rival that at Delphi. Here too stood the ancient Kiftsgate Stone, the moot place of the hundred in Saxon times.

Sir Thomas reined in his grey mare and drew in his breath at the first view of the Malvern hills and the distant outline of the Olympian mountains in Wales. The thrill of magic was in the air, and a surge of exhilaration ran through him at the thought of past revels and orgies, and what he was to perform and witness that day.

It was exactly fifty years since the traditional rustic sports at Whitsuntide had been taken in hand by the present Captain Dover's father. Captain Robert Dover had been a staunch papist, and his Games were held in defiance of local Puritan sentiment. The Puritans of the Commonwealth had responded by suppressing them, and they had not been held for the past twenty years. But now, on this auspicious anniversary, the celebrations were to be resumed. To Sir Thomas there was little to be said in favour of either of the opposing factions (save for their dislike of each other), but on this occasion his heart was Catholic. Let joy be unconfined, it sang.

All was to be as before the interregnum. The portable wooden fortification, dubbed Dover Castle, was already assembled and in place, bristling with imitation heavy ordnance and real light guns which would be fired to open proceedings and signal announcements of the various events. As the mock-royal Master of Ceremonies, Robert Dover had arrayed himself in King James's cast-off clothes, which he had obtained by courtesy of His Majesty's Groom of the Bedchamber, who lived nearby. When the king published his anti-Puritan Book of Sports, the captain had seized upon it as a mark of royal approval of his venture. He had taken to reciting a passage from it, which Sir Thomas had been to some trouble to discover and memorise for today's opening ceremony.

'And as for our good people's recreation', (it ran) 'our pleasure is that after the end of Divine Service our good people be not disturbed or discouraged from any lawful recreation,

149

such as dancing, archery, leaping, vaulting or other harmless recreations; nor from having May games, Whitsun ales and Morris dances.'

Sir Thomas was regally attired for his role. He wore his grandfather's doublet, hose and ruff, surmounted by a red cloak and crowned with a feathered hat in a style made familiar by portraits of King James. His subjects for the day now awaited him. The numbers were larger even than for the hanging of the Perrys, and growing by the minute. Word of the pre-war fame of the Cotswold Olympics had brought competitors and sightseers from far and wide.

How fitting, thought Sir Thomas, that an Overbury should preside over this historic event! He was preening himself and about to order the firing of the castle's guns when another horseman, similarly attired and also mounted on a white horse, approached at the gallop. It was John Dover and the two men stared at each other in dismay.

'I have been delayed on the road,' he explained breathlessly. 'But happily I am here in time to perform the opening in my father's name. As he most surely would have wished.'

Sir Thomas dismissed the claim tersely, without hesitation: 'It was distinctly understood that the honour should be mine, by virtue of the seniority of my position and office.'

The captain was not so easily put down. 'It may have been so understood by you, Sir Thomas, but not so by me,' he answered. 'As I recollect, the question was never so much as discussed between us. It scarcely seemed necessary. These are the *Dover* Games, permit me to remind you.'

'First and foremost they are the *Cotswold* Games,' Sir Thomas riposted. 'Permit *me* to remind *you* that they date from long before your father settled in this district. His inspiration entitled him to the personal honour of Master of Ceremonies, but a Norfolk family resident in Warwickshire can by no means lay claim to precedence in Gloucestershire.'

Captain Dover's response was a furious rattling of his sword in its scabbard. He was lost for words, but appeared about to inaugurate the day's events with a duel on horseback. Sir

Thomas stifled his alarm and hastened to offer a compromise in a show of magnanimity.

'We are under observation. Let us rather share the honour than mar the day with unseemly dissension in public. I shall make the opening proclamation and present the winners with their prizes. You shall be accorded the privilege of conducting all other proceedings.'

The argument could not be prolonged: the crowds were growing impatient, whistling and stamping. Captain Dover indicated a disgruntled acceptance, and Sir Thomas congratulated himself on achieving the lion's share of the honour while freeing himself from some tiresome duties. He raised his hand. The guns roared. The mob cheered.

At another signal a more or less respectful hush fell and he made his prepared speech declaring the 1662 Olympic Games open. The traditional proclamation was in English, but he added lines in Latin from Ovid and Horace and some sentences in Greek culled from a speech by Demosthenes. Although heard by few and understood by fewer, the oration was destined for immortality when embellished, printed and bound in morocco covers. How infinitely superior to the vacuous nothings which would have fallen from the lips of a bone-headed captain of militia!

The Games were soon in full swing and he sauntered amongst the throng in a healthy glow of self-satisfaction, little suspecting how the day would end. On his way to the sporting arenas and running tracks he paused to kiss a buxom wench scantily clad as Venus, Goddess of Love, and to throw a few pennies at the feet of an old man with a white beard who was playing the harp with his eyes shut, representing the blind Homer. Here, as celebrated in verse by England's finest poets in *Annalia Dubrensia*, were the immortals of Greece and Rome come amongst the rural swains and nymphs of Gloucestershire on this enchanted hill of sport and merriment.

The competing swains were rough Cotswold men, famed for their strength and courage. They were grappling fiercely with each other in wrestling bouts and setting about each other

151

without mercy with singlesticks, backswords or bare knuckles. Admiring womenfolk formed raucous audiences. Not many of them, alas, were slender and beauteous nymphs.

For the fleet of foot of both sexes there were long races and short races. For the agile, leaping high and leaping long. Others were competing at throwing the sledge-hammer or pitching the bar or pike-handling. The nimblest and most resourceful were engaged in the painful sport of shin-kicking, as practised in local alehouses and traditionally the special event of the Cotswold Games.

More innocent amusement was provided by clowns and tumblers and games of leapfrog. Tom Fools attended groups of ribboned Morris dancers making music with viols and bells. Quack doctors were selling dubious nostrums, and innkeepers who had abandoned their premises for the day and carried their wares uphill were being well rewarded. A maypole was the centre of attraction for dancing, and round it were jigging the fairest nymphs, wearing flowers in their hair in honour of the goddess of spring. Watching them with Ali wide-eyed at his side, Sir Thomas felt a rush of poetry to the head:

> Above the earth, beneath the clouds,
> The cynosure of thronging crowds,
> Here the young men and maidens meet
> To exercise their dancing feet,
> Tripping the comely country round
> With daffodils and daisies crowned.

This would form a graceful appendage to his printed oration. He was reciting the verses aloud for Ali's benefit when a disturbance at a distance distracted his attention and he broke through a circle of jeering spectators to investigate.

In the eye of this human storm a sour-featured Puritan divine was standing on a platform declaiming like Stentor. He was preaching against the sin of dancing, warning of the pernicious effects of Whitsun ale, and generally denouncing all the debauchery associated with these heathen frolics. His strictures

152

on swearing were being greeted with oaths. Finally, to Sir Thomas's delight, he was reduced to silence by some drunken merrymakers who invented the new game of Pelting the Puritan with Sheep's Dung.

The gentry were out in full force, congregating apart from the common folk. They were clad in their most expensive finery, buttoned and plumed; their horses groomed and shining; their carriages as polished as Sir Thomas's prose. They had come to see and be seen, and even to take part. For the gentlemen there was horse-racing, hare-hunting, coursing with greyhounds. In tents chessboards were set out and card-tables at which the ladies could play ombre and loo. Among the rich and the reckless betting on the outcome of the contests was the order of the day.

Sir Thomas joined his acquaintances for an exchange of pleasantries and gossip. His wife had come in the coach too late to hear his speech, but Sir John Keyte's wife was full of praise for his eloquence and rose in his esteem by declaring that he was more fitted to be in Parliament than any of those who sat there. It was rare to meet a woman of such mature judgment.

In the afternoon he made another speech, commending all the competitors on their prowess. He handed the champions their prizes, dispensing feathered hats, gold rings, stout belts, doeskin gloves and laced shoes, all of the best quality. There were silver tokens too, and a silver salt modelled on the castle. This, the most valued of the trophies, was awarded to the winner of the marathon and claimed by Robert Hayward, landlord of The Eight Bells, amid applause and calls for free drinks.

The Games had been a triumph. With the light fading, the no less eagerly awaited debauchery was about to begin. No day could have been more perfect. The sun had shone in splendour and Sir Thomas was standing, lost in wonder at the giant golden ball sinking behind the Welsh peaks, when a commotion broke out. People were rushing, babbling, towards a copse where the lane from Weston sub Edge breasted the rise to the summit.

A solitary rider on horseback had appeared and drew to a halt at the onset of the mob. His figure and bearing were familiar, and when he was close enough for a better view Sir Thomas was seized with one of his violent spasms of anger. Some ill-natured prankster had got himself up to represent Master William Harrison. Everyone was clustering round, gaping at him, overawed. Alarmed mutterings about Widow Perry and the witch's powers reached Sir Thomas's ears as he elbowed through the throng to remonstrate with the man.

On his approach the horseman looked up and stared around him. There was no mistaking the face. For the first time in his life the magistrate was rendered speechless: his mouth open, his tongue tied.

'I wish you a good day, Sir Thomas,' the man said. 'And the same to all you good people.' Without another word he urged his horse forward and disappeared down the hill towards the town.

The hubbub was hushed. Some of the crowd stood as though bound to the spot. Others sank to their knees and crossed themselves.

Sir Thomas's face was contorted in amazement while he struggled for words. Ali was unperturbed. He was smiling. What they had seen was the speaking image of the murdered steward. 'It *is* the murdered steward,' gasped Sir Thomas when he recovered his voice.

After nearly two years William Harrison had risen from the dead.

'In obedience to your commands,' he read aloud, 'I give you this account of my being carried away across the seas, my continuance there, and return home.'

He looked up sharply. 'My commands? When was this penned?'

'In the hours since my return, when I learned of your investigations and anticipated your summons.'

Sir Thomas uttered a humph and continued reading: 'On a Thursday in the afternoon, in the time of harvest, I went to Charringworth to demand rents due to my Lady Campden; at which time the tenants were busy in the fields and late before they came home; which occasioned my stay there till the close of the evening. I expected a considerable sum, but received only twenty-three pounds, and no more.'

The magistrate broke off to inquire: 'Was it your customary practice to carry considerable sums of your Lady's money across the country, alone and in darkness?'

'There would have been no danger in daylight, but I was delayed, as I have explained.'

'The delay could scarcely have been unexpected in view of the time of year. You must have known before you set out that the tenants would have been harvesting until late. Did it not occur to you to take your boy Perry with you?'

At mention of the name the steward winced. 'As I recollect, my wife required him to clean the hen-house,' he muttered. 'And in August the days are long.'

Sir Thomas turned to the statement again and continued reading it aloud: 'In my return home, in the narrow passage amongst Ebrington furzes, a horseman met me who said, Art thou there? And I, fearing that he would have ridden over me, struck his horse over the nose; whereupon he struck at me with his sword, several blows, and ran it into my side, while I made my defence as well as I could with my cane. Then another came behind me, ran me in the thigh, laid hold of the collar of my doublet and drew me into a hedge. Then came another. They did not take my money, but mounted me behind one of them, drew my arms about his middle and fastened my wrists

157

together with a spring-lock. Then they threw a great cloak over me and carried me away.'

Here the constable intervened. 'Perchance you still have the marks of the wounds about your body, sir?' he inquired.

'They were not deep and the scars have long since healed.'

'Then describe to me the villains who attacked you,' Sir Thomas demanded.

'They kept closely muffled, their faces well hid. I could not recognise them as any I had encountered before, but I would know them should they cross my path again.'

'Were they wearing white jackets or surcoats?'

At this the steward hesitated. 'They were wrapped in dark cloaks,' he said. 'I could not see beneath.'

Sir Thomas noted the hesitation, shrugged and read on: 'In the night they alighted at a hay-rick which stood near to a stone-pit. There they took away my money. About two hours before day they tumbled me into the stone-pit. They stayed about an hour more at the hay-rick, when they took horse again and one of them bade me come out of the pit. I answered that they had my money already and asked what they would do with me; whereupon he struck me again, drew me out, put a great quantity of money in my pockets and mounted me again after the same manner.'

'Put money in your pockets!' exclaimed the magistrate, break-ing off once more. 'Why should they do that, do you suppose?'

'They must have wished to be unencumbered themselves; so thought to use me for a saddle-bag. The coin weighed too heavily for comfort, as you will read.'

'On the Friday about sun-setting,' Sir Thomas resumed, 'they brought me to a lone house upon a heath, where they took me down almost dead, being sorely bruised with the carriage of the money. When the woman of the house saw that I could neither stand nor speak, she asked them whether or no they had brought a dead man. They answered: no, but a friend that was hurt, and they were carrying him to a surgeon. She answered: if they did not make haste, their friend would be dead before they could bring him to one. There they laid me on cushions and suffered none to come into the room but a little girl. There we stayed all night, they giving me some broth and strong waters. In the morning, very early, they mounted me as before, and on Saturday night they brought me to a place where there were two or three houses, in one of which I lay all night on cushions by their bedside.'

'This makes a sorry story, Master Harrison,' Sir Thomas observed with a long face. 'You suffered much, it seems. Have you a notion whither the scoundrels took you and why they kept you alive once they had seized your money and used you to carry theirs?'

'Those places were remote and unknown to me. The purpose of my abductors in preserving my life soon became apparent.' The steward pointed towards his statement and the magistrate bent over it again.

'On Sunday morning,' he read out, 'they carried me thence, and about three or four o'clock brought me to a place by the seaside called Deal, where they laid me down on the ground. One of them staying by me, the other two walked a little way off to meet a man, with whom they discoursed. In their discourse I heard them mention seven pounds; after which they went away together and about half an hour after returned. The man (whose name, as I after heard, was Wrenshaw) said he feared I would die before they could get me on board. Then presently they put me into a boat and carried me on shipboard, where my wounds were dressed.'

Sir Thomas looked up. 'Do I understand this aright—that you were transported across the breadth of the country to be sold to a man named Wrenshaw for seven pounds? It seems a paltry reward for all your captors' trouble.'

'They may have expected more. Or it may be that I misheard the sum.'

'And where do you suppose this Wrenshaw might be found to corroborate your tale? Did he board the ship with you?'

The steward shook his head. 'I never saw him again and would not know where to look for him, save on the quayside at Deal.'

159

Sir Thomas sighed. 'It were better for you to read the rest of it to me.' He threw the paper across the table as though his patience was exhausted and its contents offended him.

'I remained in the ship, as near as I could reckon, about six weeks,' read the steward: 'in which time I was indifferently recovered of my wounds and weakness. Then the master of the ship came and told me, and the rest who were in the same condition, that he had sighted three Turkish ships. We all offered to fight in the defence of the ship and ourselves, but he commanded us to keep close and said he would deal with them well enough. A little while after, he called us up and, when we came on the deck, we saw two Turkish ships close by. Into one of them we were put and placed in a dark hole, where how long we continued before we landed I know not.'

The magistrate held up his hand to interrupt: 'So it may be taken as gospel truth that you were shipped against your will to the Mediterranean sea, and there betrayed and sold into slavery by the ship's captain. This is a story all too common in these times, Master Harrison. We have become familiar with the adventures of travellers taken captive by the Turk or the Moor. Your tale begins very like the rest. Pray read on.' The tone of his voice expressed more scepticism than sympathy.

'When we were landed they led us two days' journey and put us into a great house, or prison, where we remained four days and a half. Then came to us eight men to view us, who seemed to be officers. They called us and examined us of our trades and callings, which everyone answered. One said he was a surgeon, another that he was a broad-cloth weaver, and I after two or three demands said I had some skill in physick. We three were set by and taken away by three of those eight men that came to view us. It was my chance to be chosen by a grave physician of eighty-seven years of age who lived near to Smyrna. He had formerly been in England and knew Crowland in Lincolnshire, which he preferred before all other places in England.'

At this point the steward paused in expectation of further questioning, but Sir Thomas was wrapped in thought. The account was so circumstantial that he was veering towards a half-belief in its truth. Why invent a reference to Crowland, of all places? He knew it for a small village with a ruined abbey, remote in fenland and famed, if at all, only for an old triangular bridge erected in honour of the Holy Trinity. What appeal could that have for a Mohammedan physician?

'The man employed me to keep his still-house and gave me a silver bowl, double gilt, to drink in. My business was most in that place for distillation, but once—'

'Stop!' cried Sir Thomas. 'A silver-gilt bowl for a slave to drink from! You strain my credulity too far.'

'Nevertheless,' replied the steward stolidly, 'that was so in truth.' He went on with his reading unmoved.

'Once he set me to gather cotton-wool, which I not doing to his mind, he struck me down to the ground and drew his stiletto to stab me. But I holding up my hands to him, he gave a stamp and turned from me, for which I render thanks to my Lord and Saviour Jesus Christ, who stayed his hand and preserved me.'

'That at least is a palpable falsehood,' Sir Thomas murmured to himself. Divine intervention necessary to repel an attack by an eighty-seven-year-old! Whatever next?

'I was there about a year and three-quarters, and then my master fell sick, on a Thursday, and sent for me; and, calling me as he used by the name of Boll, told me he should die and bade me shift for myself. He died on Saturday following, and I presently hastened with my bowl to a port almost a day's journey distant, the way to which place I knew, having been twice there employed by my master about the carriage of his cotton-wool.'

On being asked the name of the port the steward pleaded ignorance. Sir Thomas caught Ali's eye. They had journeyed together to Smyrna and would have recognised the name.

'When I came thither, I addressed myself to two men who came out of a ship of Hamburg which, as they said, was bound for Portugal within three or four days. I inquired of them for an English ship, but they answered there was none. I entreated them to take me into their ship, but they answered they durst

161

not for fear of being discovered by the searchers; which might occasion the forfeiture not only of their goods but of their lives. I was very importunate with them, but could not prevail. They left me to wait on Providence, which at length brought another out of the same ship, to whom I made known my condition, craving his assistance for my transportation. He made me the like answer as the former and was as stiff in his denial till the sight of my bowl put him to a pause. He returned to the ship and came back again accompanied by another seaman, and for my bowl they undertook to transport me.'

'Aha!' said Sir Thomas under his breath. 'Now we have the reason for the bowl!' Aloud he added: 'So Providence and the present from your master saved you at last?'

The response was the briefest of nods. The steward was not to be diverted from his prepared text.

'They said that I must be contented to lie down in the keel and endure many hardships; which I was content to do to gain my liberty. So they took me aboard and put me below in the vessel in a very uneasy place and obscured me with boards and other things. There I lay undiscovered, notwithstanding the strict search that was made in the vessel. The two who had my bowl furnished me honestly with victuals daily until we arrived at Lisbon in Portugal where, as soon as the master had left the ship and was gone into the city, they brought me on shore and left me moneyless to shift for myself. I knew not what course to take, but, as Providence led me, I went up into the city and came to a fair street—'

'Give me its name,' Sir Thomas invited. 'Describe Lisbon to me, I pray you.' He knew Lisbon too.

'I had no means of discovering its name, but I can tell you that Lisbon stands beside the river Tagus on its north bank. The quays form one side of the city's square, whence the main streets lead uphill. This street was one of those. Be so kind as to allow me to finish my statement now. It is nearly done.

'Being weary, I turned my back to a wall and leaned upon my staff. Over against me were four gentlemen discoursing together. After a while one of them came to me and spoke to

162

me in a language that I understood not. I told him I was an Englishman and understood not what he spoke. He answered me in plain English that he understood me and was himself born near Wisbech in Lincolnshire.'

Sir Thomas had intended to refrain from further interruption, but could not restrain himself from interjecting that Wisbech was but a few miles from Crowland. Was that not a most remarkable coincidence?

The steward bit his lip and read resolutely on.

'I related to him my sad condition and he, taking compassion on me, took me with him, provided for me lodging and diet and, by his interest with the master of a ship bound for England, procured my passage. Bringing me on shipboard, he bestowed wine and strong waters on me, gave me eight stivers and recommended me to the care of the master of the ship, who landed me safe at Dover; whence I made shift to get to London. Being furnished with necessaries there, I was enabled to come hither to my own part of the country.'

After a pause he continued with his peroration: 'Thus, honoured sir, I have given you a true account of my great sufferings, and of my happy deliverance by the mercy and goodness of God, my most gracious Father in Jesus Christ, my Saviour and Redeemer; to whose name be ascribed all honour, praise and glory. I conclude and rest Your Worship's, in all dutiful respect, William Harrison.'

His Worship was moved by this conclusion to brood furiously on the gullibility of those who ascribed to an Almighty God their deliverance from suffering but not the sufferings themselves. How blind and intellectually degrading was Faith!

He roused himself to discover that his respondent had handed over the statement, picked up his hat and was leaving the room, uttering a polite excuse at the door: 'With your permission, Sir Thomas, I am engaged elsewhere and must now be about my Lady's business. Much has been neglected in my absence.'

By the time the magistrate had opened his mouth to refuse permission until the examination was complete, it was too late.

He decided regretfully against creating a scandal by dispatching the constable to arrest the lady of the manor's man of business in the street.

'Shall I bring him back, master?' Ali volunteered.

'Let him be,' said Sir Thomas. 'We can resume on the morrow.'

'Unless he disappears again,' said the constable.

22

The potboy from the nearest hostelry brought food and ale to sustain the magistrate and his companions while they puzzled over the truth or untruth of the steward's strange adventures. 'Are we to believe a word of this tale?' Sir Thomas demanded, throwing himself back in his chair and abandoning formality.

Every man of superior intelligence when in contact with inferiors wears a mask (according to Francis Bacon), but not so Sir Thomas Overbury. In public stiff-necked and a stickler for observing distinctions of station, in private he was wont to descend from his pinnacles in society and intellect and treat with lesser mortals on equal terms—always provided they did not presume to respond in like manner.

Experience had taught Constable Fettiplace the dangers of overstepping the limits of the magistrate's condescension. He was aware, too, that whatever view he expressed would be opposed, probably ridiculed; so his answer was cautious.

'Master Harrison is a gentleman,' he pronounced. 'It would be wrong of me to speak ill of him or to doubt his word.'

Sir Thomas chewed on this and a mouthful of cold mutton. Was the constable sincere or frightened of giving offence to the steward because he lived in a tenant's cottage on the manorial estate? Or might it be that he was in awe of the powers of the leader of Campden's coven of Devil-worshippers? If the steward was in truth the mysterious Man in Black, as rumoured, the constable would be privy to it—as he would be privy to other Campden secrets he might not choose to divulge.

'Master Harrison is no gentleman and you are a hoodwinked

dolt,' he declared when he had swallowed the meat. 'Tell me, I pray you, why kidnappers would wound a defenceless old man whom they intended to sell. Is it to be believed that they could have transported him across the breadth of England, wounded, wrists bound, without being noticed and questioned? Why would they have run such a risk for a few pounds when they had already robbed him of many more? The account of his voyage and captivity could have come from a book. As a slave he would have had no value at his age. The tale of the silver bowl is preposterous. And what say you of his return? He landed penniless. How came he by the wherewithal to lodge and feed himself until he reached home? Where did he find the money to buy a horse with bridle and saddle, do you suppose?'

During this harangue, the constable busied himself with eating. He knew better than to speak in his defence. It was now Ali's turn for grilling. 'So what is your verdict, my young friend?'

In his role of privileged courtier, Ali had no cause to mince his words. 'Lies, master, all lies,' he said.

This provoked Sir Thomas into arguing contrary to his own beliefs. It was a method he prided himself on employing to sift evidence and arrive at the truth.

'How can you be so certain?' he demanded. 'If others have suffered at the hands of infidels like yourself, why should Master Harrison not have suffered too? The outline of his story is credible. It is the details which defy belief. Yet even improbabilities may speak in his favour. What, I ask you, would be his purpose in inventing needless references to places like Crowland and Wisbech?'

Ali stuffed his mouth with bread, drank his ale and said nothing.

'What you should be arguing,' Sir Thomas told him, 'is that a man who was born in Wisbech would not make the mistake of supposing it to be in Lincolnshire. Let me enlighten you and him and Master Harrison: it lies in Cambridgeshire.'

'Then if, as you say, Master Harrison is not a liar, it must have moved.' Ali grinned mischievously.

166

'Drink less ale and answer me properly, Infidel.' Sir Thomas punished the impertinence with a cuff over the ear.

'I was baptised a Christian,' Ali reminded him, 'and you are my godfather.'

'To my shame! But if you will not dispute with me, permit me to instruct you further in the arguments you should have advanced. Those names, like the absurd nickname of Boll, were thrown in to add a pinch of verisimilitude to an otherwise threadbare fabrication. Their purpose was to mislead me into believing what I have just argued. As for you, constable—'

An interruption rescued the officer from another humiliation. An unusual hush in the street outside drew Ali to the window. He beckoned excitedly. 'Quick, master, and you will see why Master Harrison left us so hurriedly.'

The others joined him and stared down at the procession below. It was headed by the parish priest. Behind him came a coffin on a cart pulled by the sexton, and behind the cart strode the steward with bare, bowed head. There were no other mourners, only silent bystanders marvelling at the spectacle. The creaking of the cartwheels was the only sound in what, a few moments earlier, had been a bustling market place.

'John Perry!' exclaimed the magistrate.

On the day following his return William Harrison had applied to the authorities in Gloucester for permission to take down the skeleton still hanging in chains on Broadway Hill and give it a Christian burial. The grisly sight which greeted travellers was no longer a warning of the fate which awaited murderers; it had become an awful example of the injustice of the law. The application had been promptly granted.

'A single mourner for the innocent victim of a blundering judge!' The magistrate was incensed. 'Come!' he cried, snatching his hat and cloak and running down the stone steps to the street. Below, amid astonished murmurs, he mustered his dignity and solemnly took his place beside the steward. Hard on his heels, the constable and Ali fell in behind.

One by one others were emboldened to join the cortège. By the time the church was reached several dozen mourners had gathered to pay their last respects to the wronged boy. There was little sympathy in the town for the misfortune of his mother or brother, but many pitied young John, who had taken them with him to the gallows.

Inside the church Sir Thomas glimpsed Anne Harrison, her fair hair hanging loose over her shoulders. But there was no sign of Mistress Harrison or Master Edward.

The funeral service was followed by burial in the churchyard where the vicar consigned soul and skeleton into the arms of Christ. 'Rest in peace in the bosom of our Saviour, John,' he prayed. 'Your earthly woes are done. May the Almighty in his infinite mercy grant you the blessing of life eternal!' Even Sir Thomas felt moved to say Amen.

When the ceremony at the graveside was over and all the dead had been left to their peace, William Harrison still knelt beside the open grave. Tears ran unchecked down his cheeks while his lips moved in prayer.

'We will linger here until he has finished his penance,' said the magistrate, impatient to resume his interrogation. He beckoned to the constable to join him under a yew tree which stood beside the wall overlooking the ruins of the great house. From there they could observe the kneeling figure unnoticed.

The plot chosen for the burial lay next to the mound which covered the body found beneath the terrace at Campden House. At least, thought Sir Thomas, the boy's remains had not had to wait as long as the man's for a resting place in consecrated ground—whatever good that might do for either of them.

Ali followed his gaze towards the mound. 'I pray you speak to my master about Daniel Perry,' he said, turning suddenly to look the constable in the face.

'What of him?' Caught by surprise, the constable stood flustered, his face flushed with guilt.

Sir Thomas, quick on the uptake, pounced at once. 'Did you not serve as a comrade with him in the king's army? Were you not in the fight at Naseby alongside him, you and Robert Hayward of The Eight Bells? That is what I have heard—that the three of you were conscripted and marched together from here to the battle. Is that the truth?'

'We marched first to Evesham, then on to Leicester. There we were victorious, taking the castle by storm. But what happened next, at Naseby, was too terrible to remember.' The constable was trembling and close to tears. 'It was seventeen years ago and God has not granted me a night's unbroken sleep since. Our cavalry knew well how to save themselves. They deserted us. I was one of the few on foot to escape. Robert was with me. Thousands were slaughtered. Daniel was never seen again.'

'But he had been with you on the march?' This time it was Ali who put the question.

The constable scowled at him. Ali was an unwelcome curiosity in Chipping Campden. There were black negro pages from the West Indies in the households of other gentry in the district, but none behaved with such familiarity or gave themselves such airs as this light-skinned Egyptian.

'Answer!' commanded Sir Thomas.

The constable swallowed his tears and pride. 'I did not see Daniel on the march,' he confessed. 'Not with my own eyes. The colonel had placed him under close arrest. He was facing a court-martial. A sergeant was holding him under guard at the rear of the column. That is what we were told.'

'Name the charge; and no more prevarication if you value your office.'

Master Harrison was still motionless on his knees, sunk deep in grief, like a weeper on a tombstone. His daughter, who had been standing a short distance apart, was walking towards the almonry. While the group under the tree watched and waited, the constable unfolded the story of the captured coins and the last days of Campden House.

'I would never willingly have deceived you, sir, but Robert and I promised each other with our hands on the Holy Gospels that we would never speak of the matter. Daniel being the one on sentry duty when the gold was stolen, he was judged to be party to that theft, although found dead drunk. As the other

169

members of the guard, Robert and I were to be flogged, but happily that was forgotten when the fighting began.'

'So the gold was not found, and that was the reason the house was burned—not because the commander was under orders to deny it to the enemy, as given out? And Master Harrison had the responsibility of recovering the treasure to save the house and failed? Is that correct? Forget your pact with Robert Hayward. Forget Matthew, Mark and Luke and John too. The demands of justice take precedence over Bible oaths.'

'Neither Robert nor I was privy to the disappearance of the gold. We had no knowledge of it, either then or later. I swear to that. As to the destruction of the house, we heard explosions as we were marching away. In camp at Evesham the gunners boasted they had mined and fired it.'

'Very well. Let us now be clear about this as well: after your regiment took to the road you never set eyes on John Perry's father again. Neither at Evesham nor at Leicester nor at Naseby. You have been lying about that, have you not?'

The constable inclined his head in reluctant assent.

'Then you have another and more serious question to answer. Did you not know, and did you not conceal the fact from the coroner, that the body in the tunnel was Daniel Perry's?'

'I could not be sure; otherwise I would have informed him.'

'Here we have a soldier last seen under close arrest in Campden House. There we have the body of a man executed by firing squad hidden beneath the same house. Are you so brazen-faced as to pretend that you never put the two together?'

'When we came back from the war, Robert said it would be best for his family if Daniel was thought to have died in battle. When the body was found we thought it would be wrong to change our story out of nothing more than suspicion. Think of the distress it would have caused Mistress Perry.'

'I understand now why Robert Hayward was so forward in volunteering for the jury at the inquest and why you chose him. The pair of you conspired to interfere with the due process of the law. And you one of the law's officers!'

The constable hung his head. 'I intended to speak out, but

170

Robert said: What good will it do? Let poor Daniel stay a hero, he said. Why publish a disgrace he did not deserve? Was he not a harmless creature, already unfairly shamed by his wife's black arts? I beg Your Honour, let the dead rest in peace as parson said.'

'Father and son reunited!' Sir Thomas's anger dissolved into a romantic reverie as his gaze swept over the graves where the two lay side by side. He felt his poetic nature about to take wing.

A voice brought him abruptly to earth again. It was Ali saying: 'Father and son? I pray you think again, master.'

23

Anne Harrison was running back from the almonry towards them. She was in distress, heedless of her appearance, her hair streaming behind her in the breeze.

Sir Thomas saw the girl full-faced for the first time and was struck by a flash of recognition. Where had he seen that likeness before? Of course! The fair, girlish features of John Perry! So that was what Ali's sharp eyes had detected. That was what he had meant with his 'Have you noticed Anne Harrison?' and 'Think again, master.' It was his own son that the steward was mourning.

His daughter's cries roused the kneeling man. He sprang to his feet and hurried towards the lych-gate. Sir Thomas hastened after him, beckoning to the constable to follow. Ali leapt the wall to be the first to reach the girl and comfort her. She pointed over her shoulder towards the house and the others rushed forward to discover the cause of her alarm.

Inside the house its mistress was waiting for them in the kitchen. Her face was grey as granite. Her feet were off the ground. Her body was suspended on a rope hanging from a meat-hook in the ceiling. She was swaying in the draught from the open door. A toppled stool lay nearby.

Sir Thomas at once took charge, brushing the steward aside. At his command Ali cut down the body and the constable was dispatched to fetch a physician. As soon as she was laid on the floor her husband attempted to pump air back into her lungs, but long before the physician arrived to confirm it they knew that she was dead beyond recall.

'Be off with you again and notify the coroner,' Sir Thomas ordered the constable when the physician had left. He locked the kitchen door, pocketed the key and summoned the steward into his own parlour. As an afterthought he ushered in the weeping girl and Ali too.

'What have you to tell me of this matter, Master Harrison?' he demanded sternly. This was no occasion for a display of sympathy, he judged. That the marriage had been loveless was common knowledge.

The steward betrayed no emotion. What lay behind that mask? Was there grief? Was there guilt? Or merely the stillness of shock? Plumbing Master Harrison's depths was a task to tax a Grand Inquisitor.

'What could I have had to do with it?' he replied at last. 'Who knows better than yourself how I have been occupied all this day? Condolence would be more proper than suspicion.' He spoke like an innocent accused: evenly, with a tinge of bitterness.

'I am doing my duty, no more. You and Mistress Harrison were not on good terms, I understand. Her welcome when you returned from the dead and recovered the stewardship from your son was cold, as I have heard.'

'I beg you not to address my father in that tone, Sir Thomas,' Anne protested through her tears. 'I can tell you my mother was alive little more than an hour ago. She was upset by news of the funeral. I urged her to come with me but she would not.'

At this Sir Thomas felt obliged to change his tune and express sympathy. Had there been any talk of suicide, he inquired.

'Will you take a stroll outside with me?' the steward replied. 'Alone if you please.' He treated Ali to a glare and ordered his daughter to her room upstairs. The pair of them were standing too close together for his liking.

Leaving Ali on guard outside the house with instructions to allow no visitors, Sir Thomas followed the steward through the orchard until they rounded the ruins and stood on what once had been the terrace. There they came to a halt, leaning on fragments of balustrade, each deep in his own thoughts. In front

173

of them and to left and right there was nothing but derelict gardens and the grassy hillocks of former earthworks. Beyond a ruined gateway parkland and fields belonging to the estate stretched far into the next county.

'So the poor wretch, John Perry, was your bastard.' Sir Thomas spoke without turning.

'I do not deny what is common enough. Many men beget children outside the bonds of wedlock. Most, I dare say.' He turned to look Sir Thomas in the face, but the magistrate's gaze remained on the horizon.

'Yet few beget them on witches,' he said. 'Am I correct in supposing that John was conceived during a meeting of your coven? Was he the child of a Synagoga Satanae? Did you plant your seed in that witch's womb from behind during one of those orgies on Kingcombe Plain? It has been whispered that you were the Man in Black, the Chief who was the master of those ceremonies. Falsely, I had thought.'

'You seem well versed in our ancient rites, Sir Thomas, as I would have expected.' A chill had crept into his voice and, as it seemed, into the air as well. 'That being the case, you will be aware that their secrets are not to be revealed to the uninitiated. I admit to no acquaintance with any Sabbats held in this locality and shall favour you with no answers to questions relating to matters outside your jurisdiction. All I will say to you with regard to John and the circumstances of his birth is that a man who weds a Presbyterian must seek his pleasures outside the marriage bed.'

'About John you must say more,' Sir Thomas insisted. 'His fate is assuredly a subject within my competence. Will you now admit to a conspiracy with him to conceal the real facts surrounding your disappearance? When he sought to deceive me by confessing that he had been a party to your murder, he knew full well that you were still alive, did he not? You were making use of him to cover your tracks. He was a pawn in your game, and in playing it you brought him to the gallows. It is you who bear the heaviest responsibility for the death of your own son, is it not? These are some of the questions which you

174

cannot evade. They must be answered in the furtherance of justice, however lame and late.'

Suddenly the mask cracked. The voice, always so measured, shook: 'John was the best, the truest of sons, the light of my life, and you are right to lay his death at my door. I freely confess that I killed him. But not by intent; far from it. He meant more to me than any other creature on earth, and I would give my own life to have his restored. As the Bible tells us, the Christian God is a vengeful God, and He has punished me for my transgressions by taking away what was most precious to me.'

'Word that you were still alive would have saved the boy's life. Why did you not send it?'

'I was far distant and ignorant of what was happening here.'

'Enslaved by an octogenarian Turk in Asia Minor? Spare me a repetition of that cock-and-bull tale.' Sir Thomas felt pity, but could not resist the sneer.

'Messages were sent by others who knew of my existence. The parson was bidden to inform you. He did so, but to no effect. You yourself are not free from blame in that.'

'I never swerved from my belief in John's innocence, but Master Bartholomew produced no evidence to support the truth of what he alleged. Without a signed statement his testimony was worthless. He died before one could be obtained from him, and I could do nothing to save John except speak to the judge at the assizes. The prosecution was out of my hands. I won him a reprieve at the first trial, but that ignorant, mannerless Injustice Hyde refused me a hearing at the second.' Sir Thomas spoke passionately in his own defence.

'I am told that the priest sent for you from his death-bed to make a statement, but you delayed too long in going to him.'

It was true, and against that charge Sir Thomas could offer no defence. Pangs of guilt had simmered inside him ever since. 'How was I to know that the beneficed bigot would slip away so inopportunely?' he snapped. 'If you learned of his death, why did you not send a second message? There was time enough.'

'Another message was sent before the second trial, but it was never delivered.'

'To whom then was it sent, pray? And why was it not brought to my attention?'

'Do you need to ask?' The steward cast a glance in the direction of his house. 'The message was sent to my wife, to put an end to her suspense. She should have passed it to you or the judge. It would have saved the lives of all three.'

A picture of the scene in the court-room and street in Gloucester sprang into Sir Thomas's mind: the altercation between Mistress Harrison and her son. 'Mistress Harrison had word that you were still alive and yet allowed the Perrys to be hanged for your murder!' he exclaimed, outraged. If she had not already saved him the trouble, he would have been tempted to put an end to her miserable life himself.

'She showed the affidavit to Edward and he argued that, because it was not signed by myself, it would not be admissible or credited. He wanted her to suppress it; they quarrelled until she yielded. Both hated John because of my fondness for him. For the others they cared nothing: in ridding the world of a witch and a thief they were doing God's work.'

'Did they not know John was your son?'

'I had confided in John himself. To explain my love for him. I bound him to secrecy and he obeyed me in all things. His mother's silence I bought with the promise that I would look after the boy and see that she did not starve so long as the secret was kept. But yes; my wife and Edward guessed the truth, and Edward saw John as a rival for his inheritance and the steward-ship. As soon as I learned what had occurred in my absence, I turned him out of the house. He will never live under my roof again.'

'Mistress Harrison you could not evict, but it appears that she has taken her own way out. You are fortunate in that—and in your alibi.' William Harrison's reputation for respectability was crumbling as they talked, and Sir Thomas racked his brains wondering how the suicide might have been faked.

'I confess to upbraiding her for being no better than a

murderess. I confess to threatening to expose her. But it was not I who caused her death; it was her own conscience. She and her piety! Religion came between us from the very beginning.'

In one of his swings of mood Sir Thomas abandoned all thought of uxoricide. Instead his heart warmed towards Master Harrison. How could he not feel sympathy for a man with a troublesome wife? How could his heart not go out to one who had turned from God to the Devil? He mused on the crimes and cruelties perpetrated in the name of Christianity. Islam was no less bloodthirsty. What faith could a man of reason embrace then? It was Old Nick or the Buddha. He pondered whether the coven which had met on Kingcombe Plain might be reconvened with a new Chief. An Overbury the Man in Black! He put the temptation behind him.

'Did Mistress Harrison give you no warning of what she intended today?' he asked.

'She was distressed, had all but lost her reason, but I never imagined it would come to this. The scriptures teach that self-destruction is a mortal sin. I must swear she was insane if she is to be buried in the churchyard.'

'What the Church pleases to denounce as sinful is no concern of ours,' said Sir Thomas. 'In the eyes of the law what she has committed is not a sin but a crime. In order to satisfy myself fully about its cause I shall require from you a formal—and truthful—statement concerning your whereabouts during the period between your disappearance and return. The account which you read to me this morning appeared designed to stretch my credulity to breaking point. Favour me with the truth now.'

On looking about him before replying, the steward uttered a sudden imprecation. 'The Devil take your footboy, Sir Thomas! How long has he been standing behind us eavesdropping?' For Ali had crept up behind them unnoticed.

The magistrate shook an angry fist at him. 'Did I not distinctly command you to stay by the almonry door?' The steward had been about to reveal all, he felt sure of it. The key to the mystery had been snatched from him by Ali's disobedience. That dun-

177

derhead of a coroner would arrive on the morrow to take the statement and rob him of the honour of solving what the London news-sheets were calling The Sensation of The Century. He felt fame slipping through his fingers.

Ali was not cowed by the rebuke. He beckoned urgently to draw Sir Thomas away so that the steward could not hear what he had to report. But the magistrate would not budge. 'Say what you have come to say and then be gone! There are to be no more secrets between Master Harrison and myself.'

Ali frowned and hesitated. Then inspiration came and his brow cleared. '*Habib*,' he said. '*Habib, o bey.*'

24

Sir Thomas was startled by Ali's warning to beware. So too was the steward. The expression on his face revealed that he understood the meaning of at least one word of Arabic. The implication did not escape Sir Thomas. Was this not evidence that Master Harrison had in truth made a voyage to the East? But had he done so, as he claimed, under duress?

Anxious for his daughter's safety, the steward quickly made off in the direction of the almonry. Ali was left smiling smugly. He had laid a trap for Master Harrison, and Master Harrison had fallen into it.

'You clever little disobedient blackamoor!' Sir Thomas exclaimed admiringly. 'But did you invent the danger to play your trick?'

Ali's skin was but a shade darker than his master's and he showed his disapproval of being dubbed a blackamoor by not replying. Instead he beckoned and Sir Thomas was obliged to follow until they could see the converted stables which stood on the far side of the derelict gardens.

'There is a man hiding inside.' Ali pointed towards the windows, one of which was unshuttered. 'I saw a face at that window while I was watching outside the almonry as you told me. One moment it was there; the next it had gone. I inquired of Mistress Anne and she swore to me that the house is empty.'

'Remember she is her father's daughter,' Sir Thomas told him. 'A maiden's truthfulness is not to be judged by her beckoning eyes or the shape of her bosom.'

'Mistress Anne would not lie to me,' Ali retorted indignantly.

Nor shall she lie with you, was Sir Thomas's thought, but he did not utter it. This was no occasion for word play. It was well known that those apartments were kept furnished for the Lady Juliana, who never came. 'It may be that this affair has decided her ladyship to honour us with a visit at long last,' he mused aloud. 'In that case she will have sent servants ahead of her to make the accommodation ready.'

Ali shook his head. 'Mistress Anne says her father has the keys and she would know if he had been asked for them. She says no one can enter without his knowledge.'

'Except an intruder. Or perchance a djinni.' Ali's belief in danger was growing infectious and Sir Thomas sought to allay a tremor of agitation with a jest.

'It was the face of a rogue. Maybe one of the villains who waylaid you. Shall I flush him out for you?' Ali drew the half-sword he wore for his own and his master's protection.

Sir Thomas laid a hand on the hilt of his own sword for reassurance. 'Go fetch Master Harrison,' he ordered.

The steward came grumbling. It was not fitting that his daughter should be left alone with his wife's body. Arrangements must be made for its immediate removal. In view of the warmth of the weather, he felt obliged to insist on it.

'The body stays where it lies until the coroner has made his examination,' Sir Thomas told him bluntly. 'That is the requirement of the law—and of your own interest. Unless proof of suicide is established beyond all doubt, you will be the subject of ugly rumours. Of *more* ugly rumours, I should say.'

The steward began to argue, but Sir Thomas cut him short. 'If you and your daughter would prefer to spend the night at The Eight Bells,' he said, 'I will have the constable place a guard on your premises. Now pray inform me who it is that is lodging in the stables.'

'No one, I do assure you. No one at all. They have been unoccupied ever since their conversion.'

'Why then has one of the windows been unshuttered?'

'All are closed, as you may see for yourself.' He pointed.

Sir Thomas looked up and saw, to his astonishment, that the

steward was right. All the windows were shuttered. They returned his stare blindly, like an unbroken row of lids drawn over sleeping eyes.

'One was open a few moments ago,' he spluttered, 'and my servant is sure he spied a man inside.'

The steward treated Ali to a scornful side-glance. 'Then your servant is gifted with second sight, Sir Thomas. He must have eyes which can open shutters or see through them.'

'You may be expert in magic, Master Harrison, but I for one am not susceptible to spells and delusions. I too saw the window bared.' Sir Thomas spoke angrily in Ali's defence.

'It is not possible.' The steward was adamant. But Sir Thomas, knowing him for a liar, was not convinced.

'Get me the keys,' he demanded. 'The building must be searched.'

'I have no authority to grant entry to you or any other person without her ladyship's permission.'

'My servant, I repeat, has seen a man inside. He may well be one of the robbers who assaulted me on the road to Blockley. We know that they have been here before, taking refuge in the vaults. I repeat: the building must be searched. I will answer for it myself to her ladyship, and if you obstruct me you shall answer for it to the law.'

'As you please. But my duty compels me to conduct the search myself. You have my word that it shall be done as soon as my wife's body has been laid to rest and I am free to leave my own house. I shall report to you then to satisfy the law's demands.'

'That will *not* suffice,' Sir Thomas insisted through gritted teeth. 'There must be no delay or the criminals will have fled. Is that what you intend with your "as you please"?'

Two of the most stubborn men in Gloucestershire stood face to face, both determined not to yield. For once, the magistrate's faithful footboy was on the steward's side: his master, he knew, was not courageous, but rash. To Ali the smell of danger was strong and he was about to intervene when the impasse was resolved by the arrival of the constable with important news.

181

A gruesome murder had been reported from Evesham: two men hacked to death, their mutilated bodies tossed into a ditch on the outskirts of the town. From the descriptions given it appeared that they were the two men who had ambushed Sir Thomas.

The steward favoured the magistrate with a faint smile. 'So it must have been the ghost of one of them your servant saw at the window,' he said.

The argument raged again until a compromise was reached. The steward agreed to search the building without delay, but alone. Ghosts did not frighten him, he declared, rejecting the constable's offer of assistance. Sir Thomas's suspicions were far from assuaged, but he nodded a sour assent and adjourned with the constable to The Eight Bells, where the steward promised to join them later to report his findings.

As they parted the constable had been shaking his head at the steward's folly. 'I trust Master Harrison will not get himself injured or killed,' he muttered.

Sir Thomas trusted so as well. The idea of the steward taking the secret of his disappearance with him to the grave upset him much more than the thought of the man's death.

'Constable Fettiplace has told me the news,' Robert Hayward confided to Sir Thomas as he ushered him upstairs to the room where young John Perry had been interrogated and detained.

The magistrate looked about him at the low beams and narrow window. Two years had passed since the interrogation—two years during which that innocent boy had been led away to be imprisoned and hanged and left hanging until all that was left of him, his bare bones, had been brought home that very day.

'What news?' he demanded of the landlord.

'Why, the death of Mistress Harrison and the two men at Evesham, Your Honour.'

At this Sir Thomas rounded fiercely on the constable, who was caught vainly signalling to the publican with a finger to his lips. 'Blabbermouth!' he shouted at him. 'You are employed as an arm of the law, not a town crier. Who else knows of this?'

182

'I gave strict orders to the man I sent to the coroner to keep his mouth shut, but rumours of Mistress Harrison's hanging are all over town.' The constable cringed. His attempt to saddle another with the blame brought the wrath of the magistrate on his head more heavily.

'Next time remember to tell yourself to keep your own mouth shut as well. And how dare you inform the rest of the world of the news from Evesham before informing me!'

'I told none but Master Hayward. That is God's truth, sir. I had good reason for it and'—here the constable appealed to his friend—'he will tell you what it is.'

The landlord vanished downstairs before obliging, but quickly reappeared with three tankards and a jug of ale. With Sir Thomas's permission he and the constable seated themselves and he filled the tankards. Ali, standing beside the door, was ignored but all ears.

'During the late war I and Andrew Fettiplace served in Colonel Bard's regiment,' Robert Hayward began.

'I am aware of that,' Sir Thomas interrupted. 'Also that Daniel Perry was one of your number. Also, as I have learned only today, that the body found in the vaults of Campden House was Perry's. Also that you concealed your knowledge of the identity of the corpse, although foreman of the jury which brought in a verdict of person unknown. Also that for that you are culpable—kindly permit me to finish.'

But the innkeeper was not to be browbeaten like the constable. He broke in regardless. 'I suspected the body was Daniel's. That is why I volunteered for the jury. That I confess. But tell me this, sir. How could a man be sure those bones and that skin were his?'

'So you kept silent.'

'What cause was there to rake over cold embers? The Perrys were my neighbours. They had suffered enough, God knows. Let the past be the past, I say. Daniel always wore a ring. There was none on the corpse's fingers. Had there been, I would have known my duty and spoken out.'

Sir Thomas could not hide a blush. He had pocketed the ring

with the intention of producing it when the occasion arose, remembered it and then forgotten it again. He felt in his pocket, and there it was! A keepsake crudely wrought in humble pewter. He threw it across the table. 'There!' he said. 'I had quite overlooked it.'

'Aye, that is it, or one the same,' confirmed the landlord.

'The same is not the same.' Sir Thomas corrected him sharply, always at his most aggressive when at fault. 'There must be hundreds like it.'

'That's as may be, but I remember no others in the regiment. Daniel's wife made him wear it as a charm. To ward off God, we used to say to tease him.'

'There is an inscription.' It was Ali's voice from the shadows. The others turned in surprise and Sir Thomas scowled at him. The imp had been prying in his pockets and was now speaking out of turn.

They peered at it closely and, sure enough, scratched faintly on the inside was the word, 'Ioane'.

'Joan was Mistress Perry's name,' said the constable.

'That puts it beyond doubt. Poor Daniel!' sighed the landlord. 'We were conscripted like it or not, and Daniel was no fighting man. He was accused of cowardice and blamed for the loss of gold coin he was guarding. If anyone was due to face a firing squad before the mansion was abandoned, it would have been Pikeman Perry.'

'Very well,' said Sir Thomas after a moment's silence during which the tankards were refilled. 'That is one mystery solved. Now what of the two dead men in Evesham?'

'During the war, as Your Honour will have heard, some uniforms in the armies were red, some blue, some orange,' said the constable. 'The colonels chose the colours themselves. Ours chose white because it pleased him to have the regiment called Bard's Angels.'

'So, Constable Fettiplace!' cried the magistrate with the air of a huntsman sighting his quarry. 'You are telling me—and not before time—that John Perry was likely to have been speaking the truth when he claimed to have been attacked by two men in white. You are telling me—and not before time too—that those rogues who had the audacity to attack and rob me were former soldiers from the regiment stationed here during the wars. And you believe that it is these same men who have been attacked and murdered in the next county. I thank you for that information. Until now you have been nothing but a hindrance to my inquiries.'

While the constable hung his head the landlord spoke. 'With Your Honour's permission I will ride over with the constable and inspect the bodies. Together we may recognise them.'

Sir Thomas frowned, losing himself in thought. Since the collapse of the Commonwealth and the Restoration of the king, when it had become safe for those who had fled into exile with him to return, all kinds of riff-raff were being washed ashore by the tide from the Low Countries. Was one of them the infamous Sir Henry? he wondered. Had the colonel of Bard's Angels risen from the graveyard of history, bent on further mischief and mayhem? Were these men two of his agents?

'Why do you suppose that criminals would choose to identify themselves by wearing their old uniforms?' he asked.

The other two were still scratching their heads when Ali volunteered an explanation. 'They wished to make it known why they had come.'

'Known to whom?' demanded Sir Thomas.

'To whoever stole the treasure,' Ali replied. He was staring at the landlord and the constable.

The magistrate remembered hearing that Pikemen Hayward and Fettiplace had also been on guard duty on the night of the theft. A look of suspicion crossed his face, and the two men noticed it before it could be suppressed. 'You have my permission to go and inspect the bodies,' he told them, adding after a pause: 'and Ali will go with you.'

'You will not ride home alone, master.' It was softly but firmly spoken. More of a command than a question.

Sir Thomas was not offended. He was touched by the boy's

solicitude. The others were shocked to see him stretch out a hand and stroke his servant affectionately on the cheek.

'I shall wait here for Master Harrison,' he promised. 'It is you who must take care, my Ali John.'

25

A library is a gentleman's refuge from the world. Thus Sir Thomas comforted himself as he bent over the manuscript of *Queries Proposed*, the *magnum opus* which would exalt Reason and ridicule blind faith in the superstitions of religion.

Magna est veritas et praevalebit, he wrote. Great is the truth, and it shall prevail. That was the first article of his own faith, and he was the person who would make it prevail: to the confusion of all the High Priests of Error.

But, although secluded from outside interference, he could not lock out his own thoughts. At a pause in his composition, as he groped for the *mot juste*, his concentration was broken by the intrusion of more immediate matters which would not be banished from his mind.

The most troublesome was domestic. His marriage was approaching breaking-point. After the difficult birth of their second daughter the midwife had persuaded Lady Overbury that another pregnancy would kill her. On the word of that mindless minx Sir Thomas had been denied access to the matrimonial bed and deprived of all the sexual services which it was a wife's lawful duty to provide.

He had summoned a learned obstetrician from Oxford to refute the ignorant midwife's pronouncement with a qualified medical opinion. But what had been the result that very morning? The man had arrived, insisted on an exorbitant fee, made his examination and then plumbed the depths of ingratitude by diagnosing a malformation of the womb, for which (so he said) there was no remedy. And this the womb of a woman who was alleged to come of stout child-bearing stock, who had already given birth twice, and whose three married sisters all gave birth every year to brats squalling with good health! He had only married the silly creature to get a male heir, and he had been sadly deceived.

Divorce was the only solution. But that would entail protracted proceedings in the courts if she fought it, as she would. Under the law the costs of both parties would fall on him, and he balked at the prospect of pouring money into the pockets of avaricious attorneys, amongst which obnoxious tribe her father was one of the most grasping. He would undoubtedly encourage her and employ himself and other grossly overpriced lawmongers at Sir Thomas's expense. The case would bring Sir Thomas, not fame or the sympathy he deserved, but notoriety once the metropolitan scribblers had sunk their teeth into the intimate details of a wronged husband's private life. What a juicy scandal they would make out of his fondness for Ali!

At the thought of Ali his mind moved to the other cause of distraction: the strange goings-on at Chipping Campden. It was three days since the body of Mistress Sourpuss Harrison had been discovered twirling in a draught; three days since Ali had returned alone to The Eight Bells to report on what he had learned at Evesham.

Robert Hayward and the constable had recognised the murdered men and been detained to sign statements swearing to their identity. The bodies were those of a former Captain Hill and Sergeant Conybeare of Bard's Angels. From the dead captain's fingers Ali had recovered the emerald and onyx rings stolen in the ambush of his master.

'Assuredly this proves the pair of them were thieves,' Sir Thomas had said as he restored the rings to their rightful fingers and they took the road home together. 'But where is the evidence that this captain and sergeant were responsible for the disappearance of the missing gold?'

'The constable and Master Hayward have no doubt that it was those two who hid the barrels of gold coin among the barrels of wine in the tunnel where we came across Daniel Perry's body. He must have suspected them, so they accused him of the theft and had him shot to stop his mouth.'

'That is mere speculation. It is what Constable Fettiplace and his friend would have us believe.' In the face of Ali's certainty Sir Thomas adopted a sceptical tone. 'They themselves had equal opportunity and motive, had they not?'

'That is true, but as soon as the treasure was missed all the vaults were explored. I suspected them wrongly. If they had been the ones to hide it, it would have been discovered.'

'But not if the others had hidden it? Is that what you are saying? Tell me, pray, why that should be.'

'Because the captain and the sergeant conducted the search. They were in charge of the search party. Remember the piles of barrels heaped higgledy-piggledy in the darkness, master. Every barrel could not be examined by everybody. Those two could have looked into two full barrels themselves, pretended they were empty and led the other searchers away elsewhere.'

That sounded plausible, but it was still conjecture. Sir Thomas grunted to signify that he was not yet convinced.

'If the constable and Master Hayward were the culprits,' Ali persisted, 'would they have remained in Campden living as poor men? No; they would have gone away to enjoy their riches where no one knew who they were. And if they were the guilty ones, would they not have been the victims of the two officers when they came back to look for the treasure?'

On reflection, Sir Thomas had come to accept that Ali was right. While it was true that all innkeepers were cunning knaves, Constable Fettiplace was plainly too stupid to be capable of a sustained deceit. Nor would either have sat on a heap of gold for seventeen years. They could not be as cunning or stupid as that.

If this solution to the theft had brought discovery of the gold any nearer, it would have been easier to dismiss the matter from his mind and concentrate on his Trumpet Blast To Awaken The Deluded Faithful. But that mystery remained buzzing tiresomely through his brain. Where had the gold gone, and how was its disappearance linked to the steward's? The two could not be unconnected.

There was, too, the question of Mistress Harrison's death. The coroner's jury, hastily assembled at her husband's urging, had delivered a verdict of *felo de se* whilst of unsound mind. The fig-leaf rider of insanity had enabled the suicide's body to be interred in consecrated ground. It was now lying in Christian peace within spitting distance of the remains of Daniel and John Perry.

In his mind Sir Thomas had not yet exonerated Master Harrison from criminal involvement in his wife's demise. At the very least he had driven the wretch to take her own life. The jury's verdict was reached under his influence and in deference to his wishes. The magistrate's suspicion had grown after the steward came to The Eight Bells to confirm his brazen lie that the Court House, as he called the old stables, was unoccupied. He had entered every room, he said, and all were empty.

When Sir Thomas inquired whether the furnishings were undisturbed, the answer had been a shake of the head followed by a quick departure. Here then was something else requiring further investigation, for Ali's eyes were as sharp as his wits: his glimpse of a face at the window would not have been imagined. The longer the inquiry stretched, the more Sir Thomas's misgivings about the trustworthiness of that supposedly true servant, William Harrison, multiplied.

His musings were interrupted by three soft raps on the door, a signal which identified Ali. 'Go away!' he shouted. Then he thought better of it and crossed the room to let the boy in.

Ali held out a letter. Sir Thomas unfolded it. It was from Sir John Keyte, to whom he had applied for information about the infamous Sir Henry Bard.

'The man who could wantonly destroy a noble pile like Campden House is likeliest to be the instigator of all the present mischief there,' he told Ali when dispatching him to Ebrington. 'I do declare this captain and sergeant were but his agents. They stole the gold at his command, and it is he who sent them to recover it.'

He ran his eyes over the contents of the letter. Sir John wrote that he had once met Sir Henry, and the man was 'very personable and courageous'. After the evacuation of Campden House he had been with Prince Rupert at the capture of Leicester and was said to have led the assault on the town in person. At Naseby he had commanded on the king's left flank and survived. He had then been appointed Governor of Worcester. What a career for a man who had already lost an arm in battle, commented Sir John admiringly.

'So a man who kills enough of his fellow human beings becomes a paragon of virtue in some people's estimation!' muttered Sir Thomas in disgust. His face darkened to purple as he read on.

In successive years during the war this monster had been rewarded for his crimes with honour after honour. One year a knighthood, the next a baronetcy. Finally the ravager of Campden had been rewarded by elevation to the dignity of Baron Bard and Viscount Bellomont—an Irish peerage, but a peerage nonetheless.

Sir Thomas gnashed his teeth. He had set his own heart on becoming a lord but, until that wish was granted, he affected to hold lords in low esteem. How much more so now! When the time came he vowed to be satisfied with nothing less than an earldom. Seething, he returned to the letter with a scowl.

Captured by Parliament at sea during a passage to Ireland. Imprisoned, then banished from the realm for life. Flight to the court of King Charles at The Hague. There accused of a murder. Persuaded the king the charge was false. Sent on an embassy to the Shah of Persia and the Great Moghul to raise money for the king. Stole a valuable Koran from a mosque in Cairo whilst *en route*.

Sir Thomas's reading was punctuated by mounting exclamations of anger. At the theft of the Koran he broke off with a cry: 'I wager this is the knave at the bottom of our affair.'

'Another two sovereigns on it, master?' inquired Ali.

'The same two,' Sir Thomas replied. 'I shall be glad to have them back. Why are you smiling?'

191

'Read to the end and you will learn.'

'On his journey across the Arabian desert,' Sir Thomas read, 'Viscount Bellomont was almost choked to death in a sand-storm. After an audience with the Shah he gallantly pressed on to India. There this noble soldier and diplomat succumbed to apoplexy brought on by exposure to the heat. His body lies buried in a village between Agra and Delhi.'

The letter ended with a pious epitaph on the dead ogre which further enraged Sir Thomas. It was against Reason that his neighbour should be at once so well-informed and so wrong-headed. He rounded on Ali accusingly: 'You knew of this!'

'I learned the whole story at Ebrington.' Ali confessed without shame and ducked to avoid the coins which Sir Thomas hurled across the room with a cry of 'Cheat and liar! You opened the letter!' The end of the One-armed Wonder was good riddance, but he had lost his chief suspect as well as the bet.

Ali made haste to heal his master's wounded pride with an easy question: 'Who, do you suppose, stole the treasure from the thieves who stole it first?'

'The steward, of course. Who else? He must have come across it after the garrison left, too late to save the house. No one else had access to the vaults then.'

'And that would be the reason for his disappearance?'

'What other explanation can there be? Think of the date, Ali. It was a bare three months after the Restoration. He was safe while Parliament ruled, but as soon as the ruffians who had fought for the king returned, Master Harrison must have feared for his life. The captain and sergeant came to take possession of what they had hidden. They found it gone. So they prowled the neighbourhood searching for it—and for revenge on whoever had taken it.'

'You have solved the mystery, master.' Ali clapped his hands in admiration. 'But whither and by what means did Master Harrison and the gold vanish? And once he had succeeded in escaping with it undetected, why did he come back?'

Sir Thomas was conscious that Ali was leading him on. He thought furiously and was forced to revise his judgment on the steward. 'Master Harrison was no thief,' he said, 'but truly a faithful servant. That must be so; for was he not immediately re-employed upon his return? He must have appropriated the stolen goods for the family he served, not for himself. Ergo, he would not have gone overseas, but to her ladyship in Rutland until it was thought safe for him to come home. The message that he was still alive, conveyed to me by the Campden parson, would have come from her. I suspected as much at the time, for she appointed him to the living and he was her confidant here.'

'So it is not Sir Henry Bard but the Lady Juliana who is at the bottom of it all?'

Something in Ali's tone again gave Sir Thomas pause for thought, but he concluded that this time he was not being outwitted. 'Yes,' he declared firmly; 'and tomorrow I shall ride to Brooke to confront her. The truth shall prevail.'

26

Early the next morning the coach was at the door with coachman and groom in attendance. Ever a man of impulse, Sir Thomas had decided to lose no time in journeying across the country to beard the unapproachable dowager in her Rutland lair. If he gave notice of his visit, she would be sure to send a message pleading that she was too ill to receive him.

In view of her age that excuse might well be true, but he saw no other means of resolving the mysteries of the missing money and her steward's disappearance. During a sleepless night he had determined to bluster his way into her presence. He would then force her to admit that William Harrison had purloined the king's gold on her behalf and spent two years, not in the hands of Infidels, but lying low incognito on her estate while three wretches were imprisoned and hanged for his murder. Her ladyship had much to answer for: that was his considered conclusion.

Ali had sought to deflect him from this course and was to be left behind as a punishment. Denying him the credit of a share in the denouement would teach him a lesson. When informed of this on waking his master, Ali pulled a face and had to be ordered not to argue.

At breakfast Sir Thomas went on to quarrel with his wife over the coach. She had intended to use it that day to begin a week's visit to her family in Gloucester. The arrangement had been made a month ago and she was expected.

'You may have the coach and the visit as soon as I return,' he promised. 'But you must give me your word that you will consult Dr Maybrick while you are there. He is a married practitioner, and he has been recommended to me as one who is better acquainted with the ins and outs of the female body than all those dried-up bachelors in the medical faculty at Oxford.'

'I will do no such thing,' she protested. 'Do you expect me to agree to being examined by every physician and surgeon in England until you find one who will say what you want to hear? You are a heartless brute, Thomas. I truly believe you would be pleased to see me dead so that you could marry again. Will you deny it?'

Her indignation dissolved into tears when he reasoned with her as best he could without answering either question. 'Surely you understand that I must have a male heir? The Overbury line is as old as the shire itself. We were thanes on this land centuries before William the Bastard brought himself and his low-bred Norman fellows across the sea to lord it over us.'

'The estates are not entailed,' she said, drying her eyes. 'You have two daughters to divide them between. When they are known to be heiresses, they will marry well and pass your line down through their sons. My father has told me their husbands can change their names to Overbury if that is your wish. You cannot be so cruel as to disinherit your own flesh and blood.'

Heartless and cruel! The charges were absurd. 'I am no monster,' he assured her. 'The girls will be provided for. They will have income. But not capital or estates. Those are for a male heir. You can tell your meddlesome father that I will have no sons-in-law pretending to be Overburys. There will be no name-and-arms clause in my will allowing them to inherit. If you cannot give me a son, you must give me a divorce. Tell your father that. He can draw up the settlement. You may tell him I am minded to be generous.'

There! His opening shot had been fired. Leaving the room abruptly to avoid another flood of tears, he put the miseries of matrimony behind him and prepared for the long journey. Yet it was not to be. Even as Ali was pulling on his boots, Constable Fettiplace arrived breathless from Campden and ran into the hall without ceremony to blurt out his news. The Court House was occupied!

'Another face at the window?' demanded Sir Thomas.

'No, Your Honour. A coach has been seen driving through the gates. One painted with a coronet and the family arms. After twenty years! The whole town is buzzing.'

'How obliging of her ladyship to spare me a journey! I will go to her at once.' Sir Thomas promptly issued new orders and climbed into his own coach, which bore the Overbury arms but no coronet—yet. After a few yards he brought it to a halt and, relenting, called for Ali to take the seat beside him.

As they journeyed, he rehearsed what he would say to the Lady Juliana. He would be severe with her, viscountess or no. What was she after all but a mercer's daughter? Ali listened without comment. When dug in the ribs, he responded with 'You know best, master' in a tone of voice which suggested otherwise. Sir Thomas was greatly pleased by this: he had been too clever for him, and the boy was sulking.

As soon as they were inside the gates of Campden House he saw the coach standing at the end of the drive which led to the stables. It was an exotic sight, gleaming and elegant, rising above a jungle of waist-high weeds.

With Ali at his heels, Sir Thomas crossed a courtyard and entered what he took to be the front door of the part of the building which had been transformed into a so-called Court House. Inside they found themselves in a small chamber serving as a hall. There they were met by an evil-looking, slovenly-dressed footman with the battered face of a prize-fighter rather than an indoor servant. When Sir Thomas gave his name and asked to be taken to the Lady Juliana, the man eyed him insolently and vanished upstairs without a word.

The air in the house was fetid, and Sir Thomas felt uneasy—the more so when Ali whispered that this was the face he had seen at the window. Time passed and the man did not return. Instead, after a wait which taxed Sir Thomas's patience to the full, a voice called: 'Come up, Tom, you old reprobate.'

Tom? Old? Reprobate? He stood rigid. Who among his

acquaintance would presume to address him with such vulgar familiarity? He could think of none. Mounting the stairs cautiously, he was greeted on a dark half-landing at the top by a man with straggling hair and a wispy beard who had plainly been roused from his bed.

'I have come to speak with Lady Campden,' Sir Thomas faltered.

'Then you have missed her by a hundred miles. You must make do with me instead.'

Peering through the gloom, Sir Thomas at last recognised the dishevelled speaker. The man had aged and his appearance coarsened, but this could be none other than Baptist Noel, third Viscount Campden. Twelve years ago they had enjoyed a week of drunken debauchery together, gambling and whoring in the stews of Alexandria. Eleven years ago the fellow had rooked him at cards and threatened to kill him in a duel in Damascus. His lordship was dangerous company.

They stared at each other warily. Then his lordship clapped Sir Thomas on the shoulder and led him into a small parlour. 'A glass of wine to renew our friendship!' He ordered his rough retainer to bring a bottle of the best canary.

Over the first, and then a second, bottle they exchanged reminiscences of adventures in the Near East. Lord Campden had taken refuge there after the wars, during which he had risen to the rank of brigadier in the king's defeated army. Then a vengeful Parliament had forced him to return home to fight again, this time against the sequestration of his estates.

'I was obliged to make my peace with the rebels in the end,' he said savagely, 'and at what a cost! They demanded twenty thousand pounds as the price of compounding for my own and my mother's estates. I told them they could whistle for that. Even so the settlement was ruinous enough. It was the best my lawyers could do for me. Nine thousand pounds to keep one's own property! That was republican justice.'

'But at least it rescued you from exile.'

'Not for long, my friend. I was driven abroad again by poverty, as you must know.'

197

'But here you are. You have at last been able to raise funds from your grandfather's old trading partners in the Levant.' Sir Thomas spoke what he did not believe. It was dawning on him that the Lady Juliana was not the villain of the piece. Infuriatingly, it seemed that Ali had been right once again.

Lord Campden replied bitterly. 'Most of them owed him money when he died, that is the truth. But what happened? They claimed on me instead: for goods they never sent. When I tried to make them pay up, the villains turned the tables on me.' He belched in disgust. 'But enough of my woes! What news of you, Tom? What became of that beautiful boy of yours?'

'I brought him home with me. He is well.' Sir Thomas did not wish to discuss Ali and inquired after the Lady Juliana.

'My mother is as well as can be expected at her time of life, I thank you. Although Campden is hers in her own right, she prefers to live on the Noel estate, which was my father's. She has not been here since the fire and has vowed never to set eyes on the place again. She wants to remember the house as it was when her father built it, not as our gallant comrade-in-arms, Colonel Bard, left it. That scoundrel lied in claiming that Prince Rupert ordered him to destroy it. The prince himself has assured me that he issued no such order.'

Sir Thomas commiserated and asked how long Chipping Campden could expect the pleasure of his lordship's company. 'Your arrival is timely,' he said. 'The family has been sorely missed. A manor without its lord spells trouble, and we have had that in plenty, as you will not be unaware. It was my intention to ride to Brooke Hall this very day. There is much to be discussed between us.'

'Then let us do so here and now, for I shall be departing before nightfall. This hole is not habitable, and I shall have accomplished my tasks in Campden by then. It is good to see you again, Tom. When I have taken over the management of our affairs from my mother and settled down with her at Brooke, you must come and stay awhile. The shooting and hunting there are the best in the country.'

A third bottle of canary was called for and broached. Through the haze gradually enveloping his mind Sir Thomas struggled to plan his next move. Baptist Noel, a man notorious for his brusque manner, was being uncommonly civil. It was time to seek the reason and proceed to business. 'Are you at liberty to discuss the nature of those tasks?' he ventured.

'To you by all means. They are two.' Lord Campden drained his full glass at one gulp, waited for his guest to follow suit and refilled both. 'The first,' he continued, 'is to satisfy myself that Giles has done what was required of him and to take him back to Brooke with me. I am already satisfied on that score, so you will be relieved of his presence.'

Giles? Could this be the unprepossessing servant who had received him and was handling the bottles of wine as though they were truncheons? If so, what could have been his mission? The fog lifted from Sir Thomas's mind. He could hardly believe what he was thinking. 'Are you telling me—' he began.

His host interrupted with an airy wave of the hand. 'Yes, I am. Giles is the fellow who has been serving our wine. He was a dragoon in my brigade and I have retained him in my service ever since. Uncouth for a footman, I grant you, but he has uses. He was decorated by the king himself for killing more of the enemy in battle than any other man in His Majesty's Service. When Master Harrison returned here last month and sent word that his life was still threatened by two of Bard's men, I ordered another old soldier out on reconnaissance to deal with them as he thought fit.'

'And he thought fit to cut their throats? On your orders?'

'I knew you would thank him for ridding the neighbourhood of a brace of ruffians. They even had the audacity to rob your good self, I am told.' His lordship was by no means abashed.

'I thank no man for committing murder. Nor for instigating it, my lord.' Sir Thomas was aghast.

'There I must beg to differ. Rough justice is sometimes the best, and it was a fair fight. Leaving aside the element of surprise, the odds were two against one in their favour. Giles deserves another medal, you must agree.'

199

'Giles deserves to be hanged. But in matters touching your lordship it is the innocent who suffer that fate, I think.'

Emboldened by wine, Sir Thomas had summoned his courage and thrown down the gauntlet. He was not even intimidated by the proximity of the murderous Giles awaiting his master's call in an adjoining chamber. Both men were flushed. An ugly quarrel was brewing. Sir Thomas had lost his temper, but Lord Campden was still all sweetness, keeping his under control.

'Come, come,' he said soothingly. 'We are both men of the world. Our talk here is private. I have confided in you not as a magistrate but as a friend, and I promise you further confidences if you will but calm yourself. That was my second purpose in coming—to call on you at Bourton and help clear up the affairs you have been investigating so diligently.'

He paused before continuing. 'As to the deaths of those two men, I will, of course, deny all involvement if formally questioned. They occurred in the next county, so you have no need to bother yourself or your conscience about them. Giles acted in self-defence, I dare say. But let us put those petty disturbers of the peace out of our minds and turn to the matters on which I desired to meet with you.'

'We are met.' Recklessly Sir Thomas threw another draught of wine down his throat and held out his glass to be refilled. His tongue was loosened but he would hold it, he vowed.

Lord Campden cleared his throat. 'Let me first explain that in the Levant I became saddled with debts—some imaginary, others real enough. Together they were so large that my creditors prevented me from leaving until they were paid. The dusky villains had fallen on me like vultures and stripped me bare at dice and cards. I was plucked like a pigeon and forced to live off the charity of fellow expatriates while sending urgently for funds from home.'

The cheater cheated! Sir Thomas laughed to himself. The noble lord was a madcap gambler and consummate ass. This was the idiot who had gambled away his bride's royal dowry in a day. The crafty Levantines could well have skinned him stark naked without recourse to dishonesty. 'So Master Harrison stole the king's gold,' he said, 'and brought it to you in Smyrna to obtain your release.'

'How clever of you, Tom! Did I mention Smyrna?' The tone was admiring. His lordship was still all sweetness.

'The place was mentioned in your steward's account of his adventures; which, I may add, never for one moment deceived me. Did I say your steward's account? Your own, I mean.'

'Another hit! You are too sharp for me, Tom. I warned my mother you were no ordinary Justice.'

'Of course I recognised your hand,' Sir Thomas bragged, basking in the flattery against his will. 'I knew your steward had not the learning or imagination for it. But you were ever a romancer, my lord.' 'Liar' was what he meant.

'I thought the tale a good one and well told,' his lordship boasted in turn. 'It would have gulled a lesser man than yourself. There was precious little invention in it. I took real events from here and there and twisted them together.'

'So I observed. Now, I pray you, favour me with the truth about Master Harrison and what befell him.'

'As you wish. The destruction of the mansion had blocked all the entrances to the tunnel where the gold had been hidden by those thieving officers, so he did not discover it until long after. My mother told him to say nothing, keep prowlers away and leave it where it lay. I was abroad and she could not think what to do with it. But when my predicament arose, she ordered him to take what was needed and bring it to me in Smyrna. He had made the journey in my grandfather's time, so knew how and where to take ship. It was my mother who bound him to secrecy. For fear of theft.'

'Yet he sailed with it alone across the world?'

'Not alone. Giles went with him. A sufficient guard, you may agree. It was thought that any greater protection would only serve to alert robbers. By the grace of God, the pair of them reached me safely with the treasure despite a brush with pirates. In Smyrna the settlement with my creditors was protracted by greed. Their demands rose at the first glint of gold. On the return journey I rested in Alexandria revisiting our old haunts.

Mishaps slowed our progress thereafter. In Lisbon, where we changed ships, it took an age to obtain a passage. Thus the voyage there and back, planned to take no more than a few weeks, stretched to two years.'

'During which time three innocents were hanged for Master Harrison's murder.'

'You cannot blame me for that. My mother twice sent word that our steward was alive. His confiding in his boy that he was going overseas in secret and would return within three months was the misfortune. The poor lad thought to help by halting inquiries into his whereabouts; and what better way than by confessing to his murder? The boy would have seen no danger in it until the very end, and then it proved too late.'

At the recollection of John Perry's fate Sir Thomas jumped to his feet and stalked round the room in agitation. 'Had the Lady Juliana but sent a sworn statement to me, he and others would be alive today. What excuse can you offer for her ladyship's failure to communicate with the investigating magistrate? It was her inescapable duty under the law and in common humanity.'

'She believed you had received her messages and that you or Mistress Harrison would convey them to the judge.'

This roused Sir Thomas to a peak of wrath. 'Play no more games with me, my lord. I can smell the truth. Any direct communication with me would have precipitated an inquiry, would it not? That would have uncovered your subterfuge in paying off your debts with coin which was not yours, would it not? Lord Campden, I accuse you of stealing the king's gold.'

His voice had risen and behind him, as he could see in a looking glass on the wall, the door had quietly opened and the murderous Giles stood on the threshold. He prepared to defend himself, but Lord Campden waved the man away and responded to the charge with a shrug.

'A very proper conclusion for a magistrate,' he said. 'But you err. I am no thief. What I took was no more than a small part of what the king owes to me and my family. A father, a brother, a mansion, a penal fine! What recompense did I receive for these

202

losses when His Majesty came into his own? Not one penny piece!'

'I choose my words with care, my lord. Stealing is taking another's property without his consent. Did the Lady Juliana seek the king's consent?'

'Those coins were Parliament's, not the king's. They were the spoils of war, captured from the enemy.'

'Captured by His Majesty's forces. Do not imagine, my lord, that the cause of your pleasantness towards me has eluded my understanding. You wish me to conspire with you in concealing the truth. That I shall never do. The blood of the Perrys is on your head, and the nation shall know of it and the reason for it. You must account to the law for the one and the king for the other.'

'You go too far.' It was his lordship's turn to raise his voice. He bounded to his feet in a passion, bellowing that Sir Thomas was an insolent dog and a jumped-up jackanapes. He kicked over the table between them, and bottle, glasses and wine fell to the floor.

The noise brought Ali rushing up the stairs to the rescue of his master. He was chased by Giles, on whom he rounded, whipping his half-sword from its sheath and pointing it at the cut-throat's chest. Sir Thomas called to him to fetch the constable, but Giles blocked the doorway.

The deadlock was broken by Lord Campden, who recovered his composure with an effort. 'Let your minion put away his weapon, Tom, and I will order my man to leave us.'

'Let your man withdraw first,' Sir Thomas replied.

Giles was dismissed and Ali, sheathing his weapon, took up a post on guard outside the open door.

'Move the creature away,' his lordship demanded. 'I shall have no eavesdropping on what I have to say.' He waited until Ali was out of earshot—although, at Sir Thomas's insistence, not out of sight—before resuming.

'For myself, I care not a fig what is known of this affair,' he said. 'I would gladly account to king and country for my part in it and abide by the consequences. To those who have fought in battle, there is nothing left to fear. My mother, though, is of a different mind. At her age she wants no trouble, only to live out her few remaining years undisturbed. It is she who has sent me here to beg you to accept the version of events presented to you by Master Harrison, and to pursue your inquiries no further. He will continue as steward of the Campden estate for the rest of his life, and his honesty must not be doubted. He has committed no crime, and we desire no stain on his reputation for plain dealing. This affair is now at an end. The dead cannot be brought back to life.'

Lord Campden's temper was under control again and he spoke calmly, but Sir Thomas was not to be lulled.

'I must take issue with you, my lord,' he said. 'In my philosophy truth and justice stand above all else. Without those two, human society is a jungle, inhabited by beasts. The true events in this affair must be disclosed. What crimes have been committed and what persons were responsible for them is for the law to judge. I regret the necessity of disobliging her ladyship, but the truth must be told and justice done.'

At this the dam of his lordship's restraint burst again. 'Then you will assuredly enjoy the glory of being a martyr to them,' he snarled. 'I will do you that favour, I promise you. Lest there be any misunderstanding, permit me to speak frankly—and loud enough for your boy to overhear without straining his ears, as I notice he is doing. Are you both listening?'

The tension in the air returned. Giles reappeared in the doorway unsummoned. The question went unanswered.

'All her life my mother has been accustomed to obedience and I will not see her wishes disregarded now. If they are not respected, I shall turn Giles loose on you both. He finds killing a pleasure and will take another hint just as readily as he did at Evesham. A hint only, I say; for should his responsibility for your untimely ends come to light I shall, of course, plead that he quite mistook my meaning and intention.'

For once Sir Thomas was at a loss for words. He opened his mouth without knowing what to say.

'Save your breath,' Lord Campden commanded. 'Our business is finished. On reflection you will have second thoughts about your philosophy and the priority of truth and justice. You were a non-combatant in the wars, I recollect. You tarried overseas while others risked their lives to defend the true religion and save England from the injustice of revolution. For all your fine words, life comes first, does it not?'

With the curtest of bows his lordship wished Sir Thomas a good day and retired, leaving his would-be assassin to conduct the visitor to his coach.

POSTSCRIPT

Principles must sometimes yield to necessity. The viscount's threat was too terrible to defy. When Sir Thomas published his pamphlet entitled *A True and Perfect Account of the Examination, Trial, Condemnation and Execution of Joan Perry and her two sons, John and Richard Perry, for the supposed Murder of William Harrison, Gent., being one of the most remarkable Occurrences which hath happened in the Memory of Man*, it brought him the fame on which he had set his heart. But it was neither true nor perfect.

Among the untruths was the romance which purported to explain Master Harrison's disappearance. Among the imperfections was the omission of any mention of Viscount Campden, the stolen gold or the evil lives and violent deaths of Captain Hill and Sergeant Conybeare, those stalwarts of Sir Henry Bard's regiment of Angels.

The threat to Ali was Sir Thomas's excuse for his timidity, and he promised his conscience that, come what may, he would publish a genuine account in a revised edition as soon as the Lady Juliana was dead. But the indomitable dowager's eightieth birthday came and went, to be followed in due course by her eighty-fifth, while he fretted and sickened. Her longevity thwarted him, for when God claimed her at long last and her body was borne in state across England to lie in splendour beside her father in Chipping Campden church, she had out-lived Sir Thomas.

In his last years he had become a recluse, forgotten by all except his disapproving neighbours, the Keytes and the Dovers. His master-work, *Queries Proposed to the Serious Consideration of those who Impose upon Others in Things of Divine and Supernatural Revelation and Persecute any upon the Account of Religion,* fell into instant oblivion. For want of a publisher willing to risk his liberty in the cause of Reason, it was privately printed and went unnoticed.

On top of this humiliation, domestic strife helped speed him to an early grave. As he had foreseen, the demands made by his father-in-law in the matter of a settlement were so exorbitant that he was forced to surrender any idea of a divorce. Thenceforward he and his wife, living together under the same roof, avoided each other's company both day and night. She was banished from the great hall, the parlour, the library and his bedchamber, while he never set foot in the little parlour and the solar which, with her own withdrawing room and bedroom, became her domain.

With his death came his greatest triumph: the last will and testament of Sir Thomas Overbury, Knight. The scandal which it created reverberated like the eruption of a volcano long thought extinct. News of it shook the county from Kiftsgate to Henbury and travelled like the wind to London, where all the metropolitan scribblers condemned it at length.

After providing for his wife and daughters during their lifetimes, as he had promised, Sir Thomas bequeathed the Overbury estates and his other possessions absolutely and in their entirety to 'the single comfort and joy of my life, my dearly beloved natural son, commonly known as Ali John, whom I hereby desire and enjoin to adopt the name and style of John Overbury Esquire, as will befit his station'.

The parson at Bourton declined to conduct a Christian burial service over the body of a militant atheist who had demised his ancestral estates to an heir born a heathen out of wedlock. He was adamant that he would not have his graveyard desecrated by his squire's remains. Last rites at Chipping Campden too were barred. Viscount Campden, patron of the living, was unyielding in his opposition to the body's proximity to his family's mortuary chapel. The Devil, he said, could keep his own.

With a putrifying Sir Thomas fouling the already musty air in his beloved library, the argument over his disposal was finally resolved by a hurried ceremony in the secluded hamlet of Ilmington, where his father had bought the lordship of the manor from old Baptist Hicks, and a curate without tenure was in no position to refuse.

Ilmington lay on the far side of Chipping Campden, and on the day of the funeral Ali, fancying himself in the melancholy finery of his mourning suit, decided on the spur of the moment to break the journey home. He ordered his coachman to drive through the gates of Campden House and halt outside the almonry. There he would propose what he had long intended: marriage to Anne Harrison. She was still a beauty, still unmarried, still young enough to bear him a son and heir.

Sir Thomas had forbidden him the girl, and her father, now bent and frail, would be enraged. But to Ali it seemed a fitting reconciliation that their children should be joined together in love.

At the thought of the tongues which would wag and the fury of the viscount, he smiled to himself mischievously. Now that he was acknowledged as his father's son, it would be only right and proper to begin behaving with the perversity for which Overburys were renowned.

Dismounting, he cast a glance at the ruined pile which still held its secrets, and then and there he came to another decision. What a pleasure it would be, what an act of filial piety, to confound the world by uncloaking the mystery of the Campden Wonder with a truly true, a perfectly perfect account! He would keep his father's unpublished records safe. Then one day—how was it Sir Thomas had put it?—'time, the great discoverer of truth, shall bring to light this dark and mysterious business.'